A Town with Half the Lights On

"Like a warm hug just when you need it, *A Town with Half the Lights On* will make you believe in second chances again. And seriously contemplate moving to Kansas to open a diner."

—Katarina Bivald, *New York Times* bestselling author of *The Readers of Broken Wheel Recommend* and *The Murders in Great Diddling*

"For those of us living between America's coasts and the bright lights of metropolitan areas, Page Getz's *A Town with Half the Lights On* will ring true as a church bell. This is a novel for those of us who don't move away but instead move back to reimagine, restore, and breathe life into vacant buildings and too-quiet Main Streets. This is a warm and whimsical chain letter of a novel. Kind of like opening your mailbox and finding an envelope from a long-lost friend; you can't help but smile."

—Nickolas Butler, author of *Shotgun Lovesongs* and *A Forty Year Kiss*

"Some books reach the world just when they're needed most. *A Town with Half the Lights On* is that book. This clever tribute to small towns, big hearts, and the people who make life worth living will renew your faith in humanity and make you long for a Goodnight, Kansas, of your own."

—Lucy Gilmore, author of *The Lonely Hearts Book Club*

"Big-hearted, funny, and brimming with charm, this novel will be sure to stay with readers long after they finish the last page. I know I'll be carrying Goodnight, Kansas, with me from here on out."

—Cat Shook, author of *If We're Being Honest*

"Bitingly humorous with a cast of characters that will both warm your heart and chat your ear off, *A Town with Half the Lights On* is sensational. Page Getz weaves small-town charm with candid internality, harkening for readers their own sense of home and the mosaic of people who live there. 'If you fry it, they will come!' When Page Getz writes it, we'll all want second helpings!"

—Mallory Tater, author of *This Will Be Good* and *The Birth Yard*

"This novel is perfect! It's a very funny book about an extremely serious town, Goodnight, Kansas, and its solid citizens making a glorious mess of their lives to the delight of the reader and all the while revealing our shared humanity like a necessary tonic in our soulless, cell phone–scrolling times. The wit is astounding by any measure, and the different strands pulled together masterfully, a testament to her artistry."

—Stephen D. Gutierrez, author of *Captain Chicano Draws a Line in the American Sand*

A Town with Half the Lights On

A Town with Half the Lights On

A Novel

PAGE GETZ

Published by Sourcebooks Landmark, an imprint of Sourcebooks
P.O. Box 4410, Naperville, Illinois 60567-4410
(630) 961-3900
sourcebooks.com

Library of Congress Cataloging-in-Publication Data

Names: Getz, Page, author.
Title: A town with half the lights on : a novel / Page Getz.
Description: Naperville, Illinois : Sourcebooks Landmark, 2025.
Identifiers: LCCN 2024047225 (print) | LCCN 2024047226 (ebook) | (trade paperback) | (epub)
Subjects: LCGFT: Epistolary fiction. | Novels.
Classification: LCC PS3607.E923 T69 2025 (print) | LCC PS3607.E923 (ebook) | DDC 813/.6--dc23/eng/20241011
LC record available at https://lccn.loc.gov/2024047225
LC ebook record available at https://lccn.loc.gov/2024047226

Printed and bound in Canada.
MBP 10 9 8 7 6 5 4 3 2 1

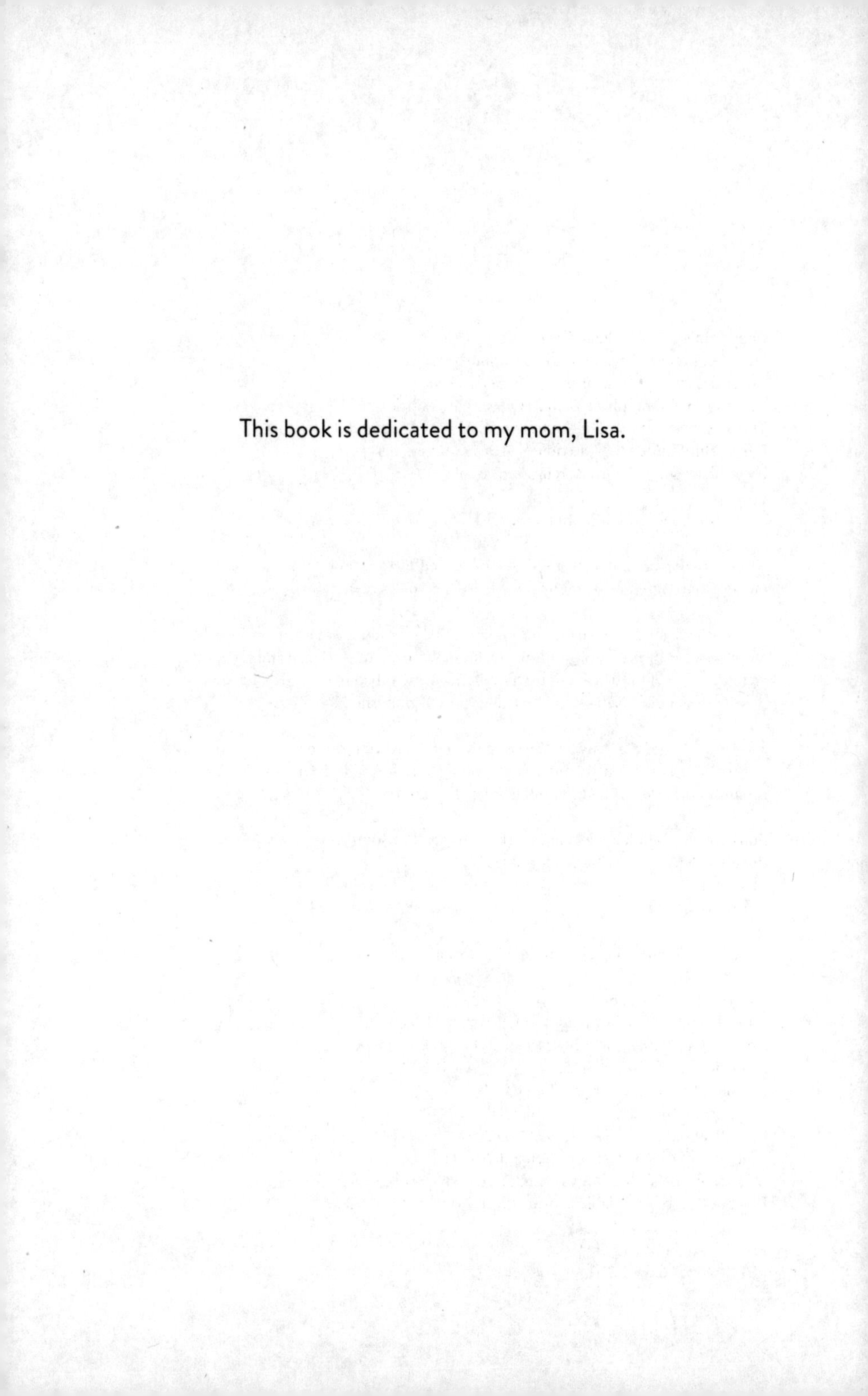

This book is dedicated to my mom, Lisa.

*No Missourians were harmed in the making of this book.

Ad Astra Per Aspera.

—KANSAS STATE MOTTO

Barn's burnt down—now I can see the moon.

—MIZUTA MASAHIDE,
SEVENTEENTH CENTURY

PART 1

Bells of Goodnight

1

A Girl on a Bench

From: Sid Solvang <brooklyncalling@zoomail.com>
To: Abbey Solvang <abbeyroadyogi@omwardbound.org>
Date: April 2, 2002

You should've heard the bells!

I've never heard anything like it. I promise this won't be another one of my five-page emails, but let me tell you, after three days of cows and mullets, we pulled into town at noon, and there were so many churches, we could hear those bells before we saw the sign that said, *Welcome to Goodnight, Kansas, where there are no strangers.*

Goodnight is so deep in nowhere, only two radio stations came in for the last mile, one Baptist, the other Southern Baptist. Harlem slept as we crossed the river into a sigh of a town, and the static broke into a crackling radio voice singing, "Sundays are for church, Saturdays are for the Gates of Mercy Flea Market: rust, dust, and the Savior's favorite funnel cakes!"

Maybe I've found the opposite of New York.

Scarlet said, "Seems like a ghost town. It's like the world turned and forgot to take us with it," and then she sort of sank into the passenger seat.

Can you believe she said *us*?

I asked how she could still see herself as one of them after being gone for 20 years, and she said, "You think you'll stop being a New Yorker once you've been here 20 years?"

I told her, "I don't plan on staying that long. Do you?"

Scarlet looked out the window the way sadness makes a person look out a window.

You know that look she gets. She answered in the voice she usually saves for marriage counseling. "Feels like I never left."

Harlem woke up as we turned onto Emporia Road, so I stopped asking questions.

Emporia Road is the main drag through Goodnight. It's a dusty, forgotten street.

Downtown is all winter-salt brick and cobblestone with ghost signs on abandoned storefronts, like a postcard with chronic depression.

I can't imagine we'll stay longer than it takes to get back on our feet, but for now, at least it's not Brooklyn. I'll take cows and mullets any day to escape the ghosts of Bedford Avenue.

Here come those bells again.

It's getting late. I'll call you when we're settled. Abbey, I want you to know how sorry I am for what happened. I promise I'll make it up to all of you somehow.

From: Abbey Solvang <abbeyroadyogi@omwardbound.org>
To: Sid Solvang <brooklyncalling@zoomail.com>

Stop apologizing. It wasn't your fault. I mean, like, technically it was your fault, but you meant well. I mean, you tried. Anyway, nobody's mad at you. I mean, everybody is sort of mad at you, but I'm not. Aunt Rachel wasn't exactly mad. She said she knew you'd find a way to fuck things up. And you know Stan and Abe never liked you, so they're always looking for a grudge. I'm sure they would've found something else to hold over you. Cousin Leah said she wouldn't have been dumb enough to take all that on.

Well, I'm not mad. But, you know, I do yoga.

Don't feel bad. Grandpa Sol raised nine children in a house on an immigrant's wage here. Right now I'm looking for a roommate because I can't afford a studio working two jobs with the MFA I'm still paying for. There's no breathing room for wrong turns in this city.

Not anymore.

From: Sid Solvang <brooklyncalling@zoomail.com>
To: Abbey Solvang <abbeyroadyogi@omwardbound.org>

One week in Kansas, and I'm mystified by the sudden influx of alpacas in my life. When we inherited the house, Scarlet mentioned it came with a few pets. I don't know why I assumed she meant cats. The mailman says Pop Bannister was known to walk around town with the alpacas on leashes.

The Goodnight Alpaca Wool Company came from Scarlet's mom's side. She told me after her mom died, Pop couldn't keep up. He sold off all but his favorite three alpacas, and now they refuse to leave the house!

I can't get a straight answer out of anyone about why we aren't allowed to take them to the Bannisters' 17 acres. Why would he insist on living with livestock when they have all that land? I can't figure out how it's even legal.

When I ask Scarlet, she says, "It's Kansas."

I don't know what that means, but she seems to think it explains something.

At least they're not food critics.

No food critics here. No critics. Just alpacas and bells.

Did you know there are 32 different types of bells?

From: Harlem Solvang <torturedsol@zoomail.com>

To: Abbey Solvang <abbeyroadyogi@omwardbound.org>

Hey, Aunt Abbey,

Oh my God, the fucking bells!

The bells don't shut up, and my dad won't shut up about the bells. He's, like, in love with them, but I'm like, I get it, they have bells here. To me, they sound like a funeral. I'm pretty sure a town like this would've burned people like us at the stake 300 years ago. They're like Stepford hillbillies. It's so creepy.

When we carried our bags up the steps of Pop's house, one of the neighbors watched us from her totally haunted Victorian porch. She was twirling her pearls around her doily collar, staring down all Amityville with her American flag whipping in the American wind against her American house.

Fuck this town.

Harlem

PS: There was one interesting thing: When we drove up the main road, there was this strange girl covered in glitter, playing a blue guitar. She had glitter from her blue fringe boots to her black tinsel braids, where it seemed like there should've been a halo, but there wasn't.

She was just sitting alone at an old bus stop looking like she'd been dropped by a UFO.

Mom said there hasn't been a bus running here for 20 years, so she wondered what the girl was waiting for. She was like, "If that's what folks are like in Goodnight nowadays, things have changed since I left."

But I think we drove through the whole town in five minutes, and there was not another speck of glitter to be found.

Dad said maybe we should go back and offer the girl a ride, but Mom said there wasn't enough room left in that truck for a Kansas flea. So we kept driving.

Letter jammed into a mason jar of prayers and placed in a closet full of 1,238 jars of prayers, written by Abilene "Honey Bee" Kennedy, April 2.

Dear Jesus,

Disco can't make a friend to save her life. That girl even scares the mission kids away. She leaves a trail of glitter everywhere she goes. When I try to get the glitter out of my carpet, it clogs up my vacuum cleaner.

Please, Lord, send a miracle, on the double.

Faithfully,
Honey Bee

PS: Please save the May Day Diner. This town can't take another broken heart.

Handwritten note on a basket of May Day biscuits left on the doorstep of 121 Northwind Road, April 2

Welcome to Goodnight!

On behalf of our town and our council, I'd like to personally extend our warmest welcome and the best biscuits in Stills County from our May Day Diner.

Like many African Americans, my family settled here just days after the Civil War ended. Missouri chased them out with pitchforks. Moses wouldn't have us, of course, but Goodnight welcomed us with open arms. Our family's been here ever since. They gave us a deal on a modest plot of land, and now it's the sixth largest Christmas-tree farm in eastern Kansas.

I hope you find the same kindness and make yourselves at home. We're glad to have you.

Warm regards,
Ford Hollis, Goodnight
council member

From: Scarlet Bannister Solvang <mystifried@zoomail.com>
To: Jules Jamison <livingthedream73@zoomail.com>

Hey, Jules,

We finally landed in Goodnight. When we pulled up to Pop's old house on Northwind Road, there was a basket of biscuits waiting on the porch with a note from an actual city councilman welcoming us to town. Can you imagine a member of the New York City Council leaving a basket of biscuits at your door? To be nice?

New York must've burned down what was left of my soul, because I forgot there were folks like that left in the world. Harlem is worse.

When she saw the basket, she screamed, "Don't touch it! It's probably a bomb!"

She's convinced our neighbor wants to kill us because the woman hasn't stopped watching us since we arrived. I told Harlem she'd better get used to being stared at if she's gonna keep wearing her hair like that.

Goodnight has changed. Downtown looks so tired. I'm worried it's turning into a ghost town, although with a monster like Goodnight American Tire Company headquartered here, I can't imagine that could ever happen.

I'm grateful we have anywhere to land after what happened. If we can sell off Pop's old tractors and trucks, we'll get by until we figure out what in the world to do with ourselves now.

We're still waiting for our last check, and I promise we'll pay you back as soon as we can. Please don't say anything to Sid. He's all bell-loving optimism with Harlem, but he's vowed never to cook again, and he hasn't slept through a night since we left New York. My dad's alpacas aren't gonna do his insomnia any favors either.

On the bright side, I think it will be good for Harlem to see there's a whole country that starts where the New York subway ends.

From: Jules Jamison <livingthedream73@zoomail.com>
To: Sid Solvang <brooklyncalling@zoomail.com

Scarlet says you're not sleeping and you've given up cooking forever. If you knew how many poser chefs will be stoked to hear you're out of their way, you wouldn't give up so easy.

Don't lose any sleep over the money you owe me; there's no rush to pay me back. If you saw the James Beard noms last month, you know

I'm sitting pretty right now. You were the only chef I backed who didn't make a killing. It's uber-twisted that of all the kitchens I've had my hand in, you're by far the most talented chef, but somehow you're the only one who didn't make it. Nobody from the academy can believe what happened. None of us saw it coming.

Remember, Sid, just because you failed doesn't mean you're not a genius. Cheers!

JOURNAL ENTRY OF SID SOLVANG, FRIDAY

We're chin-deep in dust here on the prairie. It's disorienting to be broker than I've ever been while living in the fanciest place I've ever lived. Northwind Road is nothing but fading Victorians. Pop's house has Gothic Revival windows under black gables and a steeply pitched roof. Everything is run-down, like some abandoned theater haunted by another time.

The barns are another story. It's not enough to have one—Travis had two barns. Scarlet says that's normal around here, that most people have a good barn and a bad barn, but I wonder if they also have a hundred rusting trucks and wild alpacas in those barns.

The bad barn is so full of cracks, sunflowers actually grow inside. It's crammed with everything, from Scarlet's old diaries worth almost nothing to Civil War guns worth quite a bit of something. Scarlet thinks it could take a year to sort it. She says we need the money, but I think she's looking for something. She dove into the ruins like she was searching for treasure.

You can see half the night's stars through the roof of the old barn, but no one will tear it down. To borrow the words of our mailman, Carter Bell, "Goodnight don't give up on trucks, barns, wars, and such."

Not to mention alpacas. They're everywhere.

Vertigo was Pop's favorite, so we kept the name. Harlem renamed the others Taco and Matzo. They're more affectionate than dogs, and Taco is as cynical as I am. We wake to them humming, butting their fleece into our socks, but I don't have the heart to put them out.

Ever heard an alpaca cry? I guess weeping alpacas are good company for me these days, but for the record, I'm not depressed. I'm not depressed. I'm not depressed. Even if we sold the house and everything in it, we still wouldn't make enough to go home.

What if we're actually stuck here?

Weeping Alpacas will be the name of my band in the next life.

I'm not depressed.

Goodnight Star

LOST AND FOUND, SATURDAY EDITION

LOST: Cora Bell's teeth are missing. "If you have information in regard to who stole my teeth, there's a reward. If you don't have information, don't tell me I've lost my teeth; I'm aware and so is Jesus, so you can keep your two cents and your whistle to yourself."

Editor's Note:

By "reward," Bell means pie. Please do not put yourself out looking for teeth thinking there will be a cash reward. There will be pie.

2

Save Your Casserole

From: Abbey Solvang <abbeyroadyogi@omwardbound.org>
To: Sid Solvang <brooklyncalling@zoomail.com>
Date: April 13, 2002

Nobody's heard from you. Why has nobody heard from you? I tried to call, but you never answer your phone. I even asked that narc-balled partner of yours, and he said you're not returning his emails. Don't make me come to Kansas looking for you.

Should I be worried?

From: Sid Solvang <brooklyncalling@zoomail.com>
To: Abbey Solvang <abbeyroadyogi@omwardbound.org>

All's well on the prairie. We've just had our hands full digging through old barns. I think Scarlet's father was a bit of a hoarder.

The novelty of bells is fading, so don't worry, I have no intention of staying in the little house on the prairie any longer than it takes to get back on our feet. They don't even have Manischewitz here! I just ordered a year's worth of Manischewitz wine because otherwise I have to drive an hour for it. I'm not driving an hour for 11 percent alcohol, not even for dad's Yizkor.

Scarlet discovered the local paper did a story on us before we arrived. I mailed it to you.

It's the strangest paper I've ever seen. Not exactly the *New York Times*. *The Goodnight Star* looks like any other old newspaper, all sober Courier under a waving black French Gothic banner, but it's more of a community newsletter obsessed with anonymity and mixing metaphors to a degree of comedy. Most of the paper is open letters written by residents, "a truly democratic press representing the people." The strangest thing is they keep the editor anonymous.

It's disorienting to be in a place with so much space. I don't think I ever noticed that you always seem to be in someone's way back home.

I miss it.

I'm hoping we uncover some Kansas City Wonder Motor buried under all that scrap metal in those old barns so we can sell it and come home.

WHO'S WHO AND WHAT'S WHAT, MARCH 26

Last month you may have noticed the obituary of one of Goodnight's most mysterious residents, Travis "Pop" Bannister. His historic home, the oldest Victorian on Northwind Road, has been sitting empty since his controversial death. Several of his daughters have come and gone looking after the alpacas, but according to his oldest daughter, Lynn "Skeeter" Bannister, the estate has been in limbo since, of course, being of pure Goodnightian descent, Pop did not believe in lawyers, so his last will and testament could not be found.

Until now.

An eccentric recluse, Pop Bannister wrote his final wishes first in the nearly dead Latin language, and second, he converted the letters to the quite dead ancient Anglo-Saxon or West Saxon script, circa AD 1066.

According to the Bannister family, it took some doing to find a translator willing to translate both, first transliterating the letters from ancient Anglo-Saxon—or as Skeeter referred to it, "hobbit shorthand"—and then from Latin, but finally they found Lainie Hummingbird, who minored in Latin at the University of Kansas.

"It sure seems like Daddy was trying to hide something, but who knows what was going on under that Greek fishing hat?" Skeeter said. "Everybody knows he hasn't been right for years, so we just let him keep to himself, hoarding his alpacas and rewriting his will every time one of us looked at him wrong."

Hummingbird confirmed the family's suspicion that Pop did not know Latin nor Anglo-Saxon and instead pieced the words together using a Latin dictionary and an internet website for dead-language enthusiasts, so she had her work cut out for her.

"It's been a long time coming, and hopefully the family will be able to find some closure from this," Hummingbird said. "Truth be told, after spending so much time in his words, Pop Bannister is more of a mystery than ever."

Now that his will has been translated, the big news is that Goodnight has new blood for the first time in well over a decade.

Named sole heir to the estate, the youngest Bannister, Scarlet, will return from New York to settle the estate along with her husband, Sidney Solvang, and their daughter, Harlem, 14.

Scarlet left for culinary school 20 years ago and hasn't been back since. No word yet on how long they will be here, but the Goodnight Planning Committee is on standby, ready to update the population sign should they decide to stay.

The chairwoman of the committee, Tara Rollins, said, "We've lost so many families over the years as young folks can't find work, and we're all worried sick after last month's layoffs at Goodnight American, so we're tickled pink that one of our own's come home after all this time. We're crossing our fingers that maybe they'll stay and breathe some life back into this dust belt."

LAST WILL AND TESTAMENT OF TRAVIS WILSON BANNISTER

Subtitle: This Is My Cornucopia of Bodies' Faults [*sic*]

Translator's note by Lainie Hummingbird:

The following is a translation of the last will and testament of Travis "Pop" Bannister. It should be noted Mr. Bannister did not actually know Latin. Also of note is that I studied Latin because I am a botanist, so my knowledge is limited. I was not chosen for my skill nor experience, but because I was the only one willing to take the job. Below are the rather rough results.

I, the relevant dead, Travis Wilson Bannister, being incited of sound mind, soul, and teeth, sounder than anyone in this godforsaken door of lies, yield hereby bequeath my beloved empire of alpaca, my mother's Royal Worcester china, and the Heaven weather of my estate, including the door on Northwind Road and my 17 acres of influence on Goodnight Lake, to my minimum daughter, Scarlet Anne Bannister Solvang. This forgives a much veteran debt only she keeps. Moreover, I don't have the plenty, but I'll be under the world if even alone of my alpacas or Worcester gravy boats die in the kitchens of my ungrateful seed who insist I am annihilating of natural causes.

There is nothing natural about what is episode in Goodnight, Kansas. When you follow the map I've ordained, you'll find the veritable treasury of [corpora] and keep the truth. If you keep the truth, you'll keep what to cause about it.

**It's the opinion of this translator that use of the Latin word "corpora" in this context was not intended to mean a treasury of literal bodies as a "thesaurus of corpora" could be interpreted. That's why rather than translate "corpora" I've left it in the Latin form, so as not to create a stir over what's probably a metaphor. Bannister appears to imply there's a large box, storehouse, or possibly a body of evidence to be found, not "multiple bodies" to be found as the term might suggest in a literal translation.*

In the last paragraph of the will, the most difficult to translate, it appears Mr. Bannister is asking if his body is found:

Toast it and scatter the spent love in the Moses River, where I was baptized at Harper's Crossing. Do not put me anywhere near Goodnight Lake, and when you find the [corpora], you'll keep why. If you put me in that lake, I swear on all things church, Jesus and I will be back to infest you. Math on it.

Signed,
Travis Wilson Bannister

As witnessed by alpacas: Atlantis, Bermuda, and Vertigo

Notarized on February 2, 2002 by Nora Tibley Pratt, certified notary public of Bixbin and Pratt Tax and Notary, 28 Emporia Road, Goodnight, Kansas. America

From: Abbey Solvang <abbeyroadyogi@omwardbound.org>
To: Harlem Solvang <torturedsol@zoomail.com>

Your dad sent me the newspaper article about your grandfather. If I'd known how strange he was, I would've insisted on meeting him. All those years your mom was so tight-lipped about her family, I figured they were boring, but I think we could've been great friends. What a weirdo!

From: Harlem Solvang <torturedsol@zoomail.com>
To: Abbey Solvang <abbeyroadyogi@omwardbound.org>

If you think that's weird, you should see his will. Last night I found it in the pantry where Mom hides anything she doesn't want us to find, like her secret stash of gummy bears, her mother's old jewelry, and failed recipes she can't bring herself to throw away. Of course, I was there for the gummy bears, but I found the will stashed in a rusted tin. I hid in the pantry scarfing gummies as I read it, and I was, like, instantly so obsessed with it, I ate all my mom's gummies without realizing it, so now I have to replace them before she notices they're gone!

I don't care what that translator says, I think when Pop said *treasury* he meant *treasure*. Think about it. Dad said the house has been paid off since Truman and Pop sold about a million spools of alpaca wool before he retired, so he must've been, like, kinda rich. Mom said he was so *Depression*, he saved every button he ever met and cut his own hair. Dad said his bank account was almost empty and he paid all his bills in cash. The accountant said all Pop left was a house, some land, and, of course, the last alpacas.

So where did all his money go?

If this *veritable treasury of corpora* turns out to be an actual treasury of treasure, maybe there's enough money that we can afford to come home! I looked up *veritable* in my dictionary, and it says, "being in fact the thing named and not false, unreal, or imaginary."

Veritable means *real*!

But do you think there could really be a body?

I asked Mom about it. She said she wouldn't put anything past Pop and she's in no hurry to find out what he meant. Dad said the Latin word for treasury is *thesaurus*, and we should probably not waste our time looking for something that could turn out to be a book of synonyms.

I don't care if it's a fortune, a body, or a thesaurus—either way, I want to find it. It's not like there's anything better to do in Kansas. But I don't think Pop would've gone to so much trouble over it unless it was worth something. I keep asking myself, if I had a veritable fortune, where would I hide it? I'm gonna start searching the attic in the morning.

From: Abbey Solvang <abbeyroadyogi@omwardbound.org>
To: Harlem Solvang <torturedsol@zoomail.com>

Your dad mentioned the will was all kinds of loony. He said the mailman told him your grandfather once shot a light bulb because he thought there was a hidden camera in it.

I thought *my* family had issues!

And what if the body of evidence is a *body*? Or 28 bodies! I'm less curious if the *treasury* is a treasury and more interested in knowing if the corpora is really a corpora.

We're talking about a man who took a shotgun to a light bulb.

Does it seem suspicious to you that Pop had four daughters but gave everything to your mom and nothing to his other daughters?

And where are these Bannister aunts of yours? I'm surprised you haven't met them yet.

That seems like the veritable mystery to me.

From: Scarlet Bannister Solvang <mystifried@zoomail.com>
To: Skeeter Bannister<highwater@shotmail.com>
CC: Tanya Bannister <holyroller316@prairienet.com>, Jolene Salina Bannister Cole <JC4JC@prairienet.com>

I'm guessing you've heard we're here. I don't know why, but I half expected to find at least one of you waiting for us on Pop's porch when our U-Haul hit the driveway. Then again, I keep expecting to find Pop wandering around in his tool belt, looking for something to fix.

I'm sure we still won't be done unpacking by Sunday, but if you don't mind the boxes, I'd love it if the family would come for Sunday potluck like we used to back in the day?

Feels like half of Kansas is mad at me for leaving, and I can't say I blame you. It was never my intention for my new life to erase my old one; it was just so consuming trying to scrape by, Kansas hardly felt real anymore. I could almost convince myself everything before New York was a story I made up.

Please come. I'll make the most diplomatic casseroles I can dream up between now and Sunday. Come to think of it, never mind a potluck—I'll do everything. I'll cook for you, and you can stay mad at me if you want to, but I'd rather sit across a table arguing than not have you at the table. You can bring the dogs too if you think they can handle the alpacas.

One more thing: Harlem shaved her head in a fit of gender defiance the night before picture day, so she looks like a sulking Hare Krishna. It's grown in a little, but it's still no way to make a first impression on Goodnight. I think she's in for a ride, so don't make it worse by giving her your two cents.

And please don't ask Sid what happened. He's carrying the weight of the world on his shoulders. Go easy on him. You gotta know he must be pretty low if he was willing to leave New York and take up with a bunch of alpacas and bumpkins like us!

From: Skeeter Bannister <highwater@shotmail.com>
To: Scarlet Bannister Solvang <mystifried@zoomail.com>
CC: Tanya Bannister <holyroller316@prairienet.com>, Jolene Salina Bannister Cole <JC4JC@prairienet.com>

Save your casserole, Scarlet.

There's nothing left for the Bannisters in Goodnight, and what little we had left, he gave to you. So yes, we are hell blazed Pop happened to kick his bucket on a day when he was mad at everyone in the family except you. Do you know how many Sundays we put up with conspiracy theories at the dinner table?

You step out the door one day without telling anyone where you're going or why, you don't come back for 20 years, and you're the one who gets everything?

If you ask me, that's when Pop's marbles fell out. He was never the same after you left.

You wanna do the family a favor? Sell the old heap on Northwind and go back to New York. Nobody wants you here. Don't expect to see my casserole at that table. You won't be hearing from me and my casserole.

Goodnight Star

LOST AND FOUND, SATURDAY EDITION

LOST: Mitch Minor's calico goats, Sherwood and Schrödinger, are missing. They were last seen grazing on the south side of his farm. The Minors would like to assure our readers not to worry—these are not Goodnight Lake's so-called Chernobyl goats. These goats are normal.

3

Hold on to Your Teeth

Goodnight Star

SUNDAY EDITION, APRIL 14

Mayday for the May Day

Hold on to your teeth, Kansas. It is with a heart as heavy as May Day gravy that this editor reports sad tidings for our town. After 89 years of flapjacks and Frito pie, Goodnight's oldest eatery, our beloved May Day Diner, may be closing its doors.

This morning, as waitress, Bailey Nation, hung the specials, May Day owner, Curtis Wilkes, hung a "for sale" sign in the iconic windows at the end of Emporia Road.

Between the recession and his wife's health issues, Wilkes said he's ready to retire his apron, ending three generations of breaking bread in the heart of Goodnight.

"Since this last round of layoffs at the factory, we're barely breaking even," Wilkes told the *Star* in an exclusive interview from Stills

County's favorite kitchen and the last locally owned diner. "Every time Goodnight workers take a hit, our business takes a hit."

According to Wilkes, they can keep the diner afloat for another few months, but Mrs. Wilkes's health may not last that long, and there's no one else to take the reins.

"The kids have all moved away, and now that they have families of their own, they can't just pick up and come home. There's not enough money in it to make it worth the trouble. Everybody knows that."

One of the first American diners west of the Mississippi, the May Day was opened by the Wilkes family in 1923, surviving many hardships, but it's fallen into disrepair as Goodnight has fallen on hard times again.

"It's a tragedy, is what it is," said Nation. "This diner survived the Depression, the Dust Bowl, and the Great Route 66 Snub my grandma never shut up about until her dying breath. If the May Day goes down, this town is a ghost town, end of story."

Wilkes said he was hoping to find a buyer before the first frost, but he wasn't optimistic.

Despite the failing economy and her failing health, Maggie Wilkes said she is keeping the faith and looking for condos in Arizona.

"I see the boarded-up windows, and I know we're all heartsick about what's been happening to our hometown, but the Lord works in mysterious ways, and sometimes when one door closes on Emporia Road, God opens another one in Scottsdale, Arizona."

To inquire about the May Day, readers are invited to stop by for a cup of coffee.

From: Curtis Wilkes <CW1922@prairienet.com>

To: Aspen Pottstock <aspen@pottstockenterprises.com>

Dear Mr. Pottstock,

Everybody knows you're the one man who could save the May Day. It's not exactly Red Lobster, but it's still standing. I've lost a lot of sleep worrying if we'll ever find someone who can afford to take it off our hands. I'm not out to make a profit; I know what it's worth. I'm just hoping to save its history.

I don't think anyone could've seen it coming, the hard knocks and tough breaks this town has weathered the last few years. The May Day was my family's pride and joy for decades, but on my watch, it is falling. I never was the cook my father was nor the businessman my uncles were, but I'm the last Wilkes left, and the burden falls on me to save its legacy.

When the Wilkes brothers built this diner, they laid every brick with their own hands. When the tire factory came, the diner thrived. When the Depression swept through Stills County, the May Day lowered prices. We fed the richest mayors and the poorest farmers. We served waffles to President Eisenhower, and we served cherry pie to children counting pennies on our counters.

We've given everything to keep it going, but the time has come to pass it on. I pray your generation has the guts and humility it has taken to endure the ever-changing tides.

Curtis Wilkes

From: Aspen Pottstock <aspen@pottstockenterprises.com>
To: Curtis Wilkes <CW1922@prairienet.com>

Dear Mr. Wilkes,

I don't have to tell you there's no money in the May Day. Diners are dead. If this town doesn't want to be a ghost town, it has to reimagine the future. I've looked at the numbers you sent, and I don't know how you've stayed in business this long.

There's no reason you should be paying your staff a penny over minimum wage. I don't intend to run a charity.

You want my advice? I'd level that heap and set up a franchise. Taco Bell seems like an obvious choice—or Burger King. It's no secret that the only thing keeping this town alive is the Goodnight American Tire Company. That's your customer: workers on the run. Diners are slow. Lunch breaks are shorter all the time. If Goodnight wants to survive in this new century, we have to stop functioning as a truck stop and answer the needs of the market. I made my fortune on need. I've stayed here only because my family was among the first to settle this town, but Goodnight needs to join the 21st century.

You're hanging on to a dinosaur, and you're overpaying that dinosaur by a long shot. I'm not in the market for a dinosaur. Nobody in their right mind would buy the May Day.

Aspen Pottstock

Handwritten letter found in the May Day mailbox

Dear Mr. Wilkes,

I read in the paper you're looking to sell the May Day. I would like to buy it, but I'm a little short. I was wondering if we could arrange some kind of layaway plan or rent to buy? I'll treat the May Day like the church it is. Nobody loves that place like I do.

Here's the deal: you can't sell the diner to Aspen Pottstock. Everybody knows he'll knock it down, and Bailey says he's gonna put up a Burger King. The world does not need another Burger King, but there's only one May Day Diner.

I will find the money to buy it myself even if it means I've gotta drop out of John Brown Middle School and go to work in the fields to pay for it.

Disco Kennedy

Handwritten letter mailed to Disco Kennedy

Disco,

Nice try. Everybody knows the only reason you hang around the May Day is because your mama won't let you listen to any country music at home, so you just loaf around begging for jukebox quarters all night in my diner.

I would've chased you out with my kitchen broom years ago, but Bailey likes having you around, and I'm not about to get on Bailey's bad side.

You wanna buy the May Day, then it's all yours, but you gotta pay full price. CASH.

Mr. Curtis Wilkes

Letter last seen in a bottle of root beer drifting down the Moses River

Dear Uncle Casey,

Good news! Old Curtis Wilkes says he'll sell me the May Day!

All I gotta do now is come up with the money.

I heard you can make a killing cutting grass during allergy season. I just have to find a lawn mower. Until then, Melba Dearborn said she could use some help weeding her famous heirlooms since she's revving to defend her tomato title at the America Festival.

The way I see it, the May Day is the eighth wonder of the world. Bailey would say it's her biscuits, but maybe it's just nice to have one place on this earth where nothing ever changes. Or maybe it's because there's enough Hank Williams in that jukebox to save your soul. I've spent all my winters with my forehead pressed against the glass of that old Wurlitzer, spellbound from the moment that diamond stylus falls into the rhythmic orbit of vinyl. It rides the grooves like old tires on a gravel road, and behind that static, captured in that crackling grit of vinyl, the drunk-angel voices of George, Loretta, Hank, and Tammy.

The whole world is in that May Day jukebox.

So what if you can see the China wall from space? I'm pretty sure angels watch the May Day from Heaven just to see what Tyler's blue-light special will be or to hear Bailey's what-for.

Mama worked so many nights, I would've spent my whole life alone if it weren't for that place. Last week she applied at the tire factory again, and she swears they're gonna hire her this time. She seems to think that would make us rich, but I'll take my chances with the weeds.

I'll save the May Day, or I'll die of hay fever and chigger bites trying!

From: Honey Bee Kennedy <RevelationSevenfold@prairienet.com>
To: Melba Deerborn <MelbaMayDeerborn@prairienet.com>

Oh, Melba,

Look out your kitchen window! What do you see?

You're looking at the window of Laundry Operations Assistant #4 at none other than Goodnight American Tire Company! Nine years of applications, and I finally wore them down. It didn't hurt that Assistant #2 and Assistant #3 unexpectedly retired early and their supervisor's out on medical leave.

My application was actually for the cafeteria, but the cafeteria had all the help they needed, so they asked if I knew anything about laundry. Of course, I wowed them with my knowledge of laundry and biblical work ethic.

I told them I didn't even know they had a laundry room! They said tire making is complicated and makes a lot of tire dust, so they handle the washing. "It's a bonus we provide because we care," the boss said. "This way they don't have to take tire dust home to their wives."

All I know is finally I can give up two of my three jobs, and with nights open, I can take my nursing classes again. The best part is for the first time, we're gonna have health insurance! After years of brimstone and ramen noodles, maybe the Lord has finally forgiven me and my luck is headed north. This has got Jesus written all over it because you know GATC lays folks off left and right, but somehow they're short in the laundry room. Praise God!

So, Melba, now that I'll be at the factory all day, at school most nights, and cleaning houses in between, I'm gonna need your eyes on Disco. You know what I'm dealing with.

I got a call from Curtis Wilkes. He found her sleeping behind the jukebox at the May Day again. He said she stands around begging for quarters for the Wurlitzer, which wouldn't be such a problem if she didn't insist on singing. He blamed her for scaring the customers away.

And the principal called again. He said Disco's been skipping algebra to sing drinking music in the girls' room. When he confronted her, she said she was there for the acoustics. I don't know what that means, but what I do know is high school is right around the corner, and I've got to keep her on the sunny side so she don't end up eating brimstone and ramen noodles.

All I'm asking is for you to keep your ears open for trouble. She's fortunate that boys seem to hate her. That's helpful, but you know that never stopped trouble.

From: Melba Deerborn <MelbaMayDeerborn@prairienet.com>
To: Honey Bee Kennedy <RevelationSevenfold@prairienet.com>

As your prayer partner, I feel it is my charge to remind you, sometimes we feel guilty because we *are* guilty, and maybe you got what was coming to you.

I wouldn't give the Savior all the credit on this one anyhow. If you've seen them laundry workers, you know they're old and brittle as Leavenworth.

Disco wasn't half bad at weeding at the end of the day. She's got a gentler touch than you'd expect from that mouth of hers. Anytime you wanna send her over, I'll put them idle hands to work in my garden. If her cockamamie plan to buy the May Day keeps her busy after school, that'll solve half your problems right there.

Speaking of tomatoes, I've got some Carolina Golds waiting for you, and PS, I'm telling you right now, that okra recipe Cheryl's passing around is a blasphemous waste of a good skillet.

From: Reverend Arlo Foster <humbleservant@goodshepherd.com>
To: Honey Bee Kennedy <RevelationSevenfold@prairienet.com>

I didn't see you in church this morning, and that's so unlike you, I wanted to make sure your sciatica wasn't acting up again. I tried to call, but it seems there's something wrong with your answering machine.

From: Honey Bee Kennedy <RevelationSevenfold@prairienet.com>
To: Reverend Arlo Foster <humbleservant@goodshepherd.com>

I'll tell you what's wrong with my answering machine: I threw it out the window is what's wrong with it. Of course, since we live in a ranch, a one-story tumble wouldn't have been enough to shut the thing up, so I took a hammer to it, and to answer your question, no, there's nothing wrong with my answering machine now that I don't have to listen to it anymore. I got tired of coming home to messages from the school about Disco, so I took care of it.

And yes, my sciatica is acting up, thank you for asking, but that is not why I didn't make it to church this morning. You got any other questions for me?

From: Reverend Arlo Foster <humbleservant@goodshepherd.com>
To: Honey Bee Kennedy <RevelationSevenfold@prairienet.com>

Sister Honey Bee, why does the school keep calling about Disco?

From: Honey Bee Kennedy <RevelationSevenfold@prairienet.com>
To: Reverend Arlo Foster <humbleservant@goodshepherd.com>

Since you're asking, I'll tell you.

You know I've always suspected that my Disco was born on the peculiar side, but it was a vague sort of peculiar. I figured in a town where there was more to talk about, nobody would notice. It seems this town has noticed.

The principal called to declare the girl a nonconformist on account of her mouth again, and she overheard me praying over it. I guess I got a little carried away with the Holy Spirit. You know how it is. So Disco asked, "What's wrong with me?"

I told her, "Principal says you're a nonconformist."

She asked me what a nonconformist was, so I told her, "It means you're different and you don't care."

She got a little wobble to her voice, and she said, "I can't help it."

I said, "I know. That's why I'm praying."

Arlo, that child gets more peculiar by the day. I've tried every trick in *Bible Companion for Juvenile Trouble of the Feminine Variety*, but it's been downhill ever since Disco found that blue guitar by the side of the road.

Goodnight Star

LOST AND FOUND, WEDNESDAY EDITION

FOUND: Mitch Minor's missing goats, Sherwood and Schrödinger, turned up late Tuesday. Both goats were unharmed. There appears to be no foul play, except between goats because Sherwood is in a family way. The litter is due next month, and the Minors have offered to donate them to the local 4-H kids who lost their goats to what some locals are now calling the Goodnight lake flu.

Editor's Note:

The *Star* received many letters asking what's going on around the lake. Symptoms of this so-called lake flu first swept through the eastern edge of Goodnight five years ago, claiming the lives of scores of livestock from farms that bordered the lake, but until the death of a local farmer last month, none of the symptoms reported among humans had been deadly.

Goodnight Council Member Ford Hollis said the council is working with law enforcement to organize an oversight committee to investigate the death of the farmer.

"This abstract illness is less abstract since the death toll has spread from livestock to farmers, and our citizens deserve to know the truth," Hollis said, but according to Mayor Carol Shultz, Goodnight can't afford a comprehensive inquiry.

"It will take more chili feeds than this town has the beans for," Shultz said. "We don't have the resources for a proper investigation, but we'll do the best we can."

4

Victorians of Northwind Road

Goodnight Star

LETTERS FROM GOODNIGHTERS, THURSDAY EDITION

Dear Goodnight and all relevant souls,

When I was growing up, men held doors, women were women, and to my knowledge, dogs were not allowed in stores. Children did not speak out of turn unless they were asking for it, and in my day, nobody was asking for it.

Nowadays up is down, down is up, and news is dishwater.

Ever wonder if our trusted news purveyor has been taken over by America-hating hippies printing this paper with snake oil for ink? I wonder every morning as I scan the headlines and think, *What's this world coming to?*

What is Goodnight, Kansas, coming to?

I'm referring to the implication there's something wrong with Goodnight Lake, the very watershed our most auspicious neighbor, Goodnight American Tire Company, relies on. The last thing this town needs is to scare it away by spreading the doomsday gossip of tree huggers.

You can't blame a lake for being a lake. Bacterial imbalances come and go. That's nature. Folks around the lake know it's blue-green algae season. The muck runs rampant this time of year, especially when the water's low and the temperature's high. That algae will get you sick every time, and it's been known to take out a loose dog. Nobody blames a lake for that!

Farmers can't be sloppy—letting livestock wander like common vagrants, tracking God knows what into historic houses. It's no surprise he got sick, not to mention that is no way to treat a Victorian! We've all known Pop Bannister has been sloppy since third grade when he left the 4-H gate open and let all the Guernseys out!

For this newspaper to suggest accountability lies in the water and not the citizen calls into question the judgment of this editor and our tradition of keeping editors secret, as it removes all accountability. They can write anything and not be shamed by neighbors. I think we can all agree shame and judgment are more powerful than gravity when it comes to holding a town together.

If it sounds like I'm suggesting a witch hunt, it's because I am. We need to expose the godless heathen behind this ink curtain and stop this spin cycle of liberal malarkey before it scares off the tire factory that brought a thousand jobs to this fledgling town, because it's the only thing standing between Goodnight and dust.

Cordially,

Virginia Easton of Northwind Road

From: Harlem Solvang <torturedsol@zoomail.com>
To: Abbey Solvang <abbeyroadyogi@omwardbound.org>

I can't start school until my records transfer, so I spent the whole day choking on mothballs, searching that creepy attic for Pop's treasure only to find nothing but macramé owls, broken lamps, and a thousand mason jars full of buttons and thimbles.

Meanwhile, that creepy neighbor is at it again. She's this, like, hillbilly Cruella de Vil whose ancestors probably invented racism and brunch.

By the way, I asked Mom about her sisters, and I think it almost killed her.

Her eyes aged a hundred years right in front of me, and she said there are some questions better left unasked and why waste a question mark on ancient history when I could ask a real question, like how do you bake Russian rye bread?

I'm no closer to Pop's treasure, but we have enough Russian rye bread for the whole town. How many loaves of bread would we have to sell to afford to come home?

From: Abbey Solvang <abbeyroadyogi@omwardbound.org>
To: Harlem Solvang <torturedsol@zoomail.com>

That would take a lot of bread. You might have better luck treasure hunting.

Is your dad having any luck finding a job?

From: Sid Solvang <brooklyncalling@zoomail.com>
To: Jules Jamison <livingthedream73@zoomail.com>

Jules,

I tried to call you several times, but your mailbox is full.

It's been barely three weeks since we pulled into Goodnight, and I'll put it this way, nobody's bringing biscuits anymore. One of our neighbors watches us all the time. It seems like every time we leave the house, she just happens to be standing on her porch, twisting a string of pearls around her finger. Some of the locals have taken to calling us *the outsiders.*

Finding a job isn't going any better. I know I said I was done cooking forever, but what in the world am I qualified to do outside a kitchen? I went to the unemployment office, and there were only two companies hiring in the whole town. One was construction, but they said not to bother applying unless I had experience or was 20 years younger than I look! The other was working the register at a discount store for less than $5 an hour. When I mentioned to the social worker that I was a chef, she suggested I put in an application at the Bonanza Buffet out on the edge of town. They aren't hiring, but she said, "Don't worry, line cook jobs open up every time someone catches the tummy rumbles at the tuna bar."

If you happen to come across any opportunities in New York, I wouldn't rule anything out. It's gotta be better to be a busboy in Brooklyn than a chef at the Bonanza Buffet.

If I weren't a father, I'd just pick some bad island, sell everything, and disappear, but Harlem needs braces, and we spent her college fund on the one-way U-Haul that brought us here.

I need a job.

From: Jules Jamison <livingthedream73@zoomail.com>
To: Sid Solvang <brooklyncalling@zoomail.com>

I put the feelers out, and—how should I say this—you may have to give it some time. No one wants to hire the captain of the *Titanic* to run their boat, not even as a sous-chef. It's gonna take a minute for

New York to forget what you did to your grandfather's deli. Have you considered Atlantic City? I hear there's redemption to be found there.

But things are looking up for molecular gastronomy. Remember that kid you mentored, Oliver Dean? Word on the street is he's been building on your technique and getting some attention for it. This could be good for you. Cheers!

JOURNAL ENTRY, SID SOLVANG

I can't sleep.

Jules says New York is so down on me, he can't even find me a job as a sous-chef. He suggested I try Atlantic City. JERSEY! I might as well stay in Kansas. Do I have to go back to washing dishes? I got a late enough start as it is; I can't start over again.

Meanwhile, adorable Cosby-sweatered Oliver Dean is making a name for himself with my old knives. I should be proud. I taught him everything. In those days I was so sure of myself, I liked having someone to show off for. He seemed like such an irrelevant little Gumby following me around, asking all his questions. He's not a bad kid. A decent person would be happy for him. Maybe I'm happy for him and I just don't know it.

Scarlet says I'm grieving. She put me to work in Pop's greenhouse to get my grief out of her grief's way. She said no room is big enough for that much sadness, so I took the greenhouse, and she hides in the kitchen, compulsively baking bread.

I'll save my grief for New York. There's no time to fall apart.

I've gotta find a way back to Brooklyn. My protégé is taking over, and the only place to get a job in this atomic nowhere is a tire factory. What's a chef going to do in a tire factory?

From: Harlem Solvang <torturedsol@zoomail.com>
To: Abbey Solvang <abbeyroadyogi@omwardbound.org>

You know any Latin? Mom made me clean out Pop's *TV Guide* collection, and I found a diary that belonged to him. Unfortunately, the entire thing is written in that same dead-elf English he wrote his will in. I transcribed the first line using an online alphabet, but there's no question it translates to Latin. If Pop went to this much trouble to keep people from reading it, then I'm sure there must be something in it about how to find his veritable treasure!

By the way, please don't tell my parents about this. Mom caught me reading Pop's diary, and she freaked. She was like, "I forbid you from going through any of your grandfather's things. Don't touch anything!"

She actually yelled at me, and you know she never yells except when she's cooking. So now my search is on the down-low. I'm not really in the mood to learn Latin, so I was hoping you might know it, or maybe you know someone who knows it? What language did you take?

From: Abbey Solvang <abbeyroadyogi@omwardbound.org>
To: Harlem Solvang <torturedsol@zoomail.com>

I took Haitian Creole. It's been very practical and lucrative, thanks for asking.

Learning a dead language seems like a lot of trouble for something that may not be exactly…veritable. I'm worried you're spinning your wheels. Didn't your mom say the whole town thought Pop was off his rocker? Maybe you shouldn't put all your eggs in that basket.

From: Harlem Solvang <torturedsol@zoomail.com>
To: Abbey Solvang <abbeyroadyogi@omwardbound.org>

It's the only basket I've got! I have to find a way home.

Anyway, it's too late to talk me out of it. I found a Latin dictionary in the barn, and I've already translated eleven words:

To the fortunate keeper who revivals this book, this is truth's beginning.

Unfortunately, the truth will have to wait because I start school tomorrow.

Mom says if you say it's okay and if I keep up my straight As, I can come visit you in Brooklyn, but we can't afford it until Christmas break. That's how poor we are! Maybe I could just move in with you. I swear I'll do your dishes, and I'll never complain about your weird macrobiotic mushroom steaks.

I'm not sure my parents would even notice if I left. Mom hides in the kitchen baking all day, and Dad just keeps sighing out windows like he's waiting for something.

Did I mention there are cows everywhere in this town? COWS! And don't even get me started on the alpacas. Dad is like, "It could be worse. At least they're not llamas."

How could that possibly be worse?

From: Abbey Solvang <abbeyroadyogi@omwardbound.org>
To: Harlem Solvang <torturedsol@zoomail.com>

Llamas spit on people. They are like fat alpacas with really bad PMS.

Do me a favor, and don't be so judgy with your parents. It was really hard for them in New York, and it was even harder for them to leave, but I think it was sort of killing your dad, having to walk by the deli every day after what happened.

Don't tell him, but someone's taking over the old building. It's been empty since you guys left, and everyone's been speculating over what will replace Sol's. They've got one of those construction walls around it that's all white with little pink italics that say, *It's coming!*

I don't know what pink italic nightmare is coming, but I'm glad your dad isn't here to see it. Every time I walk by, they've torn down another piece of Sol's. The dumpster in the alley is full of Dad's linoleum tiles and Grandpa's broken barstools. Did you know he built those? And I remember when Dad replaced the floors. We laid the tile ourselves because he was too cheap to hire someone even though they had more business than they knew what to do with in those days.

Your dad's a visionary. I'm so sorry for what happened. This is so root chakra, I feel the universe screaming, *Shut up before you manifest another parking ticket on your bike!*

Did you know a bicycle can get a parking ticket? That's what happens when I skip yoga. I'd better shut up and burn some white sage before I talk myself back to Prozac.

Good luck on your first day of school…

JOURNAL ENTRY, SID SOLVANG

Finally spoke to Jules. He says they turned my grandfather's deli into a cupcake shop. Not a shop, a shoppe. They charge you for the extra consonants. Jules says they're not even real cupcakes. They sell cupcake bites, whatever that means. Miniature cupcakes! They're half the size and twice the price of real cupcakes.

I heard it's doing really well.

You spend your whole life in a place, building something, thinking you mean something to the place that means something to you, and then one day you drop off the face of the earth, and the world just opens a cupcake shoppe and keeps going. Without you.

I found an unfinished birdhouse in the greenhouse and finished it. It might be the first tangible thing I've ever built. It felt so good to create something that didn't break by the weight of my hands, I went out and bought another birdhouse kit so I could build one from scratch.

Scarlet's sisters are still giving us the cold shoulder. Six cold shoulders, to be exact. I can't say I mind. I don't want to answer questions, but I can tell Scarlet's taking it hard.

From: Scarlet Bannister Solvang <mystifried@zoomail.com>
To: Skeeter Bannister<highwater@shotmail.com>
CC: Tanya Bannister <holyroller316@prairienet.com>, Jolene Salina Bannister Cole <JC4JC@prairienet.com>

I just put a fried Kansas caviar casserole in the oven, and I'm hoping y'all will drop in tonight for dinner? It's straight out of Mama's recipe box. Not the fancy company one—the good one. Harlem set the table and managed to run all the alpacas out of the house.

Will you come?

Goodnight Star

LOST AND FOUND, MONDAY EDITION

FOUND: Cora Bell found her teeth and would like to acknowledge "all the good souls who tried to help me find my teeth again. Next time I'll check the tomatoes before I send a search party across kingdom come."

There is still no sign of her missing wind chimes, which were the seventh set of chimes reported missing this year. If you have information on the whereabouts of these bells or Goodnight's rash of missing garden ornaments, GPD invites you to drop by the station for a chat.

5

Veritable

INCIDENT REPORT, JOHN BROWN MIDDLE SCHOOL, APRIL 22, 2002

Reported by: Kathleen Reno, English teacher and aspiring novelist

Bear with me, as this is the first time I've ever written an incident report. It's not that there aren't incidents, but even the boldest of crows and humblest of ceiling tiles know, come black eyes or broken bones, Kansans don't snitch. So I've never had the occasion to write one. That's not to say I'm blaming the foreigner among us.

Even though this Harlem has come to Kansas as bald as an American bullet, she's only the second strangest thing the eighth grade's seen, thanks to Disco Kennedy. I believe it would be prudent to keep these misanthropes as far away from each as is possible in a town as small as ours, and smaller all the time. But that is neither here nor there.

Let me set the scene:

As I hope you know, contrary to our namesake, John Brown Middle School is no place for rebels. When I invited homeroom to welcome a half-bald 14-year-old in combat boots and a torn T-shirt that said, *I was Iggy Pop in my last life*, I knew it wouldn't go well for the new girl.

It started when Summer Pottstock whisper-yelled, "Mrs. Reno, she has AIDS." And then, pointing to Harlem, she shrieked, "Look at her!"

I hushed her, but in the interest of public safety, I asked, "You don't, do you?"

No one could blame me for being concerned, but I realize now it was the wrong thing to say because the class nearly tore the seams out of the sky, they laughed so hard, which, much to our misfortune, caught the attention of the otherwise vaguely present Disco Kennedy.

Ordinarily Disco keeps to herself to avoid being rubber cemented to her desk again. I make a point of stationing her seat by a window, not just to prevent her talking spells, but, as a Christian, to give the poor child something to dream for, hoping she won't notice the judgment and contempt around her.

But back to Harlem Solvang.

Here are my observations of the outsider in question, based on her first week:

Harlem is more opinionated than a 14-year-old has any business being, but unlike your typical opinionator, such as Disco, she is not brave. While her convictions may be steel on paper, her heart is a humble reservoir of mashed potatoes that can't hold up to gravy, much less a rabid cacophony of eighth grade conformity. This is unfortunate because while the child can't conform, she can't speak up either.

But Disco Kennedy can. And she did.

When she saw the way the class was treating the new girl, Disco yelled loudly enough for all of Emporia Road to hear (brace yourselves, Christians): "Fuck you, you fucks! Mind your fucking manners!"

I sent Disco to the principal's office, but not before Harlem let out a terrible fit of laughter. That laughing fit couldn't be stopped, so I sent her packing for the principal too.

If Disco had a certain kind of upbringing or if her intelligence had been recognized earlier, she could've been a candidate for the gifted program. I suspect she was such a disruption that nobody thought to test her, nor take her under a wing that might've kept her on track. I hope we don't make the same mistake with Harlem. With high school looming, there's no time to lose.

Like Disco, Harlem wields an unusual intelligence that must be guided. Unlike Disco, Harlem shows promise academically. Her numbers are the highest in the class. Her transfer file from New York is impressive, and in the short time I've observed her, she learns with a furious curiosity that needs only wholesome direction. Despite her unorthodox appearance, Harlem seems quite capable of diplomacy. That's why I'm recommending her for the gifted track.

In the meantime, to my thinking, it would serve us all to keep these girls a world apart.

From: Abbey Solvang <abbeyroadyogi@omwardbound.org>
To: Harlem Solvang <torturedsol@zoomail.com>

Where have you been? You never told me how your first day went.

Was it *that* good or *that* bad? Tell me everything.

From: Harlem Solvang <torturedsol@zoomail.com>
To: Abbey Solvang <abbeyroadyogi@omwardbound.org>

My first day of school was fine. Nothing to report.

The search for Pop's treasure is going nowhere.

I spent hours translating one page of his diary, and all I discovered was a detailed report of every TV show he watched, everything he ate, and everything the alpacas ate in some random week of March 1992. Riveting, and also WHY???

Don't worry, I'm not giving up that easily.

JOURNAL ENTRY, SID SOLVANG

It took less than a week in a new school for Harlem to get sent to the principal's office. To my surprise, the school's solution is to test her for some kind of gifted track. I've never felt right about weeding kids into chutes and ladders, but Scarlet pointed out that given our finances, she'll need all the scholarships she can get if she has any hope of going to a good college.

I've got four years to get a job, make enough to pay off our debts, move back to Brooklyn, and somehow save enough to put a child through college. Scarlet's slowly been selling off Pop's old farm equipment. That will buy us a few more months, but the clock is ticking.

As Scarlet and I sat in the principal's office, I realized we've barely been in the same room since we arrived. While she's busy trying to win her sisters over with casseroles, I'm busy trying to look busy so nobody asks me an apocalypse of a question like, So what's next?

The principal warned us Harlem is falling in with the wrong crowd, but by crowd it seems he meant a little black sheep called Disco whose only crimes appear to be wearing glitter and talking too much. On the way home, Harlem asked if we were going to forbid her from being friends with Disco. I told her I was happy to hear she'd made a friend on the first day.

Scarlet said the only Kennedys she'd heard of belonged to a cultish family of homeschoolers who ran a Jesus-rode-a-dinosaur church on the edge of town. She said there's no chance a girl like Disco came from a farm like that, so maybe she's from somewhere else.

"Like another planet?" Harlem asked.

"Like Missouri," said Scarlet. "That might explain why she doesn't have any friends."

I told Harlem to bring Disco by the house sometime so we can find out what planet she came from, but Scarlet said maybe we don't want to know.

I'm not really up for company anyway.

Note passed from Disco, fourth period, John Brown Middle School, Wednesday

Harlem.

There are two things you should know before you decide if we're gonna be friends.

First, to be seen with me is social doom. Everyone in this town thinks I'm the plague, so if we're friends, they'll probably think you're contaminated. Kids will hate you or pretend they can't hear you when you talk, even when you look them straight in the eye. Grown-ups will think you're a bad person for no reason at all, and folks may run away when they see you coming.

The second thing is you can never ask me why.

I should've warned you before. I guess I forgot my

plague when we met. It seemed like you needed a friend, and I forgot who I was for a minute. I'll understand if you don't talk to me anymore, but if you would like the plague, I just got new guitar strings, which I did NOT steal, like my mama says, and I'm headed to the river after school. You know about the Moses River?

The Plague

Note passed from Harlem to Disco after fifth period

Dear Plague,

You can't scare me. Maybe I've got a plague of my own.

Did I mention my mom, like, never leaves the kitchen? And my dad is, like, phobic of kitchens. He's a chef, but if you ask him to make even a sandwich, he looks suicidal.

This morning my mom told him if he didn't start helping with dinner, she'd make him sleep in the barn. It was so pitiful. He practically crawled into the kitchen, and I'm pretty sure I heard him talking to a baguette.

You probably heard the rumor that we have so many alpacas running through our house, it's like we live in a barn. Well, it's a true story. Welcome to *my* plague!

I've got a plan to get us back to New York, but it's not going well so far.

After school I'm supposed to take some special test, but I can meet you at the Moses when I'm done, and I'll tell you about my secret plan. See you at the river.

Note passed from Disco to Harlem after school

Don't go to Harper's Crossing. Everybody goes there to get baptized, and you never know when they're gonna turn up with a bus full of church. They'll try to save you.

Also Jackson Harper owns it, and if he sees anyone trespassing who's not with a church, he won't hesitate to shoot. He always misses, but don't take your chances. Meet me north of the crossing. Nobody'll try to save you or kill you.

I live just up the street from there, and my mama's working late, so if you wanna walk over to my house for dinner, we can raid the pantry.

From: Honey Bee Kennedy <RevelationSevenfold@prairienet.com>
To: Melba Deerborn <Melba May Deerborn@prairienet.com>

I swear to John the Baptist, sometimes it seems like prayers get answered backward.

I prayed for a miracle, and do you know what God sent? I came home from work, and what do you think I found in my pantry, eating my Cracker Jacks? I'll give you a hint: it wasn't a raccoon, and it wasn't the mayor, and it wasn't no angel come to take away my troubles. No, sir.

There was a teenager who might've supposed to been a girl in a crew cut, combat boots, and a torn men's undershirt with the words *I AM DEATH* written in what looked like blood.

I told Disco, "That girl is bad news."

And do you know what Disco said?

"She ain't the bad news—*I* am."

Jesus have mercy.

So, Melba, meet me in the tomatoes with your Bible and your bourbon. Bring the good stuff, not that cheap whiskey you won at bingo the other night.

PS: Can you bring your Miracle Whip too? We're all out, and I just don't have it in me to go the store after the day I've had. By the way, you were right about the okra. That is the last time I try a recipe out of the *Ladies' Home Journal*.

Letter last seen drifting down the river in an empty bottle of Dad's Root Beer

Dear Uncle Casey,

It's lucky for me that Goodnighters never snitch because my latest battle is with Summer.

Maybe you've heard of her dad, Aspen Pottstock, since he owns our house and half of Emporia Road. Rumor has it Curtis Wilkes begged him to save the May Day and that scrooge laughed in his face, threatening to knock it down and replace it with a Burger King.

Summer is worse.

Summer Pottstock's got the face of a Cabbage Patch Kid, the voice of pepper spray, and her own fleet of henchmen in matching Banana Republic shirts.

I was hiding in a pink stall at John Brown, writing a song, when I heard Summer's henchmen henching at the new girl, Harlem. They were asking about her grandaddy's farm and her nose, which is not nearly as big as they seem to think it is. Even with barely any hair, Harlem is probably the prettiest thing John Brown's ever seen. Maybe that's why Summer hates her.

Next thing I knew, I heard Harlem crying. It sounded like all of New York was crying.

Before I could think it through, I was flying out fist first, leaving Summer with a black eye and a broken nail, but don't you know, her French manicure didn't budge.

Everybody knows rich girls can't fight, and Summer fled with her henchmen behind her.

Harlem stopped crying and smiled. "Disco Kennedy," she said. "I heard about you."

I said, "I heard about *you*."

It seems destiny has timber hitched Harlem to me with a loyalty you could take to war because that hairless wing nut has been following me around ever since.

Maybe I've made a friend in this godforsaken snake pit of a universe.

LOST AND FOUND, WEDNESDAY EDITION

LOST: Another set of chimes has gone missing from Goodnight Road. This set was from the Bells of Paradise collection in the key of "Amazing Grace." The chimes' owner, Jeanne Bloomington, warns neighbors, "Keep your eyes on your bells, folks. There is a thief among us."

If you have information on the missing bells, please contact GPD.

6

Everything You Need to Know about Goodnight, Kansas

Note passed from Disco to Harlem after homeroom, wednesday

Now that you've chosen your plague, here's everything you need to know about Goodnight:

1. That girl from the bathroom is Summer Pottstock. She's the meanest and richest girl in Goodnight, strutting down Emporia Road like a girl with a pony. Summer has no pony, but she doesn't need one with a strut like that. Once she decides she doesn't like you, none of the girls will give you the time of day. Her daddy is our landlord. He owns pretty much everything, and everyone hates him and worships him at the same time, just like Summer. The mom used to be a lawyer in Moses, but now she skis. In Colorado.
2. Everyone here is either related to someone who works for Goodnight American Tires, used to work for the factory, or is trying desperately to get a job working for

the factory. Folks act like they're afraid if they so much as look at it wrong, it'll turn into a pillar of salt, and then Goodnight will be left a ghost town like all the others. They play that hand for everything it's worth. I swear anytime someone raises half an eyebrow at GATC, they announce layoffs.

3. Everyone in Goodnight hates Moses. I mean the town of Moses, not the beardy prophet. It's something about the Civil War, which if you know what's good for you, you won't bring up. I swear the city council just stands around Emporia Road waiting for someone to accidentally mention it so they can tell you the history of the founders and why Goodnight is on the right side of history and Moses is a bunch of uptight Confederate tycoons who smell like mothballs and banks and think they're better than everyone else.
4. Everybody writes for the *Goodnight Star*. It's not just because they can't afford to pay real reporters. It's something this town invented called the democratic press. The founders thought it would catch on. It didn't, but that didn't stop them. I think they're still waiting for it to catch on 150 years later! The deal is, if you accidentally figure out who the editor is, whatever you do, don't tell anyone. It's, like, the law that if anyone finds out who the editor is, they have to get a new one, for truth or something. Folks take it, like, Eisenhower serious. Nobody has ever outed an editor, and they go to ridiculous lengths to keep it a secret, so everybody

knows that if someone pulls those covers, they'll be run out of town.

5. If you live in Goodnight the center of the universe is the May Day Diner. The menu hasn't changed in a thousand years, but they've got the best grits God ever put in a skillet.

The trouble is the owner is retiring, so he's been trying to sell it, only nobody wants to buy it except me. That's why I'm taking every odd job I can find: so I can save the May Day.

Now you know almost everything.

THURSDAY EDITION

Open Letter to Goodnight, Kansas

Dear Goodnight,

The May Day has been on the market for 19 days, and it's not looking good for Maggie's health. She can't take another winter in Kansas. Our kids have grown and moved on, so there's no one to run the diner.

If there's anyone who thinks they can save the May Day, stop by for pie, and we'll talk it over. I'm willing to make liberal arrangements, even lease to buy. Come hell or high water, we're moving to Scottsdale, and we're not taking the May Day with us.

Curtis Wilkes, owner of the May Day Diner

From: Harlem Solvang <torturedsol@zoomail.com>

To: Abbey Solvang <abbeyroadyogi@omwardbound.org>

Remember that girl at the bus stop I told you about? The one dropped by a UFO and covered in glitter? Her name is Disco. DISCO! Her real name is like Descopolis or something all Bible, so everybody just calls her *Disco*.

She taught me the Texas two-step in the Wonder Bread parking lot, so I guess I'm a hillbilly now.

I think Disco has some kind of dark past because everyone seems to be afraid of her. People run when they see her, and it seems like she hardly even notices because it happens so much.

We stopped at Food Barn the other day, so she could get the latest *Nashville Digest*. (That really happened.) As we passed the dish soap, these two ladies saw Disco coming up the aisle, and they practically ran away. Grown women!

I feel sorry for Disco, but she'd probably punch me if she knew that. She has this thing she does with her chin that proud people do with their chins. You should see her mother's chin. Her mom works, like, three jobs, so Disco's always alone, except for the Chihuahua rescues, which are blind. BLIND CHIHUAHUAS!

Gotta go. Disco wants to meet at some diner so we can two-step to real music.

In case you're wondering, my mission to find Pop's treasure has stalled. I'm thinking about asking Disco to help, since she's on a mission to buy the May Day and so far she has only managed to save $78.25. If the treasure is worth what I think it is, we can split it down the middle. She can save her diner, and I can come home.

I've gotta find that money. Mom's got her hands full clearing the barns, so she's all edgy and emo, and Dad is as vacant as half the storefronts downtown. He's like a ghost that builds birdhouses. So I guess it's up to me to find a way back to Brooklyn.

JOURNAL ENTRY, SID SOLVANG, FRIDAY

I built a sparrow house today. Scarlet says I have too much time on my hands and need to find a job. I didn't have the heart to tell her I just got rejected for a minimum wage job bagging groceries at Bargain Mart. The manager said they preferred to hire students.

He said, "It's not really a job for a man."

I filled out an application at the Bonanza Buffet, but a cook warned me, "Don't hold your breath. Applications with a Moses address go on top of the stack, Goodnighters on the bottom."

When I asked why, he said, "You know."

He shrugged and went back to the line. I went home and ordered a new birdhouse.

From: Scarlet Bannister Solvang <mystifried@zoomail.com>
To: Jules Jamison <livingthedream73@zoomail.com>

Sid's in a slump. That's a nice word for it. There's a dull ache in his eyes deeper than the Greensburg well. Would you talk to him? He stopped shaving. He wears flip-flops. He compulsively builds birdhouses just so he has an excuse to stare out the window.

We're still waiting for the last shred of our financial dignity to come in the mail. In the meantime, we're selling my dad's junk, but the trucks are rusted, and nobody wants the alpacas. They act like there's something wrong with them.

Please call Sid, and don't tell him I told you to. His confidence is in the gutter, and we don't have room for any more birdhouses.

Letter last seen drifting down the river in an empty bottle of Dad's Root Beer

Dear Uncle Casey,

Turns out Harlem is on a mission to find her grandfather's secret fortune. I never met Pop Bannister, but I noticed him around town, since he always wore a smart hat and tended to have an alpaca on a leash. People said he was strange, so I kept an eye on him—not because I was afraid, but because I figured out when folks around here say somebody's strange, it just means they talk too fast for anyone to keep up.

Like me, Harlem never met her grandfather, and nobody's ever explained why. Unlike me, nobody told Harlem she couldn't ask. She's got three God-fearing, dirt-farming aunties just asking to be asked. Everybody's heard of the Bannister sisters. Tanya's been known to pull up your Wranglers if she sees them slacking, Skeeter threatens to wash your mouth out with soap if she hears you swear, and Jolene's made her name handing out pocket Bibles every Halloween.

I told Harlem she should start with Skeeter, since she has the biggest mouth. Harlem is afraid to knock on a stranger's door, so I promised to go with her.

She said if I help her find Pop's treasure, she'll split it with me. That sounds like a better deal than tearing johnsongrass out of Melba's tomatoes until the end of days. I told her I'm in.

Since I lined up a whole month of odd jobs from South End to Emporia Road, she said she'll help me so I have more time to hunt for the Bannister treasure.

And not a minute too soon. We can't lose another piece of Goodnight. Seems like half the lights are out downtown. Yesterday I saw them boarding up the flower shop, and folks were standing around Emporia Road, crying like it was a funeral.

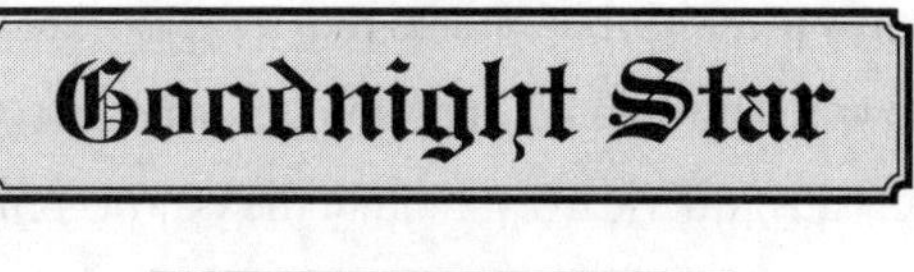

WEEKLY FEATURE, MAY 1

News from Emporia Road

Three months after the latest round of layoffs at the Goodnight American Tire Company, the recession is in full effect, and Emporia Road is feeling the fallout.

Myrtle's Green Thumb and Wonder Antiques have called it quits.

Myrtle Hall closed shop for the last time Friday night, addressing a small gathering that came to commemorate what she called "the end of an era." Her father opened the flower shop and nursery in 1946 when he came home from the war.

"There's a world of truth behind every door that closes on Emporia Road," she told the modest congregation. "I've been working in this shop since I was barely old enough to reach the register. For the first time in my life, I don't know where I'm going Monday morning."

Several council members left their chambers three doors down to attend, including Council Member Ford Hollis, a vocal champion of small businesses and tenants' rights.

"Through every turn this town has taken, we've pulled through, but this recession is something else," Hollis said. "Rents keep going up every year, and profits keep going down. Local retailers are hanging on for dear life."

Retail stores have long struggled to keep up with rents on Emporia Road. The Emporia Road Merchant's Association petitioned the owner of 70 percent of downtown storefronts, Aspen Pottstock, to freeze rents until the economy picks up, but he said rent increases are legal and necessary to keep up with the rising cost of doing business in our economy. "It would be wholly un-American to stand in the way of commerce," he said.

Loss of the historic Emporia Road storefronts will be grieved, but according to Hollis, the community can count its blessings that independently owned family businesses such as the May Day Diner and Red Carpet Video are still standing.

The council will hold a meeting May 3 to discuss downtown revitalization efforts.

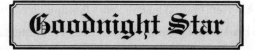

LOST AND FOUND, SATURDAY EDITION

LOST: Another set of chimes has gone missing on Little Church Road from the porch of Dr. Elliot Miles. Two more were stolen from South Church Street and another from White Church Road. If you have information on the missing bells, please contact GPD.

7

Last Night at Bingo

Letter crammed in a bottle of root beer, drifting southbound on the Moses River, May 2

Dear Uncle Casey,

My *Save the May Day* fund is adding up. Mama's pulling doubles at Goodnight American, so she's not around to see how much cash I've saved, or she'd probably take it to pay for her Buick troubles. Seems like she just works to keep that car running, but lucky for her, there are more hours than workers in that laundry room. I can't believe how hard it was for her to get a job there because it sure seems like a bunch of slackers are running that show. Somebody is always calling in sick, and they know who to call. She won't ever turn down a shift.

I talked the manager of Wonder into paying me to clean the parking lot behind the bread factory. Every morning it's covered in cigarette butts and broken glass. Mama says delinquent youth with any sense do their drinking at Cypress Park, where they can hide in the tunnels; she says these must be the dimmest-wit hoodlums for drinking in plain sight. She hates living three doors down, but I think the only good thing about living on South End is how the air smells like warm bread all the time.

Sweeping glass was dull as knee socks, so while we swept, I taught Harlem the two-step. She caught on fast. Harlem doesn't know a thing about country, but she picked the steps up faster than Tim would say he likes it, he loves it, he wants some more of it, which Harlem did not say.

I sang every honky-tonk triumph I could think of, from "Dropkick Me Jesus" to "Tear in My Beer" as I coached her through the Texas two-step, the three-step and the triple two-step. I swear we danced until the sunset fell over us like it was writing a new alphabet made of country music.

Then she stopped and looked me dead in the eyes with the Wonder Bread sign smiling as wide as a large-print Bible behind her, and she said, "You have the most beautiful voice I've ever heard in my whole life."

If I were the crying kind, I might've cried a river that drowned the whole town right then and there, but then she added, "It's a shame to waste a voice like that on country music."

Tomorrow she wants me to help her hunt for her grandfather's treasure again. I think I'll write a song about it, so keep an eye on the Moses River for another song in a bottle.

Meanwhile, I guess I'm going to Northwind Road.

Disco

From: Harlem Solvang <torturedsol@zoomail.com>

To: Abbey Solvang <abbeyroadyogi@omwardbound.org>

You aren't gonna believe where I went today! Don't tell my mom, but Disco had this idea that if we want to figure out where Pop hid his treasure, we should ask the people who knew him. So we found them in the phone book. The Bannister aunts.

I called Skeeter first, but she thought I was a telemarketer, so she hung up before I could get a word in. I called back three times before she stayed on the phone long enough to hear who I was, and then she hung up anyway.

It's not bunk enough that nobody ever bothered introducing me to my own aunts—now I finally track one down, and she won't talk to me! Mom never tells me anything, and when I ask questions, she just bakes more bread, so I don't even know why they hate us in the first place.

Disco said we should knock on their doors and demand answers. She figured we'd be less likely to get shot knocking on Jolene's door, only Jolene lives so far out, she had to dig her own well, so that just left Aunt Tanya.

It takes an hour to walk to Tanya's ranch on the edge of Goodnight. When we finally arrive, three psycho Dobermans rush the fence, like so rabid I was ready to turn around.

Tanya must've heard the commotion because she opens the screen door with like, a cigarette in one hand, and this shotgun in her other hand, and she's like, "If you think I won't shoot a Girl Scout, you must've missed the sign." She points to a hand-carved birch arrow that says, *Trespassers will be shot. No exception for Girl Scouts nor Bible-thumpers!*

Disco's like, "We're not Girl Scouts. My name's Disco. This here's your niece, Harlem."

So Tanya lowers her shotgun, but she stares at me for so long, it seems like maybe she's still thinking of shooting. Finally she's like, "If your mama sent you to talk me into coming to her Sunday dinner, you can tell her it's never gonna happen."

And I'm like, "I just wanna ask some questions. My mom doesn't know I'm here."

My voice shakes so hard, I think she feels guilty, because she invites us in for Dr Pepper.

Tanya has one of those smoker's houses that look like some cranky chain-smoking pioneer found an empty acre, unloaded his collection of ashtrays, and then built the whole house around them. Even her bathroom has an olive-colored shag toilet seat with a brass ashtray that looks like a birdbath perched on the tank.

Anyway, Tanya tells us to take a seat on this, like, rumpled velvet duck sofa. She sits on the edge of an easy chair with an ashtray built right into the maple. She has an impatience around her, and with this, like, anthrax voice, she goes, "What do you wanna know?"

So I'm like, "Do you think Pop might've been hiding something?"

And she's like, "What are you getting at? You mean a secret?"

And I'm like, "Not a secret. Something else. Something real."

And Disco's like, "Something *veritable*."

That kills what's left of Tanya's patience. She's all, "That's why you came out here? You never thought to look up your aunt before, and now you turn up on a scavenger hunt?"

That's it. She shakes her head like we broke something, and she shows us the door.

As we walk home, I ask Disco what I should do.

Disco gets a look in her eye that makes things seem possible.

She's like, "Guess we'll try Jolene, but it's too far to walk. I'll see if we can hitch a ride with Reverend Arlo. He'll give anybody a ride."

Disco was right. He's picking us up Saturday. When she told him it was part of her plan to save the May Day, he said he'd give us a ride anywhere!

From: Sid Solvang <brooklyncalling@zoomail.com>
To: Abbey Solvang <abbeyroadyogi@omwardbound.org>

You heard from Harlem? She's been disappearing at all hours, and when she comes home, she goes straight to her closet and blasts Velvet Underground so loudly, it scares the alpacas.

When I ask where she's going, she acts anxious and guilty.

I took one of those online surveys to find out what's wrong with your teenager, and it said there's a 97 percent chance she's on drugs. She checks most of the boxes—mood swings, avoids eye contact, antisocial behavior at school, isolation at home. Then again, she was born rolling her eyes, and she's dressed like a heroin addict since the day she refused to go to kindergarten if we didn't let her pick her own clothes.

What do you think?

From: Abbey Solvang <abbeyroadyogi@omwardbound.org>
To: Sid Solvang <brooklyncalling@zoomail.com>

So the dude who scraped through high school stoned and dropped acid at his own bar mitzvah is worried his straight-A, honor roll daughter whose idea of a good time is reading in her closet while listening to her father's collection of Velvet Underground is on drugs?

Hilarious, Sidney.

Get a life. Get a job. Harlem's not on drugs.

Instead of spinning your wheels on narc surveys, maybe you could spin those wheels looking for a road out of Kansas.

From: Tanya Ann Bannister <holyroller316@prairienet.com>
To: Skeeter Bannister <highwater@shotmail.com>

Just between us, what do you reckon Pop meant by "a veritable treasury"?

From: Skeeter Bannister <highwater@shotmail.com>
To: Tanya Ann Bannister <holyroller316@prairienet.com>

Between you, me, and the outhouse, I wouldn't be surprised if that Lainie Hummingbird had Pop all wrong and maybe that geezer had a body or two lying around. The man could hold a grudge. Remember that shit list he kept taped to his Frigidaire because he was afraid he might forget who he was mad at? Did you see how many names were on it?

I don't figure he had enough nickels to fill a treasure chest anyhow. That man wouldn't pay full price for a can of Dollar Holler baked beans. Why do you ask?

From: Tanya Ann Bannister <holyroller316@prairienet.com>
To: Skeeter Bannister <highwater@shotmail.com>

But if he had something worth something, where you reckon he'd hide it?

From: Skeeter Bannister <highwater@shotmail.com>
To: Tanya Ann Bannister <holyroller316@prairienet.com>

I see what you're getting at, and you've watched too many movies.

Didn't Pop spend all his money on some Y2K bomb shelter? You wanna go on a wild goose chase that lands you in a bunker of Spam, be my guest. I'm going to bingo.

From: Tanya Ann Bannister <holyroller316@prairienet.com>
To: Jolene Salina Bannister Cole <JC4JC@prairienet.com>

Don't tell Skeeter I asked, but what do you figure Pop meant by "veritable treasury"?

From: Jolene Salina Bannister Cole <JC4JC@prairienet.com>
To: Tanya Ann Bannister <holyroller316@prairienet.com>

Funny you should ask. You won't believe who knocked on my trailer this morning. I'd just settled into my coffee and my paper when I heard the unmistakable sputter of Reverend Arlo's Ford. I figured he came on the meal train, but when I looked through the curtains, there he was on my porch with that glitter child from his church and none other than Scarlet's girl, Harlem!

And what was she asking about? Veritable treasure!

Well, you know what I had to do. I told her the only true treasure is the kingdom of Heaven, and I was happy to be the one to give her directions there.

To my surprise, Arlo said that wouldn't be necessary, that the girls had come to do the saving, not to be saved, only the thing that needed saving was a diner.

They think Pop might've had a secret fortune hidden somewhere, and they're gonna use it to save the May Day, only they've gotta find the fortune first.

I'm sure I don't have to tell you, but that diner nursed more than a few broken hearts, and if those booths could talk, they'd tell you they love you.

Now, that's a cause I can get behind. Harlem isn't half as weird as she looks. She's polite and smart as a whip. I don't care what Skeeter says—I think it's high time we paid Scarlet a visit.

From: Tanya Ann Bannister <holyroller316@prairienet.com>
To: Jolene Salina Bannister Cole <JC4JC@prairienet.com>

Last night at bingo, I mighta brought it up with Skeeter not for the first time, and she had a story to tell. Turns out Harlem ain't the only Solvang turning up on doorsteps.

She said Scarlet herself rang the doorbell, and Skeeter almost didn't recognize her with hair straight as arrows and looking like a funeral, she wore so much black.

I couldn't make heads nor tails of what went down, but Skeeter was fit to be tied over some incident involving Crisco.

Skeeter made me promise not to give Scarlet the time of day, but Jim's hours got cut at the factory again, so we could use the cash if you think there's something to this treasure hunt.

From: Harlem Solvang <torturedsol@zoomail.com>
To: Abbey Solvang <abbeyroadyogi@omwardbound.org>

Do you think it's weird that I have three aunts I'd never met in my whole life?

On the drive home in Arlo's truck, I had a little too much time to think, and it hit me how it's kinda weird I have three whole aunts I'd never met. It always seemed normal before, like everyone in New York misplaced a family and couldn't remember where they left them, but now that I've seen their shag-carpet toilets, smelled their ashtrays, and wiped my feet on their *Precious Moments* welcome mats, I can't help wondering why my mom never brought me here.

Seems like weird family is better than no family.

Then again, Reverend Arlo made me promise not to ring Skeeter's bell. I asked how it could possibly go any worse than it had gone with Tanya. He said the difference between Skeeter and Tanya Bannister is Tanya would aim a shotgun at me, but Skeeter would pull the trigger.

Maybe we won't need her. Jolene gave us a list of places she thought Pop might've hidden something. The first was Vertigo's roost! It's really just an oversize doghouse in the barn with a homespun sign that says *Welcome to Vertigo's Roost*, but Jolene said Vertigo was his favorite alpaca, so that's the place to start.

From: Abbey Solvang <abbeyroadyogi@omwardbound.org>
To: Harlem Solvang <torturedsol@zoomail.com>

It *is* weird you have three aunts you've never met, but it's weirder you met one at the other end of a shotgun. Somehow that seems to answer the question of why your mom never bothered to introduce you!

JOURNAL ENTRY, SID SOLVANG, TUESDAY

Scarlet sold a stockpile of antiques she found buried in the bad barn, so we can coast a little longer, but the future looks so bleak, I applied for a job as a janitor at Wonder Bread. Carter Bell warned me the factory is on a shoestring budget since sugar-bread sales are down, so it took some humbling to apply for a job cleaning a crumbling factory possibly on the verge of bankruptcy. There was nowhere to sit, so I had to fill out the application on the floor. When I handed it to the manager, he skimmed it and shook his head.

He handed it back and said, "You've got no experience."

I told him I have plenty of experience cleaning, but he said not to waste my time.

"We've got a stack of three dozen applicants with a custodial background."

Carter stopped by the next day on his route even though we didn't have any mail, and I told him what had happened. He thought it was hilarious I was rejected for a minimum wage job mopping Wonder floors. He said they probably just didn't like me because he said, "I know for a fact they hire teenagers out the gate."

I asked if he could get me a job at the post office, but he said the pile of applications for government jobs would reach Coffeyville if they laid them out.

As we stood on the porch talking, we heard Vertigo scream, so we followed the commotion to find Harlem and Disco urgently digging around the barn. When I asked what they were looking for, Disco swaggered. "What are *you* looking for?"

I told her I wasn't looking for anything.

She said maybe I should be looking for something, and she asked me what kind of birds my birdhouses were made for. I told her the truth: the birds don't seem too interested in my birdhouses. She asked why I keep making birdhouses for no birds. I didn't have an answer.

Carter said, "She's got your number."

Harlem was hiding something up the sleeve of her hoodie. I wanted to ask what it was, but instead I went inside and built another birdhouse.

From: Harlem Solvang <torturedsol@zoomail.com>
To: Abbey Solvang <abbeyroadyogi@omwardbound.org>

Jolene was right about Vertigo's roost, but Pop didn't make it easy. Disco and I crawled around that haystack for an hour searching, and we almost gave up when she noticed there was a panel of wood that didn't match in the corner. We poked at it until it gave enough that we could see there was something behind it. We managed to rip off the panel, and inside there was this weird rolled canvas paper. Unfortunately, it's more cryptic than Pop's hobbit journal. It's just lines, shapes, and squiggles that don't seem to mean anything. There's the tiniest hobbit scratch along the margins, but the barn leaks, so the ink is smudged, and it's almost impossible to read.

When Vertigo realized we were snooping in her roost, she threw such a tantrum, Dad came running with the mailman, and they chased us out of the barn with their questions.

The mailman was like, "Y'all are gonna get scabies crawling around in here."

That's not a real thing, right?

Anyway, we took the canvas back to my closet and blasted my chronic-depression playlist while we took turns staring at the meaningless shapes and translating Pop's diary. Pop finally stopped rambling about *Gunsmoke* reruns and started ranting about making right some debt to my mom. He wrote in circles of guilt, and I don't know what he's talking about, but I can't ask Mom. She'd be furious if she knew I was snooping through his stuff again.

After two hours, we were so bored of Latin, we took up howling to Radiohead.

We discovered howling is good, but screaming is better.

We're gonna do it again tomorrow.

You know anything about a debt to my mom?

From: Abbey Solvang <abbeyroadyogi@omwardbound.org>
To: Harlem Solvang <torturedsol@zoomail.com>

It's nice to hear you've found someone to scream in your closet with you.

I've never heard anything about a debt your grandfather had to your mom. Maybe he just meant a mistake?

No one tells me anything because everyone thinks I can't keep a secret, but that's only because they don't know how many secrets I'm keeping! Like your quest for treasure—or dead Kansans or a secret thesaurus or whatever.

Scabies are real, by the way. Go take a shower.

JOURNAL ENTRY, SID SOLVANG, SUNDAY

Every Sunday, Scarlet cooks all day and insists on setting the table for her sisters, and every Sunday, the food gets cold before she'll admit they're not coming.

Tonight I finally worked up the nerve to ask about their bad blood. She didn't answer, but her sigh was so aggressive, I dropped the subject.

I thought I was getting away with something when we

first met at the academy and she suggested we promise never to ask questions about our pasts. She sold it casually, like some "Be Here Now" whim. In those years I'd spent so many nights wandering in the alley behind CBGB with a head full of acid and some random drunk on my arm, it seemed a Kansas farm girl couldn't possibly have more to hide than me, but over the years, I could tell there was something unsettling her soul.

I pressed her to talk about it in marriage counseling a couple of years ago, and we bickered over it until the counselor pointed to a coral embroidered chancery sign above us that said, "Do you want to be right, or do you want to be married?"

Scarlet sighed.

I said, "Can't we be both? Why can't everybody be right?"

That inspired another of Scarlet's marathon sighs that could mean agreement or looming divorce, or it could mean she was thinking we should stop at that sushi place up the street to split Tokyo Delight Combo Six and let ourselves be exhausted. Whatever it meant, we stopped going to marriage counseling after that. On the way home, we stopped for sushi, and as we waited for our rolls, Scarlet said, "What the fuck is 'happy' anyway?"

We laughed—really laughed—and for a moment, I was sure we were happy.

Letter last seen drifting downriver in an empty bottle of root beer

Dear Uncle Casey,

Seems like our search for treasure is getting somewhere, but I couldn't tell you where. It takes so long to translate, there's no way we'll find whatever it is before Curtis's deadline to sell the diner, so I had to come up with a faster plan.

You've gotta be 18 to buy lottery tickets, and you've gotta be 18 to sell your blood, so I was running out of ideas.

Then it came to me last night like a flash of a thousand Nashvilles.

We were doing our Friday-night screaming, which is louder than our Thursday screaming, and it was crossing into the howling neighborhood when Harlem's dad said we should take a break on account of all the screaming scaring Vertigo.

Harlem was like, "Why are the alpacas even in the house? Seriously, WHY?"

Sid said he didn't know how they kept getting inside, but he didn't have the heart to put them out. That got me wondering, what kind of man lets three deranged alpacas run things?

Harlem says he's weird, but I think a man with three alpacas has a heart that can't say no, so I tested him. I asked if we could dye the white ones blue. He said he'd think about it.

That settled it. I said, "Mr. Solvang, Harlem tells me you know something about diners. Maybe you could give me some business advice about mine."

"It wasn't a diner." Harlem shot me an expression meant to shut me up. "It was a deli, and you weren't supposed to mention it, remember?"

Sid took on the look of a sad puzzle, so I said, "I think it's time you met the center of the universe. Why don't I buy you dinner?"

When we walked in those jingling May Day doors, I could see the way his eyes lit up at that warm pink neon caught in the steel-quilted counter. Sid was a goner.

As we stepped in, Patsy Cline poured from the speakers, singing "You Belong to Me," and it felt like the May Day herself was singing to us.

That's what gave me my genius idea. I wrote a song about it I'm calling "I Couldn't Save My Soul, but I Can Save the May Day Diner."

Goodnight Star

LOST AND FOUND, TUESDAY EDITION

FOUND: The search for Constance Ahlberg's missing reading glasses is over thanks to the Good Samaritans of South End.

LOST: Melody Hahn's souvenir Hawaiian bamboo chimes disappeared late last night.

"I don't know why anyone would want my chimes," she said. "I just got them at a Hawaiian flea market. They weren't hardly worth a thing, just a keepsake from my honeymoon, so I'd appreciate it if they were returned. No questions asked."

8

If You Fry It, They Will Come

JOURNAL ENTRY, SID SOLVANG, TUESDAY

Disco and Harlem dragged me out of the barn and into what Disco calls "the center of the universe." The May Day Diner is a humble truck stop where you can still get a cup of coffee for a quarter and peppermint candy with your handwritten bill. There's a "Please Wait to be Seated" sign where no one ever waits to be seated and a gum bank next to a shelf lined with every kind of map you could need to get from one end of the country to the other.

They were running low on maps of Kansas, because Goodnight isn't listed on the regional maps, only the state map—an injustice they like to point out to each other.

Everyone seems to know everyone at the May Day, and no one ever hesitates to tell you exactly what they think about anything, from the price of gas to the new and controversial bridesmaid-red geraniums planted outside City Hall. Everything's on the table, from Darwin to vegans, two subjects I've learned never to mention anywhere else in the state of Kansas.

All the booths were taken when we arrived, so we sat along the counter on red swivel barstools that shined like maraschino cherries. Just as we opened our menus, a waitress with wild hair and wilder eyes tore off her apron and started waving it madly at a couple of overdressed missionaries who ran for the door like the devil was right behind them.

Satan might as well have been behind them because it was Bailey Nation. She had a face that looked like it'd seen better days, but I'm sure it hadn't. Her jangly earrings glittered behind vo-tech bangs that shot up like mall fountains, landing over eyes lined with too much mascara and not enough sleep as she raged, "Keep your Holy Spirit to yourself before I take your tonsils out with my teeth! Go back to Moses, you highfalutin Hula-Hoops!"

Disco yelled, "Bailey! Leave them poor Mormons alone, and come meet Sid Solvang!"

She sauntered over as she tied her apron strings back together.

"Bailey's a legend," said Disco. "God never made a better waitress. Even with a hangover that'd kill a Missourian, she'll still clock in on time."

"This town would be lost without me," Bailey said. "How's your mama, Disco?"

She didn't wait to hear about Disco's mother. That's just something people say here. Disco explained later, "In fancy cities, like Wichita, folks ask how you're doing. Here they ask how your mama's doing, but nobody ever tells you how their mama's doing, unless she's sick. Then you'll hear about it."

Bailey poured a cup of coffee for me, though I hadn't asked for any, and she said, "Only two kinds of people in this world, you know: them who take orders, and them who give 'em."

I asked which one she was.

"Neither," she said, blowing a bubble in a decadent, angry method of punctuation that seemed aimed at me. But then she pulled out a notepad and said, "So, what can I get for you?"

When she returned to the kitchen, there was electric banter between her and Tyler the cook, interrupted by a thrashing of dishes. I got the feeling there was some kind of violence or love happening in the kitchen. Before I could decide which, she had returned and Tyler was hollering, "Order up: two over easy," hitting a little brass bell in the window.

To my surprise Harlem knew everyone who worked there.

Disco said, "That's because I pretty much own the May Day, except for the money part, so nobody minds that I've been giving two-step lessons to Harlem after school."

"Who says nobody minds two hooligans fox-trotting through my diner with the rhythm of a tornado?" Tyler said through the kitchen window.

"Who says tornadoes don't have rhythm?" Disco countered.

I must've gotten on Bailey's bad side because everything I said seemed to offend her. She nearly chased me out with the Mormons, but Old-School Omelet Number 3 was worth the abuse.

As she cleared our plates, she said, "You didn't eat your bacon. What's wrong with you?"

Harlem told her Scarlet's watching my cholesterol, but Bailey was no less offended.

She said, "You didn't drink your water neither. That ain't

got no cholesterol. What's the matter, New York, you too good for tap water?"

Then she shook her head and walked away, leaving the bill between us.

Check-in from Bailey to her probation officer
From: Bailey Nation <hellrazor@shotmail.com>
To: Tallayla Parks <onedayatatime@stillscountycorrections.org>

Dear Tallayla,

I'm sure you've heard about the Solvangs by now. I guess everybody's heard about them, since it ain't every day someone new moves to Goodnight. It ain't even every ten years.

Anyway, one of them came into the May Day last night. He couldn't have been a day over 50, but you wouldn't know it. He reminded me of one of them square grandaddies who smell like a medicine cabinet and give candy to any kid who knocks on the door.

He's nothing like I imagined from all the rumors.

Solvang asked for the specials, so I told him the blue-plate special was noodle pie. That bridge-shopping fool asked what noodle pie was. Tallayla, you ever tried May Day noodle pie? It's sort of like spaghetti pie, only this recipe's straight out of the recipe box of Satan, a.k.a. Curtis's mama. Someone should do the world a favor and burn the ink off that travesty before we scare off what's left of this town. Just 'cause someone drops dead from bad kidneys don't mean the world gotta carry on with their noodle mistakes.

So I warned Solvang, "It's like something your kids would make you on Father's Day if they was drunk and mad at you. Trust me, you don't want that."

Solvang closed the menu and asked what I recommended. I told him Old-School Omelet Number 3 is the best omelet there ever was, and maybe he's sharper than your average butter knife, because he ordered it, no questions asked. But then that lunatic had the nerve to ask for a bagel!

I lowered my bifocals so he'd know I meant business, and I said, "I don't know who you think you are waltzing in like the king of France looking for bagels."

The sucker started to apologize, so I laughed, but don't you worry, Tallayla, I don't owe nobody amending 'cause I told him, "Welcome to Kansas," and I said it in my Sunday voice, if I believed in Sundays, which I don't, but if I did, that Sunday voice would impress Jesus.

He must've liked Old-School Omelet Number 3 because he came back the next day, and he gave me a birdhouse and then asked me what else is good.

Truth be told, I'm about beside myself that there are new balls in town for me to bust. I could tell right away that Solvang's balls can take more busting than your standard balls. It gives me a certain respect for New York if all the balls are as sturdy as his.

Yours truly,

Bailey

From: Tallayla Parks <onedayatatime@stillscountycorrections.org>
To: Bailey Nation <hellrazor@shotmail.com>

Now that you've gotten the gossip out of your bones, maybe you could talk about your side of the street. I heard you chased the poor Mormons out of the May Day again. Don't they have enough trouble without you scaring the freckles off their souls? I heard you threatened to beat them with a Hula-Hoop? Maybe you don't owe Solvang an apology, but I think you oughta make it up to the Mormons.

Sounds like whiskey to me. Let me remind you that just because you're off the hard stuff doesn't mean you can drink your balance in Southern Comfort. When was the last time you went to a meeting? You need a ride? Then again, if you can walk to the liquor store, you can walk yourself to an ass-saving meeting. Your liver will thank me.

LOST AND FOUND, THURSDAY EDITION

LOST: The Minors have misplaced their goats again. This time it was Thurgood and Amelia. If you know the whereabouts of either, please contact GPD.

LOST: Braley Scott's collection of craft-kit wind chimes have gone missing. They're the first reported missing on the south side.

9

How to Get on the Devil's Good Side

JOURNAL ENTRY, SID SOLVANG, FRIDAY NIGHT

I spent most of my nights this week at the May Day with Harlem and Disco, since they've fused themselves together like two gummy bears melting in the dashboard sun.

Seems like you can see the whole town from the May Day windows, and there's something about a Friday sun that lands on Emporia Road differently. Feels new and unexpected, like hope.

Tonight I met the diner's owner, Curtis. He was slumped at the far side of the counter over his crossword. Bailey says Curtis always looks hungover, but he never actually is, which is funny since Bailey never looks hungover, but she always is.

We'd just ordered, and Bailey was kvetching at me for buttoning my shirt in a style that suggested I was inclined to shoot a president, when Curtis looked up from his crossword as if we were continuing a conversation.

"I'll bet you didn't know I knew your wife before she ran away and left us all in the dust," he said. "I've known Scarlet

Bannister since she was a freckle of a girl selling popcorn canisters door to door. She come to my front porch at least a hundred times slinging cheese logs and Christmas ribbon for the school."

I told him she doesn't talk about growing up here and that if I ask too many questions, she gets in one of her moods, so it's never come up.

He seemed to continue his conversation without me. "A different kind of man would raise the price of hush puppies to keep up with the times," he said. "My wife reminds me of that every summer when the money barely stretches far enough for a vacation at the Holiday Inn in Reno, and all she wants from life is two weeks in Bermuda, but that's not how I was raised."

I told him I didn't think there was anything wrong with Reno.

"Everything's wrong with Reno. That's what I like about it," said Bailey. "Ain't no Branson, but it ain't no Vegas neither."

I wasn't sure what that meant, but it didn't seem like I'd ever get on Bailey's right side, so I nodded in agreement. Bailey went back to waving a paper fan, Curtis yawned into his crossword, and I must've smiled because that's when Disco spun that maraschino barstool around like this was the moment she'd been waiting for, looked into my soul, and said, "You know this place is for sale, right?"

I told her I didn't know that.

She said everybody knew it because it was in the paper. "Don't you read the paper?"

When I told her I read the *New York Times* every day, she said, "Well, that's your trouble right there."

Harlem punched Disco in the elbow and said, "Don't tell him the diner's for sale! We'll never get out of the seventh gate to Hell if he buys it!"

She shook her head to an increasing degree of alarm, but Disco kept talking. "They're gonna close the May Day if they can't find a buyer soon," she said. "I've been saving up to buy it myself, but I'm a little short. I'd be willing to step aside if you wanna be the one to rescue it."

The whole diner looked a little brighter as I imagined what it could be. Harlem must've seen the dusted neon in my mind, because she turned to ice.

"Never," she said. "I can't believe you'd even think about it. How are you gonna run a diner when you're so busy hiding in barns, waiting to die in flip-flops, that you can't toast a Pop-Tart for your own kid?" She slipped out the door, abandoning an uneaten plate of onion rings.

Disco chased after her, and I sat stunned, realizing how my life must look through the eyes of a 14-year-old girl. I scanned the diner to see if anyone heard her indictment.

Bailey stopped waving her paper fan at herself and turned the fan on me.

"I've heard worse." She slid an airplane Bacardi out of her apron, passing it under the counter. "Tornadoes and teenagers strike us all equal, and you'll never get an apology out of neither. I've got three teenagers at home, and I'll take a twister any day of the week."

Bailey wasn't the only one who heard it, but to my surprise, it softened the space between everyone in the diner that night.

Curtis told me about his son's sixth rehab and a niece on crack, and he insisted dinner was on him. One by one the May Day stragglers shared war stories of surviving adolescent theater, from stolen trailers to Texas cults, until I could smile again.

Goodnight got a little warmer, and the world got a little smaller that night.

Harlem hasn't apologized, but since that day, Bailey never lets me leave the May Day without a basket of her famous biscuits, on the house.

From: Disco Kennedy <lostblue@prairienet.com>
To: Harlem Solvang <torturedsol@zoomail.com>

Please stop avoiding me and hear me out.

I'm not saying we should give up our search for Pop's treasure, but seeing how it's taking a while, I have a genius plan that'll save the May Day AND get us out of Goodnight!

Bailey told me there was a half dozen wallets interested in the diner, but after getting a closer look they all backed out because they said the May Day is too much trouble. They said the diner shows its age, and to fix it would eat their budget for a chef worth paying. None of them thought Tyler was worth keeping even though half his menu is voted the best in the county every year by the *Star*, the *Democrat*, the *Gazette*, and *Merle's Truck Stop* blog.

They all came to the same conclusion as Aspen Pottstock—level it, franchise it. One of them suggested we embrace the location and put up a Love's Travel Stop!

So my genius plan is I'll give your dad my whole *Save the May Day* fund toward buying the diner. We can fix it up and make it what it used to be. We'll make it so good and sturdy, nobody would dare knock it down. Sell it or keep it, if it's good enough, you can raise the money to go back to New York, and you can take me with you.

Handwritten letter found in a half-finished birdhouse on the good barn workbench

Dad,

Bailey offered me five dollars if I'd apologize to you. I didn't take her money, but it got me thinking maybe I was kinda, like, horrible. I'm sorry I freaked out on you. I shouldn't have implied birds hate you and mailmen only talk to you because they have to. I was just scared of getting stuck in Goodnight.

You're not as embarrassing as the other dads, and your shirts don't really look like they're made of recycled bowling shoes like Bailey says, but you should probably burn those flip-flops.

If you wanna buy the diner, maybe it's not your worst idea.

JOURNAL ENTRY, SID SOLVANG, MONDAY

Tonight at the May Day, Disco laid down her spoon and announced, "Enough of this. Curtis, you should sell Sid this old pile. I'm sure he could read the paper and boss folks around just as good as you."

"Listen to that mouth." Curtis coughed. "Disco Kennedy, you better watch yourself, or I'll send you home with a mouth full of Ajax, and you know your mama will thank me for it."

Disco said, "I like the taste of soap, and Ajax is my favorite."

"I'm sure you've had plenty." He shook his head the way old men do when they see civilization crumbling in the eyes of a teenager. Then he got what Bailey calls a thinking look, and he said I had the grip of an honest man, but he wanted to know what I think I know about running a diner. I figured I had nothing left to lose, so I told him the truth.

I told him everything.

He took "a minute with the Lord," coughed awhile, and said, "The Bannisters meant well, even if Pop was stark raving mad, but I won't hold it against you if you wanna buy it."

Maybe I've seen a light at the end of this tunnel, and that light is a pink neon heaven called the May Day Diner. It's not just the opposite of New York; it's the opposite of irony itself.

Something entirely what it is. Salt of the earth.

Letter to Jacob Wilkes at the Sunset Home for Widows, Un-wived, and Under-wived Men

Dear Uncle Jacob,

I think I've finally found someone to buy the May Day. It's a bit of a gamble with the devil, but before you judge, you should know the only other interest was Aspen Pottstock, who offered half our asking and tried to talk me into replacing our family legacy with a Burger King.

At least this Solvang character is a straight shooter, even if he's shooting his own left foot with a mouth that don't know how to dress a turkey.

He told me outright, "I ran my grandfather's deli out of business. It was doing really well for 84 years before I took over for my father, and in two years I killed it."

I said, "Let me get this straight. Your grandfather and your father built 80 years of regulars, and in two years, you ran them all off?"

He said that's exactly how it went.

I asked how his father took it, and Solvang said it killed him. "It broke his heart, and it killed him, and then my mother was so distraught, it killed her too, only a year later."

I said, "So you killed your family's business and your parents, you pretty much killed the American Dream, and now you'd like me to entrust you with the legacy of my family's diner?"

He said, "Yes, I guess so."

I laughed so hard, I caught my whistle cough, and I asked where the weather went south.

Solvang didn't miss a note. He started going on about flying too close to the sun and not knowing how to leave well enough alone. He said, "I'm not a chef. Scarlet's the real chef. I should've given her the kitchen and left the menu alone, which is what I plan to do with the May Day if you sell it to me. Like they say, if it's not broken, don't fix it."

Of course, the menu's about the only thing that ain't broken at the May Day.

I might've signed the heap over on the spot, but that mosquito bite of a waitress, Bailey Nation, came back to clear the counter, and she said, "Only two kinds of folks in the world: them who say *no,* and them who say *yes*. Of course, that don't count folks who say *yes,* but they really mean *no,* and folks who say *no,* but they mean *yes.* Curtis here is a hard maybe."

"I think you're a yes. You're a yes that says yes and means it," that Disco kid said to Solvang, while his daughter was shaking her head.

I can't get to Scottsdale fast enough.

Solvang said he'd go home and talk it over with his wife, so I'm not holding my breath. I'm asking you to put a word in with the Lord because if this works out, maybe there's hope for this town. The way I figure, Solvang's gotta do better than a Burger King.

At the very least, a man that down's got something to prove.

From: Sid Solvang <brooklyncalling@zoomail.com>
To: Abbey Solvang <abbeyroadyogi@omwardbound.org>

Talk me off the ledge. I had this idea, and you've got to talk me out of it before I squander what's left of our savings and risk destroying our whole world. Again.

The diner is for sale for so cheap, they're practically giving it away. They say if someone doesn't buy it, there's a plan to level it and replace it with a Burger King. You'd understand what kind of tragedy that would be if you ever spun on those barstools and took a bite of a warm May Day biscuit while the waitresses fought over the jukebox, but no one dared rush them. So far as I can tell, the waitresses rule Kansas, and the rest of us are just lucky to get a booth.

Disco offered me a mason jar crammed with her life savings if I'd go in on buying the May Day. Of course, I told her to keep her money, but it got me thinking that last check was coming, and Scarlett can't stop cooking anyway. We've got a freezer full of her wasted genius because Harlem has suddenly gone vegan with a vengeance and she cooks for herself. Scarlet said she's willing so long as she never has to leave the May Day kitchen, so we've got ourselves a chef. Neither of us has had luck finding a job anyway.

If we save the diner, it won't just spare the world another Burger King. Maybe we can make enough money to get back to New York.

Last night, I asked the owner about it, and as I left with Disco and Harlem, I had the closest thing to a burning bush I've ever witnessed. I got a warm feeling that something good was watching me. I turned to look back at the May Day and I swear it was looking back at me.

Its pink neon lit up the stainless steel quilting like the Heaven of kitchens was dreaming, talking in its sleep, saying, *Sid Solvang, this is your diner. This is your destiny.*

I told them, "I'm going to buy that place. I don't know how, but I'm going to do it."

Disco said, "Maybe Curtis will let you pay in alpacas."

Harlem asked how many alpacas it would take to buy an old truck stop.

"Can't hurt to ask," I said.

I found myself whistling all the way back to Northwind.

When we arrived at the house, Scarlet was standing at the mailbox, smiling.

Our last check had come.

So, Abbey, talk some sense into me before I start taking orders from a pink neon sign.

From: Abbey Solvang <abbeyroadyogi@omwardbound.org>
To: Sid Solvang <brooklyncalling@zoomail.com>

I don't see any better offers in Brooklyn. As long as this plan of yours brings you back to New York, who am I to argue with a pink neon sign?

PART 2

Breaking Bread

10

The Best Thing Since Glitter Guns and the Grand Ole Opry

From: Sid Solvang <brooklyncalling@zoomail.com>
To: Abbey Solvang <abbeyroadyogi@omwardbound.org>

My apologies for not getting back to you earlier. It's been a whirlwind since we bought the May Day, not to mention school starts soon. Harlem will be off to Goodnight High, something I can't wrap my mind around.

Meanwhile, Scarlet's been dreaming up the menu, and I've had my sleeves up, fixing everything that was broken, which was almost everything.

The clock is running, and the math is daunting, but we can afford to stay shut down for a month longer while we get the diner ready.

We still have to seal the leaks in the roof, replace the griddles, and rewire the ceiling fans, but tomorrow we paint! Bailey organized all the waitresses to help us so nobody misses a paycheck. They've been such good sports, I'm giving them a raise.

I love this place.

From: Abbey Solvang <abbeyroadyogi@omwardbound.org>
To: Sid Solvang <brooklyncalling@zoomail.com>

Don't love it too much.

From: Tallayla Parks <onedayatatime@stillscountycorrections.org>
To: Bailey Nation <hellrazor@shotmail.com>

What's the story with your new boss? I'm stuck in bed again with that god-awful flu, so I've got nothing better to do than read your gossip. Don't leave anything out.

From: Bailey Nation <hellrazor@shotmail.com>
To: Tallayla Parks <stillscountycorrections.org>

Nothing to tell. All I can say is the man is true to his word. I got a raise, Goodnight kept its grits, and the May Day's getting bagels. We're not talking Sara Lee.

Maybe the whole world ain't so shot to shit as we thought.

Note in an empty bottle of root beer last seen trapped in a beaver tumble on the river

Dear Uncle Casey,

I haven't written in a while because I've spent every day helping to fix up the May Day.

Harlem and I planted coral bells in the flower beds outside the diner that have been empty for a thousand years, if you don't count dandelions.

I've spent every night in Scarlet's kitchen. That's Harlem's mom. Sid doesn't want to change the menu, so

Scarlet's trying to change up the old May Day recipes "just enough to make it different without being different."

She lets us try everything, and then she asks us what we think of it. Some of it's good, and some of it's plain strange, but Scarlet says that's how she gets ideas: by mixing things that don't usually mix and seeing what happens. I think she hears recipes the way we taste songs, like each flavor is part of a chord. Some of it is flashy and mean like a seventh, and some of it rings like a wind chime of thirds, golden red with sprinkles of purple, like frankincense. The Solvangs eat as weird as they talk, but it's better than sitting alone and eating frozen dinners with those god-awful stiff mashed potatoes that never seem to cook all the way through.

It's nice to finally have something weirder than me in this town. Nothing I say scares Harlem. She says she's seen everything, since she's been taking the New York subway her whole life, and I'm starting to believe her.

I haven't made up my mind about Harlem's dad. He reads the *New York Times* every day, so I asked him why he still reads a newspaper from a town he doesn't even live in, and he said, "I guess I'm not all here. Maybe as long as I know what's going on in New York, it's like I never really left."

I told him, "Well, that's just pitiful, but I can't blame you. If I was you, I'd save every penny you make selling waffles to get out of here."

"That's the plan," he said. "But it's gonna take a lot of waffles."

I told him he should have a little faith. Their waffles are really freaking good.

Scarlet claims Sid's the better chef. She said if he goes to bed imagining a flavor, he dreams up a recipe in his sleep, but Sid said he doesn't do that anymore, and then he looked like he might crack if we didn't stop talking about waffles.

I don't care what anyone says—I think the Solvangs are the best thing since glitter guns and the Grand Ole Opry. I wrote a song about them called "The Best Thing Since Glitter Guns and the Grand Ole Opry."

Disco

From: Harlem Solvang <torturedsol@zoomail.com>
To: Jolene Salina Bannister Cole <JC4JC@prairienet.com>

I hope you don't mind, but I found your email address on Mom's laptop. Please don't tell her about this, or I'll be grounded for a month. I'm not supposed to snoop, but she didn't really give me a choice since she never tells me anything.

You probably heard my parents just spent all our money on the May Day. Now I figure it's up to me to find a way home. Disco and I have been saving up for New York, but there's not a lot of work to be found.

My dad paid us to help him finish painting the diner, but now that the walls are done, he's moved on to fixing things. We tried to help, but I kept losing tools, and after Disco almost set the kitchen on fire, he sent us home.

If there's money to be found, it could save us years of crappy jobs, but the search for Pop's treasure stalled in Vertigo's roost. I went back to translating his diary, but the only secret he ever mentions is some kind of debt to my mom. Do you know anything about it?

From: Jolene Salina Bannister Cole <JC4JC@prairienet.com>
To: Harlem Solvang <torturedsol@zoomail.com>

I heard the good news that somebody saved the May Day, and I was delighted to discover it was your family. This town loves that diner, not just because without it, we'd have to cross the bridge to get a decent flapjack, but also on account of there's not really another place for folks to gather anymore. Even Skeeter was proud to hear the news, though she'd never admit it.

As for some kind of debt, it must've been translated backward. As I recall, it wasn't Pop who owed your mama, but your mama who owed Pop. I never knew any details, but your mama ran away. She was gone an awful long time, and when she finally came home, she didn't stay 24 hours before she fled to New York without a word to any of us. Pop took it hard.

If there's a debt between them, that's the one.

From: Scarlet Bannister Solvang <mystifried@zoomail.com>
To: Skeeter Bannister<highwater@shotmail.com>

I know you're still not speaking to me, but I'm asking you to put your grudge away for five minutes. I haven't slept in days.

Maybe you've heard the news that we bought the May Day. For the record, it didn't come out of any secret fortune. As far as I can tell, there is no fortune to be found. We paid for it with what was left from selling our life in Brooklyn. It's the only money we had left, and we poured every last penny into the May Day.

I'm such a nervous wreck about our opening, I toss and turn all night. Sid's worse. He woke up trembling last night. He started pacing the floor in a daze of worry, walking in circles and talking to the windows like he couldn't even see me, saying, "What if no one comes? What if no one comes? What if no one comes? What if no one comes?"

He woke the alpacas and didn't seem to notice them, even though Vertigo was walking the floor right behind him and Matzo kept looking up trying to figure out who he was talking to. Taco just watched like he knew exactly what time it was and wanted no part of it.

The truth is, that's all I've been thinking. What if no one does come? What if the May Day falls apart like Sol's did? It would kill Sid to go through all that again, and what would that do to Harlem to see her father fail twice? She'll be crushed, and that will kill me.

Talk me off the ledge, Skeeter. Did we make a mistake coming here?

From: Skeeter Bannister<highwater@shotmail.com>
To: Scarlet Bannister Solvang <mystifried@zoomail.com>

Of course, you made a mistake coming here. This town is running on fumes, and you drove right into them, but maybe something good will come of it. You had to find some way to make a living, and somebody had to keep the May Day running, so it might as well be you. Just don't be serving no plates on fire like they do at the Chili's up in Olathe. It's off-putting serving anything that looks like it was baked in the devil's oven.

You were always too sensitive for your own good, and somehow you managed to find yourself an old man more sensitive than you. That's something. But you're honest. That means something in this town. You serve an honest omelet, and Goodnight will forgive a lot.

Don't worry about folks coming. This town's too curious and

hungry not to give it a chance. It's not like there's any competition. Nobody can afford to eat in Moses anymore. I think they raise the prices just to keep us on our side of the river. And Lord knows we've all caught the rumbles slumming it at the Bonanza Buffet enough to try anything.

Tell you what: I'll drag Tanya and Jolene and whoever else ain't at Civil War Camp that day, if you promise to save us a booth. My sciatica can't take anything but a booth.

JOURNAL ENTRY, SID SOLVANG

I finally fell asleep at a decent hour last night, only to dream that no one showed up to the opening of the May Day. All the booths were empty, the same way Sol's looked those last weeks before it closed. I couldn't sleep the rest of the night.

The whole thing seems impossible. What was I thinking?

It's one thing to fail in New York, but to fail here... There will be no coming back from it.

I'll have to sell the diner to Aspen Pottstock for nothing. He'll put in a Burger King, and everyone will blame me. Harlem will have no money for college, so she'll end up strung out on Ozark bathtub meth. Scarlet will run away with Oliver Dean, and they'll open a wildly successful surf and turf bistro in the Village inside a performance art gallery, and they'll have inside jokes about how much I hate the word "bistro" and never understood performance art. They'll use their fortune to fund rehabs, PhDs, and sailboats to rescue Harlem, who will sober up, knit Shetland wool sweaters and move to places where everyone wears white pants. Scarlet will give me the house out of pity because I'll end up washing dishes at the Bonanza Buffet, living among kvetching hordes of alpacas, and every Hanukkah I'll get a Shutterfly Christmas postcard from New York with a picture of them and our future grandchildren in matching Fair Isle sweaters, under a mauve cursive banner that ends in "CHEERS!"

Mauve! Cheers! Sweaters!

They will be sailors, I will be a busboy, and someday Taco, Matzo, and Vertigo will die in my arms, one by one, until I have nothing but crumbling birdhouses to keep me company.

I can't sleep.

From: Harlem Solvang <torturedsol@zoomail.com>
To: Abbey Solvang <abbeyroadyogi@omwardbound.org>

My parents have gone off the deep end. It was my first day at Goodnight High today, and I'm not sure either of them even noticed. Dad was up all night, so he was in a state this morning.

He and Mom rushed out the door without even taking one of those horrible pictures they used to take every first day of school. Dad was asking Mom a million questions about sweet corn chowder, and Mom said unless he wanted them to be the first couple ever to cite irreconcilable chowder as their reason for divorce, she suggested he keep his identity crisis out of her recipe box, but he was all worked up, saying he thought they were veering too far from the May Day menu and we're gonna be run out of Kansas. She said he's the one who killed Sol's, and she's not about to let him kill another one. They drove off ragging so hard, they forgot to say goodbye.

I started walking to school with Disco, but their church boss,

Arlo, spotted us on the road and offered us a ride. I hesitated because turning up for my first day of high school in a minister's wheezing truck was not my first choice, but Disco whispered, "There's no use trying. Nobody can say no to Reverend Arlo."

That man never stopped whistling. We played name that whistle for six blocks, but I did all the naming because Disco didn't say a word. Arlo must've thought she was ashamed of the truck because he told us if we think of trucks as ironic, it won't bother us showing up on our first day of high school in a '77 Ford F-350 smelling like diesel.

We pulled up to Goodnight High just in time to see everyone we hated from middle school sprawled across the steps of the old sandstone building.

I hate my teachers, I hate my classes, and most of all, I hate the students. Disco had a worse day than I did. How are we gonna survive four years of this?

From: Abbey Solvang <abbeyroadyogi@omwardbound.org>
To: Harlem Solvang <torturedsol@zoomail.com>

Poor Harlem. If I had any money, I'd hop on a plane and come visit, but my latest girlfriend stole my rent money and took off with the drummer from my other ex-girlfriend's band. Who gets dumped for a drummer? Apparently me.

So now I'm house-sitting for extra cash, but it's not so bad because the Sagittarius house sitter next door invited me to her naked yoga class tonight.

I wish I had some advice on getting through high school, but I don't remember mine. I'm pretty sure I was drunk from the first miserable toga party until graduation. I'm not recommending that. If I hadn't been such a lush back then, maybe I wouldn't be living in a heatless studio above China2Go, smelling like a wrong turn and soy sauce.

Aren't you guys opening soon? Maybe things will calm down after that.

Letter slid into a bottle of root beer, last seen drifting southbound down the Moses River

Dear Uncle Casey,

The May Day is almost ready! We finally finished painting the last wall of the diner Friday night. I tried to talk Sid out of painting over the yellow smoke stain with white. I suggested neon blue, but he said he promised old Curtis he wouldn't change anything too much at least until he's beyond the Golden Gates of the hereafter.

I told him I'm sure once Curtis is poolside in Scottsdale, he won't care what color we paint the diner, but Sid got graveyard eyes and said, "I'll keep my word, even if it kills me."

I think he's nervous about opening. Harlem says he walks the floor all night. You can't get away with that in those old Victorians. Those creaky floors'll wake every devil for a mile.

While we waited for the paint to dry, I danced through the diner with my blue guitar, singing to the Solvangs until Harlem threatened to cut the strings off. She yelled, "My ears are gonna commit suicide if they have to listen to another round of 'The World Needs a Melody.'"

I told her the truth is I can't stop, but I think my voice broke in half when I said it.

We scrubbed that place down from the rafters to the checkers to be ready for tomorrow, and when we dusted that old neon sign, the whole diner shined pink.

Sid let me turn off the neon sign for the night, and he said, "Disco, you've done it. You saved the May Day."

So, Casey, will you come to my opening? Mama wouldn't be caught dead there, so you don't have to worry about running into her, and Scarlet's pie is worth the cost of diesel.

Maybe I'll see you there?

ADVERTISEMENT, SUNDAY EDITION

THE MAY DAY DINER INVITES YOU TO OUR GRAND REOPENING AUGUST 30.

It's been a hard year.

Unprecedented layoffs, war looming over soaring gas prices,and the high cost of living are taking a toll on our town.

The May Day family extends our hand to make the load a little lighterby offering discounts to laid-off factory workers and veterans.

Welcome Goodnight's own Chef Scarlet Solvang,putting her own touch on the classic menu–everything you loved about the May Day, only with bagels.

Welcome back, Goodnight!

11

The 26 Birdhouses of Sid Solvang

Local Headlines, August 31, 2002

Moses Register: May Day refurb gives Moses a reason to cross the river

---

USADinerReview.com: New May Day is ode to old May Day: NY chef elevates KS menu

---

Emporia Road Merchants Association News: Solvangs bring hope to Emporia Road

---

Stilwell Democrat: Stills County's favorite diner gets a makeover; locals celebrate

---

MerlesTruckStopBlog.com: Tastiest truck stop in KS promises new destination for foodies

---

Goodnight Star: Best grits in America just got better; May Day triumphs opening night

Goodnight Star

RESTAURANT REVIEW BY ROVING FOOD CRITIC CLARISSA BRENDEN, AUGUST 31

Chef Scarlet Solvang had me at Born-Again Noodle!

Everybody knows there was one dish on the old May Day menu nobody in their right mind ever ordered twice—Arlene Wilkes's noodle pie. Curtis kept it on the menu only as an homage to the dish his late mother created to get them through the Depression, and even when it was the blue-plate special every third Tuesday, I don't know anyone who came in for the dish.

That's why it was pretty sharp to offer samples of the reimagined noodles. What was once a starchy culinary crime is now a delicate Italian potpie fit for Sardinian kings.

It's beyond this eater how anyone could take something so bad and make it so good.

Of course, we had to order the grits because nobody would believe May Day grits could get any better than they already were. Lo and behold, those grits were so savory, so complex, it could well be the closest thing to a religious experience I've had outside a church.

My husband and I attempted to split blackened cherry pie for dessert, but it was almost obscenely tasty. We had to order a second slice to prevent bloodshed or divorce.

The rebirth of this diner should make all of Goodnight proud. Scarlet Solvang took a menu nobody thought could be any tastier, and she found a way to make it a heck of a lot better!

Goodnight Star

LETTERS FROM GOODNIGHTERS, AUGUST 31

Dear Goodnight,

I decided to give the May Day a chance, not entirely because a new ill-fated casserole recipe nearly burned my whole kitchen down, but maybe I was a little curious on account of all the gossip over these outsiders. I was happy to see the menu hasn't changed much, and although it's true the roof doesn't leak now, and there's a fresh coat of paint on the walls, it hasn't lost its charm. Same old jukebox, same bossy waitresses, same sparkling red barstools, and the same frosted booths where I had my first sundae.

What surprised me most was that even though the menu had the same dishes, everything I tried was worlds better than it used to be. You'll be glad to know that Goodnight's own Scarlet Bannister is the cook, not the husband, though he seemed pleasant enough.

They even offer discounts to laid-off workers, which was appreciated since Goodnight American threw my husband to the unemployment line after 22 years of loyalty to that company in the last round of layoffs.

All I can say for the May Day is if every dish on that menu is as good as the ones we had last night, maybe we need to throw the Solvangs a parade, instead of judgment.

Sunday Mulligan, mission leader, Ninth Street Good Shepherd Baptist Church

JOURNAL ENTRY, SID SOLVANG, AUGUST 31

We survived opening night at the May Day. Within an hour of opening the doors, half the booths were already full and every counter stool was taken. Not too shabby for our first night.

The bells didn't stop jingling until well after nine, and even Bailey was in high spirits. Her teenage daughters and her probation officer came by to heckle her, and she seemed to revel in the kitchen theatrics between Scarlet's genius and Tyler's irreverence.

Scarlet saved a booth for her sisters. To my surprise they were the first to show up for the dinner rush, and they brought their entire families, including a whole battalion of cousins dressed for Civil War Camp. Tanya said she couldn't tell if Scarlet's Reuben was the best thing she'd ever tasted, or if her expectations were just so low, anything would be a step up.

Skeeter insisted she makes a better Reuben than God, ask anyone, but she ordered a Frito pie to take home, so we must've done something right.

Jolene left a tip so high, it made Bailey blush, but she left it in a pocket Bible because apparently that's what Jolene does. It might kill her to know Bailey said she collects all the Bibles people constantly inflict on her because the pages make for good rolling papers.

I was just so relieved the Bannisters showed up for Scarlet. Maybe they don't hate us as much as they want us to believe. Or maybe they were just hungry.

As they left, Skeeter nodded and said, "Not bad, Solvang. We might actually come back."

Everyone seemed sort of buzzed by the night, except Disco. Her eyes stayed on the exit, like she was waiting for someone. Whoever it was, they didn't come. Her eyes never left that door. At the end of the night, she was so sullen, I offered her a sundae, but she wouldn't take it.

It didn't help that Harlem had abandoned her at the counter. During the rush, Harlem went back to see if she could help, and she didn't leave the kitchen until the last plate was served.

The last ticket of the night was for a mob of teenage girls who drank their weight in coffee and ate enough fries to keep Rudolph's potato farm in business for another season. Bailey chased them out the door and turned off the neon sign. The lights fizzed out, and we all looked at each other in exhausted, ecstatic disbelief.

It felt so good to rush through the smoke, sizzle, and hustle of a kitchen again. I'm so tired, I might actually sleep. I can't believe I get to do this again tomorrow. I can't wait.

From: Scarlet Bannister Solvang <mystifried@zoomail.com>
To: Jules Jamison <livingthedream73@zoomail.com>

I got your message, but it's too late to call you back.

To answer your question, yes, Sid's back in the kitchen, but he still insists he'll never be a chef again. He says the reason May Day is going well is because he kept his hands off the menu.

I keep asking him to add a few new dishes, but he refuses.

We got into it in the middle of the May Day the other night, so now all the waitresses know our business. I made the mistake of asking if he'd come up with a special next week and he put on this feminist monologue in the kitchen that was such BS, I thought one of the waitresses was going to slap him. He said it's a shame I spent so many years in his shadow and that the only reason he ever got more attention than me at the academy is because I'm a woman and kitchens are patriarchies, so it's his responsibility to step aside and let me shine, blah, blah, blah.

Of course, that part is true, but I told him, "Nice try, nobody's buying it."

It seemed like he might cry. He said, "I'm cooking again. What do you want from me?"

So I said, "Sid, you know good and well the difference between being a cook and being a chef, and you need to get over yourself."

He said, "I couldn't if I wanted to. I don't dream dishes anymore. I lost it."

The waitress told him to man up, and the cook threw us both out of "his kitchen" for getting in his way.

Sid's right about one thing: the May Day is doing pretty well without his bells and whistles. At this rate I don't see anything stopping us from saving enough to come home.

LETTERS FROM GOODNIGHTERS, SEPTEMBER 7

Dear Goodnight and all relevant souls,

I, for one, do not approve of selling the May Day Diner to outsiders. We wouldn't sell the heart of Goodnight to Moses, and I don't see how this is any different.

I am also vehemently opposed to the new geraniums outside City Hall. As we all know, red is Satan's favorite color, and it makes our sturdy God-fearing town look like it's being run by a bunch of dime-store heathens. Join me at the next council meeting to implore our civic leaders to remove these flashy monstrosities and replace them with more reasonable and godly flowers such as white lilies. Or maybe some pleasant hydrangeas.

What this town needs is someone keeping score besides Jesus.

We need an alliance of real Americans keeping watch. Are you a *real* American? Do you disapprove of outsiders and geraniums taking over Emporia Road? If you've had enough of radicals planting devil flowers and running our economy into the ground while outsiders hang us out to dry, meet me at Eisenhower Park, high noon tomorrow.

Virginia Easton of Northwind Road

LETTERS FROM GOODNIGHTERS, SEPTEMBER 9

Dear Goodnight,

Yesterday I attended a gathering of concerned citizens in Eisenhower Park, and what I heard sounded real good to me. I will not be taking my business to the May Day Diner. I don't appreciate them offering handouts to the unemployed who need jobs, not waffles. I don't like the implication by outsiders that our tire factory has not done right by its workers.

If we want this town to survive the recession, we must keep Goodnight American in Goodnight. It's a business, and businesses have to make sacrifices. Sometimes that means layoffs. Just be glad we have a factory holding this town together.

Boone Kelmsworth, distribution manager, Goodnight American Tire Company

LETTERS FROM GOODNIGHTERS, SEPTEMBER 9

As farmers market season draws to a close, don't forget your neighborhood farms.

Every farm bill has its foibles, but this latest one hits Goodnight hard. The *Moses Register*—or should I say, the *Monsanto Register*—claims the 2002 Farm Bill is here to save the world, but don't let them pull that Bible wool over your eyes while crop-insurance companies make out like bandits and family farms are taxed to pay for subsidies we don't qualify for. Yet again small farms are left with empty pockets and barns full of surplus with nowhere to go.

Sarah K. Thomas, Thomas Farm

LETTERS FROM GOODNIGHTERS, SEPTEMBER 10

Dear Goodnight,

I've heard there's a surplus of crops around town from the latest subsidy cuts.

The May Day would like to do our part to help. We can offer a fair rate to buy whatever surplus you have. If you've got corn, we'll make corn on the cob. If you've got tomatoes, we'll make spaghetti. It doesn't matter so much what you have. We can adjust the menu around it.

There's just no reason for our kitchen to rely on national restaurant suppliers when Kansas farms are hurting to sell.

Stop by and see us at the May Day, or give us a call and we'll bring the truck.

Kindly,

Sid Solvang

Goodnight Star

LETTERS FROM GOODNIGHTERS, SEPTEMBER 12

Dear neighbors,

That Solvang fellow is at it again. He and his wife turned up on our doorstep and offered to buy direct from our ranch, save us a trip, and cut out the banks. Well, he's speaking our language. We walked through the farm, and he seemed to know his stuff. He said he didn't care for middlemen, so why don't we just bring whatever we've got to spare and they'll bend the menu around it? I've never heard of such a thing, but it sure beats the House of Pancakes out on 69. Denny's is only ten miles up the road, and they've never offered to buy our soybeans.

Maybe we ought to hear the fellow out. It seems to me that some of the Solvangs' critics in this town have been perfectly content to take our money. Nobody's ever asked the farmers what we think about the price of beans. I guarantee you'll get an earful if you do.

Alls I'm saying is there are elements in this town who have made quite a fortune off our misfortune. The Solvangs aren't one of them.

Mitch Minor

From: Sid Solvang <brooklyncalling@zoomail.com>
To: Chef Katz Selznick <NYA@culinaryscience.edu>

Hi, Chef,

There's no time to explain, but the CliffsNotes version is I've got more soybeans than I know what to do with and more on the way. I've got a stream of hard red winter wheat coming faster than Scarlet can mill it and the sweetest corn straight off the stalks of Eastern Kansas. Between you and the rest of the academy, I'm hoping you have connections in the Midwest that might be interested in buying directly from farmers, Alice Waters style.

At the very least, if you know any chefs in KC, we can hook them up with a fresh local source about an hour south at a fair price. You know anyone who might be interested?

From: Chef Katz Selznick <NYA@culinaryscience.edu>
To: Sid Solvang <brooklyncalling@zoomail.com>

Do I know anyone? I know everyone!

I've reached out to some friends in your area, and if you've got farms, they've got tables. If you have regular sources and drivers who can deliver, I know a number of chefs who would be more than happy to take some of that off your hands.

How much surplus are we talking about? Have you heard of the new school lunch initiative to replace prepackaged with fresh food from local sources?

The farm-to-table movement is catching fire right now. I can give you a list of public and private grants to support networks connecting farms to regional schools, if you can get it there.

Give me a call.

CLASSIFIED ADS: JOBS SECTION

Drivers Wanted. The May Day is looking for drivers to deliver from Stills County farms on a home-daily schedule. Local routes to Goodnight High, John Brown Middle School, and Nation Elementary. Regional routes include KC, Lawrence, Wichita, Lincoln, and Jefferson City.

From: Rita Younglund <RYounglund@gpsfs.edu>
To: Sid Solvang <brooklyncalling@zoomail.com>

Dear Mr. Solvang,

My department received your query about connecting Goodnight farms to our school cafeterias, and we are very interested. There are a number of new grants available, just send contact information for the farms you mentioned, and we'll take it from there.

On a personal note, I read the paper. Thank you for what you've done for this town.

Rita Younglund, director of Goodnight Public Schools' food services

Goodnight Star

LETTERS FROM GOODNIGHTERS

Dear Goodnight,

You have to admit the Solvangs have brought a certain charm to Northwind Road. Of course, being city-souled, Sid Solvang can't keep a tomato garden alive to save the Pope, but he always feeds the birds, and I think Jesus holds a certain place in His heart for folks who feed the birds. Sid Solvang has more birdhouses than anyone could count, unless it's a long winter, and then you'd count 26. This is a man of 26 birdhouses. Imagine what kind of heart is behind that much birdseed.

But Solvang isn't just feeding birds. I've heard small farmers all over the county talking about the man who's picking up the slack from the new farm bill snow job. What would've died on the vine is now en route to restaurants from Branson to three capitals. He lined up buyers in so many restaurants, he was able to hire workers laid off from GATC last spring as drivers.

Enough of this talk of outsiders.

This town has always been an open door, dating back to the war between brothers, but we are skeptical people, and it has kept our town true since the day we drew a line between Moses and Goodnight, between greed and compassion, between injustice and abolition, the day Moses Road became Goodnight Road, so test your skepticism with truth.

Are you following the Shepherd or the innkeeper?

I'm sure I can count on each of you to search your soul and weigh your conscience with the same vigilance you've deployed on Solvang.

If not, maybe you'd benefit from Sunday's sermon: "Mind your own Bible's dust and your own soul's rust."

I'll save you a seat and a muffin.

Reverend Arlo Foster, Ninth Street Good Shepherd Baptist Church

JOURNAL ENTRY, SID SOLVANG, SATURDAY

What do you do when you figure out you're the bad guy?

At the very least a fraud.

Everyone says I saved the May Day. A local minister wrote a letter to the Star carrying on about what a mensch I am. Yes, I started reading the Star. It's impossible not to if you want to know what's happening in this town.

But I'm no mensch. I can't help thinking they'd all hate me if they knew I was just trying to save my own birdhouse. And it's Scarlet's cooking everyone's in love with, not mine. Of course, she won't tell them that. She'd fake her own death to avoid a spotlight. When I try to give her credit, they think I'm being humble. Has there ever been a humble New Yorker?

The Goodnight City Council came by the diner tonight after a town hall meeting. They raved that the town owes me a debt of gratitude for rescuing the May Day and how grateful they are we chose to stay in Goodnight. How could I tell them we're not staying? They were so kind I couldn't bring myself to tell them I just needed a job and no one would hire me and that the second we clear our debts, we'll sell it and be back to Brooklyn faster than Bailey can say, "I'll wear a hairnet when the Queen of France wears a hairnet."

Just a few months ago, I couldn't get a job bagging

groceries at Bargain Mart, and now I'm serving the city council. "City" is the wrong word. Also, it's not so much a council as a recipe-swapping rabble of gossip-drunk onion ring enthusiasts who take themselves very seriously.

Councilman Ford Hollis has the earnestness of a redwood, which he told me is his favorite tree. He rambled about civic responsibility and Christmas trees and how trees support each other through their roots, and by the end of it, I loved him and I loved trees a little more.

It feels like a betrayal to leave these people and their trees.

12

Too Good for Crisco

From: Skeeter Bannister <highwater@shotmail.com>
To: Scarlet Bannister Solvang <mystifried@zoomail.com>
CC: Tanya Ann Bannister <holyroller316@prairienet.com>, Jolene Salina Bannister Cole <JC4JC@prairienet.com>

The kids might know me as Lunch Lady, but the district knows me as Boss. That's not because I am the boss; it's because the superintendent is afraid of me and because I know everything that goes down in Goodnight schools. Rita hunts with all the lunch ladies, so I heard about your old man's secret plan to save the farms by inflicting sprouts on our local youth.

I'm not saying I forgive you for leaving, getting the house, or for forgetting where you're from for 20 years, but what I'm saying is crank the leaf on that ugly table, set a place for three more, and mind your alpacas. Your sisters are coming to dinner, and we're bringing the dogs.

From: Harlem Solvang <torturedsol@zoomail.com>
To: Abbey Solvang <abbeyroadyogi@omwardbound.org>

You should've heard them.

The Bannister aunts (and their dogs) finally came to dinner. It was so strange seeing them all at one table. They sigh as much as Mom does. Even their dogs sigh. Tanya has like 16 different gasps depending on what law of the Bible she thinks we broke. Jolene is nothing but eyes, and Skeeter is the boss. She walked in jaw first with the air farm girls get when they spend too much time with horses and started bossing everyone around.

She demanded an apology for the *Crisco Incident.*

Apparently Mom came to her house months ago to beg her to come to dinner. Skeeter was like, "She almost wore me down, but then that pagan went through my pantry, stole my Crisco, and when I gone looking for it, I found it in the trash."

And Mom was like, "I flushed it. It's poison."

Skeeter was all, "She thinks she's too good for Crisco now that she's been to New York."

And Tanya was like, "You a vegetarian now?"

Dad told them we just don't eat red meat, which Skeeter took to mean we killed Jesus or something because she got so worked up. She was like, "People who don't eat meat hate America." And then she was coughing through her biscuit, going on about, "If we didn't eat cows, there'd be so many, they'd take over the streets, then what would you do?"

Aunt Jolene—who barely spoke all night, but just kept nodding like she agreed with whatever anyone said—finally opened her mouth for the first time, and you know what she said?

"See, you should thank us for eating cows so they don't take over the streets."

Dad got that lost ghosty look he gets at Scrabble, but Mom started laughing, and she was all, "Thank you for eating the cows so they don't take over the world."

The minute the last piece of pie was gone, Skeeter stood, all murder-eyed like that mural of John Brown over the capital, and said, "Harlem, make yourself scarce—there's business."

I was kinda freaking out because I figured they were gonna tell Mom about my search for Pop's treasure and I'd be in trouble for snooping, but Mom hasn't said a word about it, so I don't know what business they were talking about.

What the hell is Crisco?

From: Abbey Solvang <abbeyroadyogi@omwardbound.org>
To: Harlem Solvang <torturedsol@zoomail.com>

Nobody knows what Crisco is. I don't even think Crisco knows what Crisco is.

I'll have to call you later. I'm sick as a vegan dog. I'm going out with this actress/dog walker/cranial-sacral homeopathic healer/etc. and she put me on a detox cleanse where I can only drink this, like, paprika lemon juice, so I feel like I swallowed a manic-depressive tornado. I'm like deathly sick, but Zara says once I get over the dying part, I'm going to feel better than I've ever felt. Obviously she's insanely hot for me to give up manicotti and coffee. She's a Capricorn, and you know I'm powerless against Capricorns.

I can't wait to hear how your dad fared at family dinner with the Bannisters!

JOURNAL ENTRY, SID SOLVANG, SUNDAY

Scarlet's sisters finally came to dinner. They could be New Yorkers with the velocity of kvetch at that table.

When dinner was over, Skeeter shooed Harlem away and started in.

"Scarlet, when you left, we didn't know if you were dead or alive for months," she said. "When you finally called from New York, Pop swore you'd never last a month there."

"Nobody dreamed you'd be gone for 20 years," said Jolene.

Skeeter said their Grandma Mary told them not to ask questions because when somebody leaves a place that fast, there's a secret, and the bigger the hurry, the darker it is.

"She figured you were hiding a bun in your oven," said Tanya. "Aunt Dana blamed heartbreak, but Aunt Christy suspected somebody had done something terrible to you, because she said folks don't stay away that long over love gone south."

"What is it?" Skeeter asked. "Why'd you run away?"

"I didn't run away," said Scarlet.

"So a spaceship beamed you up and spit you out in New York?" said Skeeter.

Scarlet looked smaller by the second. "What did Pop tell you?"

Tanya said, "All he told us was y'all had a fight, and you took off in the middle of the night. He said you were too high and mighty to fit in this town."

"He didn't tell you where I was?" Scarlet asked.

"How would he know?" Tanya said.

"How would any of us know?" Skeeter huffed. "You know

Aunt Rita had your name on every church prayer list from here to Moses for 21 Sundays before you finally called from New York, only to tell us you were never coming back! You have no idea what you put us through."

Jolene leaned closer, and in her softer way, she said, "What happened?"

"It wasn't—I didn't—" Scarlet's voice cracked under the weight of the room. The grief between sisters was unmoving and unmovable, a brooding grief. I pictured it as angry pasta—tagliatelle in black squid ink, maybe, Himalayan black salt, roasted cherry tomatoes, minced shallots in black garlic sauce.

Scarlet cleared her throat. "That's it," she said. "We had a fight and I left."

"That's the whole story?" Skeeter's chin stiffened.

She didn't buy it. None of us did.

"Pop was right. I was too high and mighty for Goodnight," said Scarlet.

"But you're still too good for Crisco, so why'd you come back?" Tanya asked.

Scarlet looked at me and hesitated.

"We had to," I said finally. "We had nowhere else to go."

As the words fell into the room, there was a new grief on the table, and it was mine. I could feel my shape change in their eyes, the hazy geometry of family hierarchy shifting with me at the bottom. To my surprise, they seem to like me better now that they've seen the shape of my gutter.

As they left, Scarlet asked them if they'd be back next

Sunday. Skeeter laughed, looked at me, and kept laughing as they sauntered out the door.

After the table was cleared and the dishes were washed, Scarlet went to work on a wild yeast starter she'd been saving for sourdough, and she baked into the night.

From: Tanya Ann Bannister <holyroller316@prairienet.com>
To: Skeeter Bannister <highwater@shotmail.com>

You think Scarlet's hiding something?

From: Skeeter Bannister <highwater@shotmail.com>
To: Tanya Ann Bannister <holyroller316@prairienet.com>

I'd bet my George Foreman grill on it. I'll betcha I can crack that code in seven Sundays. There's no way Scarlet's telling us the whole story. Wanna grab lunch at the May Day tomorrow?

Note passed from Disco to Harlem after first period

The Wonder folks asked if we could sweep the lot again. They can't pay as much as last time, but they said we can take all the Wonder Bread we want. You free after school?

Note passed from Harlem to Disco after class

When I told Dad we were looking for odd jobs, he offered me an actual job at the May Day! All I have to do is help in the kitchen, and he's gonna pay me! He said I'd better start saving money now if I don't wanna drive a John Deere tractor to college.

Forget Wonder Bread. Come by the diner.

LOST AND FOUND, THURSDAY EDITION

FOUND: The Minors' goats Thurgood and Amelia were found wandering South End. According to Mitch, "I blame Cleveland. That Tennessee fainter will eat anything, but she stays close to home. The trouble is Cleveland is inclined to eating fences, Thurgood is inclined to leaving, and the rest are in the habit of following Thurgood anywhere that troublemaker goes."

FOUND: A brass skeleton key washed up on the western bank of Goodnight Lake on Tuesday. The key is rusted and half the size of a standard key, fit more for an antique safe or hope chest than a door. Verne Bennett's goat, Lincoln, fished it out of the mud, and he turned it in at GPD station in a ziplock bag, "to prevent the spread of the lake."

Bennett said, "I can't be too sure if the key's got the lake flu or not. I can tell you since Lincoln dragged that key out of the water, he hasn't been right, but no wronger than the rest of us who share the lake for a backyard."

13

On the House

Goodnight Star

LETTERS FROM GOODNIGHTERS, OCTOBER 29

Dear Goodnight,

It's been seven months since the last round of layoffs at the tire factory. What happens every time we have layoffs? Workers who don't get fired end up doing twice the work for the same money. GATC has frozen wages for the eighth year, but I don't see management taking the hit. They say they can't give us more because the economy isn't what it was and times are hard, but it's no secret profits are higher than ever and the bosses' salaries keep going up.

I work too long and too hard to be struggling to make ends meet. The only grocery store in my neighborhood keeps raising the price of milk and bread. I'd bake my own bread if I weren't working a second job at night. Who has time to raise their own yeast when we're all working night and day? Something's gotta give.

A Goodnight American worker

Memo: To all Goodnight American Tire Company Staff
From: GATC Management

It has come to management's attention there have been a number of complaints regarding workload and wages at GATC following restructuring efforts.

These are trying times for American tire manufacturers, and we've had to make tough choices. Among our sacrifices was the reorganization of units into smaller, more-agile teams in order to compete with overseas markets. The bottom line is we're competing with countries where workers are paid less for a day's work than GATC workers make in an hour. Closer to home, the average wage at GATC is substantially higher than the countywide average.

For the company to achieve marketplace success, more tough decisions will have to be made. We face increasing operating expenses, from the skyrocketing cost of raw materials to pensions and the soaring price of health care. Despite these challenges, we're energized and confident in our global position going forward. Our success is your success, and we urge you to exercise discretion representing the GATC family. Sharing information can result in unintended consequences. Thank you for your cooperation.

From: Sid Solvang <brooklyncalling@zoomail.com>
To: Reverend Arlo Foster <humbleservant@goodshepherd.com>

Dear Reverend Arlo,

They say you're the one to talk to when it comes to getting people fed around here. Since the day our doors opened, our counter has been full of laid-off workers who only drink coffee. I'm sorry it took me this long to realize they order coffee because it's all they can afford.

Arlo, we have so many leftovers by the end of the night… I offer it to our staff, but they eat free, so by the end of a shift, they don't want to look at another key lime pie. By closing time, we have piles of homemade biscuits, stuffed baked potatoes, and pies that won't keep.

I offer it to laid-off workers who come in to stare at the classifieds and sip coffee all day, looking for work they won't find. I've told several of them who seem really hard up to come by at the end of the night and they can have their pick of leftovers, but no one will take me up on it. They seem offended and humiliated that I would acknowledge their situation. These are family men, and I hate to think they're going home to empty pantries every night.

There are so many perishables left, and it's a crime to waste them when there are people going hungry in this town.

I understand the churches offer food to the community. Would you be interested in our perishables? At the very least, if you know any families we could give to directly, maybe they'd be more comfortable taking food if it came from the church.

Kindly,

Sid Solvang

From: Reverend Arlo Foster <humbleservant@goodshepherd.com>
To: Sid Solvang <brooklyncalling@zoomail.com>

Dear Sid,

We have the same problem at the Good Shepherd. The folks who need help most won't take it. We have a pantry of canned food, but most folks are too proud or embarrassed to take anything. We've started throwing church dinners every few days, inventing reasons to serve food just so we can feed them without them realizing we're trying to help. If any of them caught on that we were doing it to help them, no one would show up.

What if you wrote a letter to the *Star* talking about wasting food? Maybe if you told people what kind of food is getting thrown out, you might appeal to their practicality. Everybody knows our pantry is full of nonperishables that will last forever. Canned creamed corn and lima beans are one thing to walk away from, but no one wants to see a key lime pie thrown out.

Just one word of caution: watch your language about sounding too green, or you may be accused of being a tree hugger, and then nobody will take your pie.

You could have Bailey write it. That woman could sell blue to the sky. Folks might show up just because she told them to. Maybe she can scare them into taking your biscuits.

Rev. Arlo

LETTERS FROM GOODNIGHTERS, SUNDAY EDITION

Dear Goodnight,

We've got trouble at the May Day. The trouble is we have more key lime pie than anyone can eat, but we can't make half a pie, so the other half bites the dust.

You know what else we can't get rid of?

Biscuits!

You know who makes those biscuits?

Those are *my* biscuits that we are forced to toss in a dumpster for the rats. You know what else those rats are having for dinner? Here's half the leftovers I fed to the rats last night:

A quarter of a chocolate crème pie, Tyler's meatloaf that won the meatloaf bake off two years ago at the America Festival, Scarlet's macaroni casserole—yes, the one with bacon. And remember my ambrosia salad with the rainbow marshmallows that's better than anything your mama ever made in her entire ambrosia life? I fed half of it to the rats last night. You know what ambrosia means? It's Greek for *immortality*, means it lives forever, but you know what [doesn't] live forever? Ambrosia salad.

It's a tragedy that Goodnight refuses to take pie when somebody offers free pie.

What's the matter, Kansas? You too good for key lime? What about French silk? You have any idea how good these rats are eating all because this town refuses to help us out?

Now, I know what some of you are thinking. You think we're trying to trick you into taking charity. Well, it's not charity when we give it to the rats, so why should they get all my biscuits? It makes me sick to think we've got rats in our alley eating better than the rest of this town.

I know you, Goodnight. You don't wanna take something for nothing because your daddy told you to pick yourself up by your bootstraps, but you can't pull yourself up by your bootstraps if you've got no boots.

Now, we don't have boots, but we've got biscuits. I made them myself, and I know you [aren't] gonna turn down my biscuits now that you know what's what.

I will see you at the May Day.
Yours truly,
Bailey Nation

LEAD STORY, MONDAY EDITION

Emporia Road Faces Public Health Risk

The Public Health Department has been looking into concerns about a growing population of rats reported in downtown Goodnight.

Council Member Ford Hollis said the rats have long been an issue, but that in recent months, there is an increasing number of rats drawn to the dumpsters behind the May Day Diner.

"The trouble with rats is they are a public health hazard because of all the germs they carry," he said. "It's a sanitation risk for all of us."

The local inspector's office has confirmed there is no evidence that the rats have penetrated the inside of the diner and that the rat droppings are confined to the alley where the diner's dumpsters are located.

May Day owner Sid Solvang has addressed the cleanup, but he said there is a simple solution to prevent attracting rats, and he's asking the public for help.

"The problem is we're just producing more food than we can sell before it expires," Solvang said. "It's long been a practice of restaurants to share their leftovers when expiration dates loom, but we have no one to share our leftovers with."

Hollis said it would be a great service to public safety if there are any families willing to take some of the leftovers off their hands so the May Day dumpsters won't keep drawing varmint to Emporia Road.

"If you are able to help solve this public health crisis," Solvang said, "just stop by the May Day with a sturdy bag and an appetite."

Letter received by mail at the May Day, Tuesday

Dear Mr. Solvang,

I heard about your trouble with rats. There are folks on my street who can't find work, and we'd be willing to take some of that food off your hands to help you with your rat trouble.

The problem is most folks around here don't have cars, and we live on South End, where there's no bus anymore. We had the same trouble with the churches. It's an hour's walk to church row, but the hour back is the problem. It's too far to walk home carrying groceries. I tried it twice when we were really hard up, and they loaded two bags full of food for my family, but don't you know the bags broke, and all those groceries fell right into a gutter of sleet. It's happened to every one of us who walked the three miles for bread.

Nobody around here's gonna complain about not having a ride to get free food. It's hard enough to admit you can't feed your kids without having the humiliation of watching your free food roll down the street while the whole town drives by looking down on you.

Let me make something clear: We're not poor. My

husband and I worked at GATC. He went on disability for cancer last year. I was laid off a month later. We've hung on to the house, but they took our trucks. He's still sick. I'm cleaning houses, but it's hard without wheels. What I'm saying is nobody's eating bonbons in this house. We don't take handouts. So I wouldn't ask if it weren't a public health crisis like they say, but since you've gotta get rid of food, I thought you should know there'd be plenty of takers if someone could bring it to South End.

Raina Freeman

From: Raina Freeman <freebirdy@shotmail.com>
To: Lexy Gunner <craftycat@shotmail.com>, Sam Heck <balls2walls@shotmail.com>, Colt Watts <coltjolt@prairienet.com>, Briana Janson <bribaby@prairienet.com>, Denise Shelby <Dimondz@shotmail.com>, Daisy Hayes <hazeydazey@ksmail.com>, Megan Starkey <DontWaitUp@fresheartlifecoach.com>

Get over here right now, and bring Tupperware! You're not gonna believe what just turned up at my door. That May Day guy showed up on my porch with his daughter, both holding armloads of free food from the diner. There's enough here to feed the whole block. And it's good! There's pickled okra and angel cake and potpies and so many fucking biscuits!

When they left, they asked if they could come back sometime and maybe we could help them find folks who can take food off their hands. They said it would really help them out—you know with the rat trouble—if they had a place to bring leftovers. I sent them over to Old Ruby Robinson's house around the corner. I wish I could see her face.

I gotta go. Get down here before my kids eat all the pie!

Note passed from Disco to Harlem during math

The sun's out, and I'm headed to the river after school. Wanna come?

Note passed from Harlem to Disco two minutes later

I can't go. I promised my dad I'd help him at the diner. I guess word spread he was delivering free food, and now everybody's asking for it. It's kind of fucked up how many people around here are hungry.

Tonight we're gonna be over on your side of town. Why don't you come with us?

From: Harlem Solvang <torturedsol@zoomail.com>
To: Abbey Solvang <abbeyroadyogi@omwardbound.org>

It happened again.

Disco and I were helping Dad and Bailey load the truck for a delivery, and these pilgrim kids took one look at Disco, gasped, and ran away! Usually she barely notices, but this time she was like, "I don't wanna kill your business tying my horse to the May Day. I'm gonna go."

And Dad's like, "The May Day tied its horse to you."

Disco got all emo and took off anyway. Bailey said the kids were Kennedy cousins, but she said Disco doesn't know that, and if I ever say anything, she'll break my second toe. I don't think she meant it, but I'm not taking any chances.

PS: Dad spent all our money on bells, and now we can't come home for winter break!

From: Abbey Solvang <abbeyroadyogi@omwardbound.org>
To: Sid Solvang <brooklyncalling@zoomail.com>

What's this I hear about you being too poor to come home for the holidays? Harlem says you spent all your money on bells. What does that even mean?

From: Sid Solvang <jewyorker@zoomail.com>
To: Abbey Solvang <abbeyroadyogi@omwardbound.org>

Yesterday they took up a collection from the merchants on Emporia Road to save Goodnight's oldest bell tower. They have to recast the bells and the collection came up short, so they sent the bell founder himself door to door asking for more. All this to say, we spent our savings on bells, but I promised Harlem we'd get her to Brooklyn without us for Christmas—or solstice, or whatever you pagans are doing with your Decembers.

Meanwhile, I'll be stuck here trying to find dreidels at the Dollar Holler.

From: Abbey Solvang <abbeyroadyogi@omwardbound.org>
To: Sid Solvang <brooklyncalling@zoomail.com>

Not to be a downer, but I feel I should remind you that you planned to move back to Brooklyn the minute you saved enough money to get out of there. I'm a little worried the corn brainwashed you and now you're spending your savings on bells. BELLS, Sidney?

Have fun at the Dollar Holler, spinning dreidels with the corn children.

From: Sid Solvang <brooklyncalling@zoomail.com>
To: Abbey Solvang <abbeyroadyogi@omwardbound.org>

I didn't forget. Now that the May Day is steady and Goodnight's bells are in order, I see nothing to stop us from saving money. It's only a matter of time before we're back in Brooklyn.

14

News from Emporia Road

Goodnight Star

LEAD STORY, NOVEMBER 13

More Trouble for Emporia Road

There's a wrecking ball coming for the Hallelujah Hotel, and it seems nothing can stop it.

Despite its designation as a historic landmark, the building has been condemned, and according to Council Member Clovis Geary, "No one can afford to fix it. It's just too much of a liability to leave it standing, and it's too costly to bring it up to code."

The building was boarded up late yesterday, after a routine visit from the local inspector's office found evidence the structure was no longer sound. There were municipal code violations ranging from electrical issues to fundamental stability issues in the foundation.

"It's been a long time coming," said Mayor Carol Shultz. "I'm surprised it's survived this long. I think we all knew it was only a matter of time."

According to the Emporia Road Merchants Association, as the only lodging in Goodnight, the Hallelujah Hotel was the highest source of revenue on Emporia Road, and the loss will hit Goodnight hard.

Demolition was postponed temporarily while the Preservation Commission reviews the case, but according to a statement released by the inspector's office, "The hotel is unfit for human habitation and given the severity of damage, it is unlikely and economically unfeasible that these violations can be overcome without funds the city just doesn't have."

Council Member Ford Hollis spearheads the task force to save the hotel.

"I don't know how this town will survive the loss of the Hallelujah," he said. "We need a Hail Mary for the Hallelujah."

Note passed from Harlem to Disco during homeroom, November 13

My parents are making me go to some annual spaghetti thing. Dad said the whole town has to go, and the city council asked the May Day to sponsor it, so I can't get out of it.

Is the whole town really gonna be there? Does that mean you're going?

Note passed from Disco to Harlem, 10 minutes later

Yes, it's the spaghetti feed at the mayor's farm. Yes, the whole town goes. No, I don't go.

From: Harlem Solvang <torturedsol@zoomail.com>
To: Disco Kennedy <lostblue@prairienet.com>

Did you hear what happened tonight?

You know that awful neighbor across Northwind who stares at us? She showed up with a bunch of protestors waving Bibles and American flags! All of Kansas was just trying to keep the spaghetti sauce off their jeans when this lunatic starts ranting, "The *Star*'s been taken over by devil-worshipping communists trying to kill Jesus and destroy Goodnight!"

So I was like, "Communists don't believe in devils, so how can they worship them?"

It was kinda funny until she got all Mr. Burns and pointed to us and said, "Why are we letting outsiders take over our spaghetti feed?"

Then the cops came running because they heard somebody set an American flag on fire, but they weren't lighting flags on fire—they were lighting newspapers on fire.

Somebody yelled, "Let them burn. It's just newspaper."

But Lainie Hummingbird was like, "Why is it a crime to burn a symbol, but it's not a crime to burn words—the very essence of freedom of speech?"

So they called her a hippie, and everybody took sides.

Finally Dad brought out Mom's mud moon pie, and of course, Goodnight chose free pie over controversy. The protestors stuffed their faces with whipped nutmeg and went home.

The sad thing is my mom had actually left the kitchen for once, and after all that, I don't think we'll ever get her out of that kitchen again.

By the end of the night, everyone acted like the whole thing hadn't happened, but something's definitely up because I saw Ford and Dad huddled behind the barn, whispering.

Apparently the protest was over an article in the *Star* about working conditions being unfair at the tire factory. Has your mom ever mentioned anything about that?

From: Disco Kennedy <lostblue@prairienet.com>
To: Harlem Solvang <torturedsol@zoomail.com>

Mama is too proud to ever admit something's hard. I think that's how they get away with killing so many miners. If you admit your boss is killing you, you're a weak commie, and people would rather hand over their lungs on a black platter than be called a commie or admit anything is hard.

Goodnight used to have a paper mill and a steel plant. When they shut down, so many folks were left out of work that now they'll do anything to keep GATC running.

But that's old news. I'm more curious what your dad and Ford were whispering about.

From: Harlem Solvang <torturedsol@zoomail.com>
To: Disco Kennedy <lostblue@prairienet.com>

I have no idea what Ford and Dad were talking about behind the barn. If I had to guess, I'd say it was birdhouses and Christmas trees.

I asked Bailey about the protest, and she was like, "Folks play Monopoly with thieves, and when they get robbed, they blame Satan and keep rolling."

No wonder Pop went off his rails in this town. We've gotta find a way out. I think it's time we get back to our treasure hunt.

Letter handed to Sid Solvang by Goodnight's most trusted mail carrier, Carter Bell

Dear Mr. Solvang,

I've enclosed the figures on the Hallelujah Hotel, including the inspector's report I mentioned last night. I realize I caught you off guard at the spaghetti feed when I suggested you buy the Hallelujah, but I want you to know my suggestion couldn't be more in earnest.

Our council is impressed with what you've done to turn the May Day around. I'm more impressed with your efforts to bring food to neighbors in need. I heard it was you who paid the balance to repair the bell tower. That's the selfless leadership it's going to take to save the hotel.

Our council has been meeting behind closed doors, trying to find a solution, but we're not having any luck. A member of upper management at the tire factory approached us with an offer, but it is not a fair one, given how much revenue the place was bringing in even in its most deteriorated state. Also, he's from Moses.

Word around town is that if you could afford to leave, you would. As you'll see from the numbers, an investment in the Hallelujah could be your ticket back to New York.

It will take a significant investment to get the building up to code, but once it's back in business, I guarantee it will make a handsome profit. The trouble is the daunting number of repairs required to lift the condemned status. We're prepared to set up a lease-to-own plan to minimize your start-up expenses, but as far as the cost of bringing the building up to code, I'm afraid it will require a bank loan, unless Pop Bannister had some secret fortune. There's a small handful of people in this town with the clout to secure a loan of that magnitude, but as far as our council can figure, you're the only one with no history of exploiting our constituents.

There is more potential for profit in the Hallelujah than you can imagine, and it's paramount that we keep it in safe hands.

One more thing: Cheryl is wondering if she can get your wife's recipe for moon pie?

Warm regards,
Ford

Letter handed to Council Member Ford Hollis by the hand of Carter Bell

Dear Ford,

I've looked over the numbers you sent. I think you've got the wrong idea about our situation.

People around here seem to think we pulled into Kansas in a golden chariot, but the truth is we came with almost nothing. When we left Brooklyn, we'd lost everything. I'm grateful I've been able to keep the May Day going with what little we had, but there isn't more.

My heart goes out to you, but as much as I'd love to

help, we don't have the kind of money it would take to save the Hallelujah.

Kindly,
Sid

Handwritten note slipped under the locked door of the May Day after hours

Sid,

I'm going to speak plainly and beg your discretion, as I cannot afford a scandal with an election year looming.

Just between us, no one who would do right by this town can afford to buy the Hallelujah. So-called pillars of our town have done Goodnight no favors. Pottstock raises rents as high as the law lets him, keeping hardworking folks in a constant struggle.

He may have deep roots and deeper pockets, but it's no secret he plans to surrender the hotel to the wrecking ball. He's worked every angle, trying to prove it's not worth saving. He has the Preservation Society in the palm of his hand, promising them first dibs on architectural salvage if they sign off. His plan? To tear the Hallelujah apart, sell it in pieces, and put in a budget motel. It won't matter how little charm it has, because there's no competition. If you know Pottstock, you know that won't stop him from charging as much as he can get away with.

You can see my predicament. Lord knows you can't

stand in the way of the free market in this town without committing political suicide, but so many who would vote us out for speaking up are the very ones whose rents will starve them to the breadlines to save the free market.

The council is weighing options, and all of us agree (with utmost discretion) you're one of the few businessmen in this town who have done right by us. Folks here don't have the credit nor assets to secure a loan of that scale, but we're hoping you do. We're prepared to make liberal arrangements to make this happen. Goodnight needs a break, and I believe you're it.

Ford

From: Harlem Solvang <torturedsol@zoomail.com>
To: Disco Kennedy <lostblue@prairienet.com>

Last night I found my dad looking at this long dusty parchment paper sprawled across the kitchen table. I asked what it was, and he said it was some kind of map that came with Pop's deed for his land on the lake. He said they wanna sell it because none of the Bannisters want it and it's nothing but 17 acres of wilderness. Mom said when she was a kid, they raised alpacas there. She figured they let it go when her mother got sick because they had to downsize and move what was left of the herd to the barn. She said not to get my hopes up, that they aren't selling it so we can move back to Brooklyn; they need the money for something else; and they can't tell me what it's for yet. I asked why they didn't sell it in the first place, but Mom said she couldn't until she was sure her sisters didn't want it.

Dad showed me little ink waves that made the border around the Bannister acres, but the map was bigger than that. It was an old parcel map of the whole north end of Goodnight with the lake running through it.

The more I looked at it, the more I felt like I had seen those shapes before.

I waited until Dad went to bed, and then I dug out the canvas we found in Vertigo's roost.

You won't believe it—we were holding it upside down. When I turned it over and held it up next to the parchment, there was no mistaking it. The shapes matched. That canvas is a hand-sketched map of Goodnight, and those shapes aren't random at all. The long lines make up the Moses River on one side and Goodnight Lake pointing like an arrow to a cross!

Disco, what we found in the barn is a map, and there's a very clear cross—like a tipsy blue X somebody knocked over in the middle of those 17 acres.

Dad's meeting a real estate agent on the land tomorrow. I asked if we could go with him, and he said he didn't see why not.

From: Melba Deerborn <MelbaLynnDeerborn@prairienet.com>
To: Honey Bee Kennedy <RevelationSevenfold@prairienet.com>

You know where that daughter of yours was yesterday? I'm sure she'll never tell you since it involved a certain lake and a certain family of oddballs. I spent an hour at that lake with none other than Disco, Sid Solvang, and his infidel daughter.

Sid needed an agent because he wants to sell the Bannister land. Apparently nobody told the Solvangs what happened to it!

Not that I'm saying anything happened, but I figured everybody heard the rumors.

When we arrived, Disco and Harlem ran off like they were chasing something.

I'd never been to the Bannister land before. You wouldn't know to look at it that anything's wrong—not that I'm saying anything's wrong. Sid asked what I thought the 17 acres was worth. I told him, I said, "Sid, I'm gonna level with you: there ain't nobody in this town gonna pay a nickel for this land on account of the lake flu."

And do you know what he said? "What lake flu?"

What lake flu?

I couldn't believe my ears. I asked why he thought everybody calls it *Chernobyl Lake.*

Get this: he thought it was because Kansas hates communism so much, we blame Russia that the lake is ugly. I see why folks can't make up their minds about this guy. Nothing he says makes any sense, but I honestly think he didn't have a clue about the lake flu.

But that's not the half of it.

We heard a commotion through the trees, followed by the kind of screaming teenage girls do in the face of death or pop stars.

We followed the screaming and found Harlem and Disco huddled over something. Above them there was something painted in black on this old birch tree, something like an arrow. A black arrow pointing straight down.

As we got closer, I could see they were digging something out of the ground like a shallow grave under the arrow. Oh, Honey Bee, my heart nearly stopped. All I could think was there must be a body, only when I looked closer, I saw it. They pushed the dirt aside and pulled out the corner of a wooden box. It was ornate, like the kind of pawnshop hope chest nobody who shops in a pawnshop can actually afford.

It had chains wrapped every which way around it and a rusty brass lock covered in dried mud. We searched around for a key but didn't find one.

Now I know a thing or two about hiding things. There are two reasons to hide something: you either hide it because you want it hidden, or you hide it because you want it found.

This box wanted to be found.

While I was standing there, a migraine from the Seventh Gate came on. You don't suppose I could've caught the lake flu just from being down there an hour, do you?

From: Honey Bee Kennedy <RevelationSevenfold@prairienet.com>
To: Melba Deerborn <MelbaMayDeerborn@prairienet.com>

I ain't one to gossip, but I wouldn't believe a word that came out of that Solvang's mouth, pretending not to know about the lake! He's probably trying to cover his tracks because you busted him trying to peddle poisoned land.

I'm sure you don't have no lake flu, but if I was you, I'd take a long shower, and I wouldn't ever go back. As for Disco, I'll be having a word with her.

Whatever happened to the box they found?

From: Melba Deerborn <MelbaMayDeerborn@prairienet.com>
To: Honey Bee Kennedy <RevelationSevenfold@prairienet.com>

No idea. They couldn't get it open, so Sid took it home. I wouldn't have touched that box with a Swiss fishing pole, but Harlem and Disco were hopping around like jumping beans at a revival, hollering, "We found it! We found it!"

Harlem was waving an artsy-tartsy paper like a treasure map. That box sure didn't look like any kind of treasure to me, but maybe you can get some answers outta Disco.

From: Disco Kennedy <lostblue@prairienet.com>
To: Harlem Solvang <torturedsol@zoomail.com>

What do you think all those hobbit papers mean? They had that important smell, like carbon paper and gravity. Pop sure went to some trouble to hide that box, and he went to twice as much trouble to make sure we'd find it, so I've got some theories. You don't have to be fluent in hobbit to count to four, but so much for our ticket out of Goodnight.

The worst part is our mason jar escape fund stalled at $748.35 since we stopped working for cash and started hunting for treasure. I can't believe we're right where we started. Not only are we not getting out of this town anytime soon, but I'm not getting out of my room for a week. When I got home, Mama grounded me!

I asked her what I did wrong, and she said, "I think we both know."

I was too afraid to ask what she meant in case I had done something and forgotten.

So what's your dad gonna do with all those files?

From: Harlem Solvang <torturedsol@zoomail.com>
To: Disco Kennedy <lostblue@prairienet.com>

Dad gave the files to that hippie translator from the community center, but when he asked how long it will take her to get through them, she whistled. That can't be good.

Handwritten letter marked "SENSITIVE" slid under Ford Hollis's door

Ford,

I'd hoped if I could sell off those empty acres we inherited on the lake, maybe we'd come up with enough to buy the Hallelujah, but it turns out there's something wrong with the land, and no one will buy it. The agent seemed to think everyone in Goodnight knew about this.

Goodnight lake flu. Maybe you've heard of it?

If this lake flu isn't weird enough, I found a strange box there. When I managed to get it open, it was full of records and what appear to be water tests. There are pages of medical and industrial jargon, but the notes are written in the same dead languages Pop's will was written in.

Before I put myself in debt to save your hotel and we go to the trouble of translating 200 pages of rune-garble, is there something you want to tell me about the death of Pop Bannister?

Sid

Handwritten letter found under Sid Solvang's door

Sid,

I figured you heard the rumors. The truth is nobody knows if there's really something wrong with the lake. All I can tell you is that, yes, there is a mysterious illness going around. For some time, livestock have been dying or exhibiting peculiar patterns—like the Bannister alpacas, a.k.a. "the Chernobyl alpacas"—but there's no science proving it does or doesn't have anything to do with the lake. Goodnight American Tires monitors the water since the factory virtually sits on top of it, and all their environmental tests come back clean.

They suggested it could be some kind of bird flu because the lake is a migration hot spot.

There's been enough speculation that the council formed a committee to look into it, but it's all on the down-low because everyone is afraid it'll scare the tire factory away if they discover there's something wrong. We can't afford to lose those jobs and the tax revenue.

I'm leading the committee, but most of the council is pretty convinced the culprit is some kind of bacterial imbalance from natural algae. Our council is entirely volunteer, and we don't have a lot of resources, not to mention there's concern about property values falling over gossip, as you witnessed firsthand today, so the mayor has asked us to proceed quietly and with caution.

So far that means silently in slow motion with no budget.

Maybe that chicken scratch you found will have some answers for us all.

Meanwhile, maybe we can get together tomorrow to discuss your ideas on the Hallelujah?

Ford

Goodnight Star

LOST AND FOUND, MONDAY EDITION

LOST: The Hobbes family has lost their kitten, Spoon. The gray calico was last seen wandering the eastern alley behind Emporia Road on Sunday. There is no cash reward, but Tommy Hobbes has offered a free tire rotation to anyone who helps them find the missing cat.

15

Ain't Jesus Red?

Note Passed from Harlem to Disco before homeroom, Tuesday

Is there something you wanna tell me? I cashed my check, so I stopped by your garage to pick up our New York jar, but I noticed only my money was left. Why'd you take yours out?

Note found in Harlem's locker, one hour later

I was hoping you wouldn't notice. Mama finally complained to Pottstock about raising rent after Christmas, so he raised the rent early, and we're short. She took every penny I've saved, and she said there will be no more allowance until she can find a way to make rent.

Mama said things would be different now that she's working at the factory, but she's working longer and harder than ever. I wrote a song about it called "Working 9 to 5 to 9 Again."

She even took the couch apart, looking for dimes, so

there was no chance I was keeping that old mason jar out of Dodge. I'm sorry.

Note passed from Harlem to Disco, three minutes later in shop class

I wish you'd told me. Maybe you could work at the May Day with me. We've been so busy lately, I'll bet Dad would hire you. Want me to ask?

Note passed from Disco to Harlem, 15 minutes later

My mama would have to sign off for me to get a real job since I'm a minor, and she'd never let me work for your family. Melba told her your dad's communist because he gives food to poor people. I don't know why when the church helps poor folks it's God's work, but when anyone else helps them, it's socialism? Why is Jesus the only one who gets to be a communist?

I'll find a way to put some money in that jar.

Yesterday I went door to door asking if I could make a little money shoveling snow, but everybody said the same thing: Pottstock raised all the rents, so nobody has a nickel to spare.

When's your dad gonna get the papers from the hobbit box translated?

Note passed from Harlem to Disco, five minutes later

Does it matter? There's no money in it. Just dusty papers. I can't believe he's actually paying to translate them, and I can't believe we wasted so much time looking for that dumb box.

By the way, I'm pretty sure what your landlord did can't be legal. Let me ask my dad.

From: Sid Solvang <brooklyncalling@zoomail.com>
To: Honey Bee Kennedy <RevelationSevenfold@prairienet.com>

Dear Ms. Kennedy,

I hope you're not offended, but Harlem mentioned your landlord raised your rent illegally and I'm concerned. It seems like it could be a simple lawsuit, maybe even small claims. My cousin is a lawyer back in Hoboken, and I'd be happy to ask her about it if you want.

Kindly,

Sid

From: Honey Bee Kennedy <RevelationSevenfold@prairienet.com>
To: Sid Solvang <brooklyncalling@zoomail.com>

By my clock, lawyers are crooks, and there's no sense in paying one crook to out-crook another crook. Besides, I'm too busy to think about it, so how am I gonna find the time to do something I can't find 22 seconds to think about?

I prayed on it, and someone on the night shift called out for the week on account of gall bladder trouble, so I'll be working swing shift until we're set.

No need to worry on our account. We've taken plenty of punches. As for that serpent landlord, the Lord took down Rome, so he can handle a golfer who's afraid of his own wife.

Goodnight Star

LETTERS FROM GOODNIGHTERS, TUESDAY EDITION

Dear Goodnight,

Anybody else's rent go up again?

Maybe this town is too polite to call out the vampire among us on account of him being a church man, so it's up to me to address the ski-goggled bloodsucker riding around Moses with his sun tea and loafers, planning world domination from a golf cart.

My auntie lives in one of Pottstock's "luxury" condos. Every time it rains, the shingles fall off. One time a mess of them came flying so hard, it nearly killed the dog. He knocked down a neighborhood of sturdy bungalows to put in those dog-killing eyesores.

When the richest man around buys up the town and then raises rents so he can buy up more of the town, that [doesn't] sound Christian to me, but none of you've got the biscuits to say something. This leech ain't stopping 'til he owns the whole town and can't none of us afford to live in it. Now Aspen Pottstock wants the keys to the Hallelujah? NO.

Yours truly,

Bailey Nation

From: Aspen Pottstock <aspen@pottstockenterprises.com>

To: Mayor Carol Shultz <mayor@goodnight.gov>

This Solvang character is becoming a thorn in my side. It's bad enough he's turning the May Day into Moscow, but now I'm hearing from the rumor mill that the council is courting him to bid on the hotel. I was told the Hallelujah was mine for the taking. What is going on?

From: Mayor Carol Shultz <mayor@goodnight.gov>
To: Aspen Pottstock <aspen@pottstockenterprises.com>

Mr. Pottstock,

Given the years you've demanded this council let business be business under your motto, "the market is the market," I'm sure you understand the position we're in.

Certainly there's no harm in entertaining all offers. Ford Hollis has had a bee in his bonnet over the Hallelujah for years, and as much as I'd love to reject any idea out of Ford's bonnet, honestly, he's right on this one. What family doesn't have history with the hotel?

You could sweeten your offer. You can't pretend you don't know what it's worth.

From: Sid Solvang <brooklyncalling@zoomail.com>
To: Council Member Ford Hollis <FHollis@goodnight.gov>

I walked by the hotel on my way home from the May Day tonight, and I stopped to take a closer look at those steep gingerbread gables and Gothic Revival windows of the Hallelujah all boarded up and waiting for the wrecking ball.

That hotel seemed to follow me home, and I couldn't sleep all night. I just kept thinking that someone has to do something.

I've discussed it with my wife, and though it's quite a gamble to take on more debt, we're willing to take the risk.

We've talked to the bank, and we're ready. I understand you may have incentives for contractors willing to help. We'll need whatever they can offer. It will take every penny we have and more we don't have to get the doors of Hallelujah open again.

16

Meet Me at the May Day

From: Council Member Ford Hollis <FHollis@goodnight.gov>
To: Sid Solvang <brooklyncalling@zoomail.com>

The papers are signed, the contractors are ready, and zoning has given us the green light.

When word spread that you saved the Hallelujah, so many folks offered to help, it was really something. We've got electricians, plumbers, contractors, and the world's most opinionated roofer offering services at cost, and in some cases, entirely free, to rescue the hotel.

City Hall received so many calls from folks offering to help—even regular people offering to paint or clean up—it's almost restored my faith in humanity.

www.PrairieChat.org Private Chat Room

MELBA has entered the chat.

HONEY BEE has entered the chat.

HONEY BEE: You there?

MELBA: Did you hear about the Hallelujah?

HONEY BEE: The hotel?

MELBA: Somebody bought it.

HONEY BEE: Who?

MELBA: That Solvang.

HONEY BEE: I didn't think anyone would ever buy that old thing. The roof's caving in.

MELBA: I heard he took out a second mortgage to pay for it.

HONEY BEE: Seems like a shame nobody around here could buy it.

MELBA: Better him than Pottstock.

HONEY BEE: That's a lot of money to pay for a headache. It's gonna take a world of work to put that place back together.

MELBA: He's done pretty well by the May Day. Bailey says he's decent to work for, and he pays better than Curtis did.

HONEYBEE: Whatever happened with that box y'all found?

MELBA: I don't think Lainie finished translating it. It must've been 300 pages.

HONEY BEE: You going to Jazzercise today?

MELBA: Depends. You got anything to drink?

HONEY BEE: Come on over.

Letter to Sid and Scarlet Solvang from Molly Miller, received by mail, Saturday

Dear Mr. and Mrs. Solvang,

I heard what you did to save the Hallelujah Hotel, and I wanted to thank you. My grandparents met working there as teenagers, and that old heap meant everything to this town.

You said you wanted to do right by this town, and by my watch, you've done right by us as few have. From now on, when I need biscuits, I'll be taking my business to the May Day, and if my grandchildren ever actually come back to visit, we'll be putting them up at the Hallelujah.

Molly Miller, retired schoolteacher

JOURNAL ENTRY, SID SOLVANG, SUNDAY

We've barely started renovations, and there's already a waiting list to stay at the hotel.

Ford wasn't exaggerating: local contractors offered such generous terms, I thought there must be some mistake. Everyone is so relieved the Hallelujah isn't about to be replaced by a Super 8, strangers are coming out of the woodwork offering help.

The last time there was this much expectation around me, the whole thing fell apart so apocalyptically, I'm afraid to get my hopes up, but I have to admit it gives me a little skip in my step when I walk down Emporia Road and see the pink neon of the May Day, to think I had something to do with keeping those lights on.

If the Hallelujah turns out half as well, we'll be set, but there's a long road ahead to restore those bones. I can't wait to tear the boards off those windows and get some light in there.

It reminds me of an old Kastor's Drugstore I used to

pass every day on my way to the academy. I dreamed of fixing it up and converting it into a restaurant. It sat empty long enough the building fell into disrepair and squatters, but somehow no one ever knocked it down. After class, I'd take the train by it on my way to work as a fry cook and imagine my grand opening: the ribbon cutting, the sound of corks popping, the buzz of the most cynical palates in the world won over. I passed it and dreamed it so many times, it felt like it belonged to me.

Now when I go near a kitchen, it feels like I'm trespassing on the shadow of my former self, a better self, a chef. But I've lost it. I used to dream new dishes in my sleep. Since Sol's went down, my nights are dreamless.

I keep telling myself I don't need a James Beard Award nor a Michelin star—I've just gotta do better than a budget motel. Pottstock sank the bar so low, I shouldn't feel this much pressure. But I can't sleep. My not-depression has been replaced by not-anxiety.

Ford says once we get the hotel up and running, if it does as well as he believes it will, it won't take a year to save enough money to go home to Brooklyn. Of course, now when we go, we're going to have to find a place with room for three alpacas. We've all become quite attached.

Note passed from Disco to Harlem before homeroom, Monday

I heard we're supposed to get snow overnight. I need to start refilling the mason jar, and I'm thinking we can make a killing shoveling sidewalks. Wanna meet after school to make a plan? This time we'll keep the jar at your house so my mama can't get her mitts on it!

Note passed from Harlem to Disco after homeroom

Did you forget I have a job? I have to work every day this week.

Now that we're not totally broke, my parents said I can spend winter break with my aunt in Brooklyn. Mom found a cheap ticket on the red-eye Friday night.

Why don't you meet me at the May Day so we can hang out before I leave?

Note passed from Disco to Harlem before homeroom Tuesday

Sorry I couldn't make it last night. The heat keeps going out, so my mama made me stay at Melba's while she was at work, and that bossy poodle wouldn't let me out of her sight for a minute. Of course, it turned out to be a trick. Reverend Arlo and his wife just happened to come by, and next thing you know, the Bibles were out, and there was Lean Cuisine for all.

Note passed from Harlem to Disco, after homeroom

Did you know there used to be a cooking club at school?

You know Jatori and Lindsay, those kinda homespun girls from my IB History class? I guess Jatori's dad is a cook in Moses, so she grew up in kitchens too, and Lindsay's mom catered before she had five kids. They came by the May Day last night, and when they found out I've been cooking there, they asked if I'd be interested in bringing back the cooking club.

Wanna do it with me?

Note passed from Disco to Harlem, one hour later

Everybody knows Lindsay is still afraid of the dark, and Jatori wears too much yellow. I don't trust anyone who wears that much yellow. You never have any free time as it is; I don't see why you'd wanna give yourself another thing to do.

When do you leave for Brooklyn?

From: Abbey Solvang <abbeyroadyogi@omwardbound.org>
To: Scarlet Bannister Solvang <mystifried@zoomail.com>

Scarlet!

Before you panic, don't worry, Harlem arrived at LaGuardia on time this morning. She's been asleep ever since. We'll be having pizza for breakfast as soon as she wakes up, obviously.

The real reason I'm emailing is to warn you. I don't want to call because I know Sid will pick up if the phone rings this early.

Does Sid still subscribe to the *Times*? You have to keep him away from the newspaper today. Burn it. Feed it to the alpacas. Tell him a baby tornado swooped down and swallowed it whole. Don't let him read the *New York Times*!

From: Scarlet Bannister Solvang <mystifried@zoomail.com>

To: Abbey Solvang <abbeyroadyogi@omwardbound.org>

It's too late. At this very moment, I'm looking out my kitchen window and watching Sid behind the barn setting the *Times* on fire in my dad's old Sears grill. He has such a look of doom on his face, I'm almost afraid to ask. I have to be in the May Day kitchen in 20 minutes, but maybe I can call you after the morning rush. It should be slow this close to Christmas.

Maybe you can tell me why a grown man would set the *New York Times* on fire.

17

Nobody's Business

From: Abbey Solvang <abbeyroadyogi@omwardbound.org>
To: Scarlet Bannister Solvang <mystifried@zoomail.com>

Here's the story: There was a night when Sid was still at the academy and a bunch of us went out drinking. He was trashed and rambling about his dream restaurant. He dragged us on the train to that boarded-up old Kastor's Drugstore. You remember the one where the workers wore those hideous yellow smocks? It was across from the place with the chopsticks that gave you splinters, but they had good wonton soup. Maybe he doesn't remember that night. He was so drunk, we practically had to carry him back to the train. He'd drawn these tragically specific blueprints of his vision for the building. I'm pretty sure he carries it in his wallet to this day.

What does this have to do with today? This morning there's a feature in the paper about it. Someone from the academy is opening a restaurant in that very same building!

I don't mean to sound all Y2K, but maybe Sid should be on suicide watch.

JOURNAL ENTRY, SID SOLVANG, SATURDAY

Of all the crack houses in New York.

Of all the abandoned buildings he could've chosen, Oliver Dean picked my corner, my displaced dream to open his restaurant, Ein Sof. There's an article in the Times this morning about the promising young chef taking New York by storm with his ultrahip innovative twist on molecular gastronomy.

Can fate be sadistic? It's enough for me to question if there is some malevolent force in the universe, keeping watch, keeping score, taking notes, and somehow I've gotten on its bad side. Surely I'm being punished by a cruel Restaurateur God of New York.

Does every dream hang in the air waiting for someone to take it, and if they can't, it just waits for a faster hand to snatch it out of the dream ether and build it like some cornfield for baseball ghosts? Did everyone who took that train have a dream for that corner, but only little punk-ass Cosby-sweatered Oliver Dean had the mental health to realize the dream I was so close to but just couldn't reach?

There's a photo in the Times of Oliver, tribal-inked arms folded with skepticism under the carelessly rolled sleeves of his whites, looking like an accidental rock star standing in front of the very same drugstore-crack house-fine-dining kitchen that was meant to be mine. They left the ghost signs and graffiti, only painting the doors and windows with the chic black of Downing Street. Exactly as I pictured it. It's almost like I dreamed the dream so precisely, it was hovering as a cloud over the Lower East Side, just waiting for someone *to steal it. No, not stolen, not even God or fate; it's just real estate. That sad corner screamed "gentrification."*

I can't help thinking I must've mentioned it to him; it's too uncanny. But I've racked my memory and I'm certain I never mentioned it, not to anyone. The vision seemed too decadent, too much a pipe dream, too embarrassing to speak out loud.

If ink could kill, I'd be lying dead under the New York Times food section. Instead, I've gotta hold it together long enough to whip something up in the kitchen. Scarlet is working, and Disco will be here any minute.

From: Disco Kennedy <lostblue@prairienet.com>
To: Harlem Solvang <torturedsol@zoomail.com>

You picked the right Christmas to go back to New York. The windchill's brutal tonight, and they say it's only getting worse.

Your dad called this morning to invite me to hang at your house because he heard our heat's out yet again, and of course, Aspen Pottsfuck won't return our calls since he's on another skiing trip. Mom's been picking up extra shifts at the tire factory because flu season's tearing through the laundry room something awful, and she won't ever turn down work, so I was home alone when your dad called. I was too cold and bored to say no.

I don't know what happened between the time your dad hung up the phone in his normal sickly optimistic way to the moment I arrived, but by the time I got to Northwind, it was like a funeral the second I walked in the door. Something had changed.

Your mom was at the May Day, the alpacas were sleeping under the kitchen table, and would you believe your dad was actually cooking? I could tell there was something on his mind, and I was surprised to see him in the kitchen at all because I've seen how he gets. But there he was, staring into a pot of soup like that soup was breaking his heart.

I asked him if he'd gotten over his phobia of kitchens. His face crinkled up all New York–y, and he said he wasn't afraid of kitchens, that it was more like he was mad at kitchens, but he was too sick of leftovers to keep up with the grudge at least for the night. Anyway, he said he wasn't really cooking, just throwing a soup together with whatever he could find.

I'm not a soup person since I don't like vegetables or barley or potatoes or noodles or anything I can't eat with my hands, but I took one taste of this soup and couldn't believe it.

I told him, "This soup is, like, the best thing I've ever tasted in my entire life. You have to put it on the May Day menu!"

He said, "I don't cook anymore."

So I said, "But you have to! It's like a miracle on a spoon. I could write a song about it."

Your dad smiled so crazy town, I thought maybe he was thinking of something else, like maybe there was a puppy in the room I hadn't noticed. But there was no puppy, just some mad soup, tasting like a miracle, and your dad smiling like he just found Jesus or Jesus's puppy.

And he was like, "All right, Disco Kennedy. Write me a song about it."

I asked him why Scarlet does all the cooking at the May Day if he can cook like that.

He got all dark and was like, "I'm done cooking."

And I was like, "I don't think you are done."

Then he got really dark, like he was gonna yell at me, but instead of yelling, he sort of whispered—which was way weirder, and he was like, "I'm done, and I can't talk about it."

I tried to make a deal that if I wrote a song about his soup, he'd put it on the menu, but you'da thought it wasn't his menu to change with the way he acted like I'd asked him to rewrite the Bible. And he said no. Just like that. "No. I just can't do it."

And I was like, "Sid, you could be on the Food Channel with this soup. You could, like, win an Oscar for best soup, it's so good."

And he was like, "It's just dinner."

So then just try to guess what happened next.

I'll give you a minute to come up with a guess. Time's up.

Here it is: your dad went from missing a shingle to the whole roof flying off. He started crying!

CRYING, Harlem!

Your dad was crying like someone had stolen Jesus's puppy!

OHMYGOD, it was SO AWKWARD. So now I'm gonna have to freeze to death at home or eat Lean Cuisine with Melba Deerborn every night because I can never be in the same awkward room with your awkward dad again, no matter how good his soup is.

So don't ask me to meet you at the May Day when you get home.

When are you coming home, by the way?

And while I'm asking questions, are you gonna tell me why soup makes your dad cry?

From: Harlem Solvang <torturedsol@zoomail.com>

To: Disco Kennedy <lostblue@prairienet.com>

The story about my dad is boring and kind of stupid. You don't want to know.

Also, he swore us all to secrecy.

I'm supposed to stay in Brooklyn until New Year's, but I'm really homesick. I never thought I'd miss Goodnight as much as I've missed it. I actually miss Emporia Road. I miss how you can smell the May Day kitchen from down the street. I miss the fight over the geraniums at City Hall. I miss that weird gossip rag that thinks it's a newspaper.

I miss the sun tea on every porch and the suncatchers in every window, even though there's no sun to catch most of the time. I miss slipping free pie to the farmers and taking leftovers to South End to give to all those families that are too proud to take the "wealth-fare."

And you! I miss the May Day almost as much as I miss your yodeling-glitter-tornado self. I can't wait to get back in that kitchen.

From: Disco Kennedy <lostblue@prairienet.com>
To: Harlem Solvang <torturedsol@zoomail.com>

Did you hear Moses is getting a Krispy Kreme? Mama and Melba are going to the grand opening. I think the whole town is going. So that's the big news you're missing.

You should come to my house as soon as you get home because I'm still avoiding your dad. Maybe we could take the guitar down to the river and scream with the crows. It's been a while since they've heard your scream. And for the record, I do not yodel.

JOURNAL ENTRY, SID SOLVANG

When a child called Disco makes you cry, that's got to be some kind of bottom, right?

But it didn't feel like a bottom. It felt like something else.

I made a soup for Disco yesterday. It was nothing. I've thrown together dishes with a thousand times more complexity, more refinement, more thought. This was just something I threw together to feed a child because it was 16 degrees outside and I felt bad she spent the night before eating frozen dinners with Melba Deerborn.

But Disco loved it. She really loved that soup.

Last night I dreamed I was walking through a heavy mist by the river, and there was an empty white plate drifting on the water. I reached down to pick up the plate. Just as I touched it, I woke up. And I woke up thinking about thyme.

Of all the seasonings, thyme is my favorite. It's understated, but it's medicinal. It's sober and volatile at the same time. Most folks don't know that about thyme. Scarlet salvaged the thyme in Pop's little greenhouse, but she really didn't have to because wild thyme grew behind the barn all summer. When we first met, Scarlet slept with thyme leaves under her pillow because she said it kept her nightmares away. She apologized for it, but I remember thinking why would I marry someone who didn't sleep with thyme leaves under their pillow when I could marry someone who did?

That plate seemed to want to tell that story.

I started sketching out a dish built around wild thyme. I couldn't bring myself to actually take the recipe into the kitchen. I don't know if I'll ever be that brave again. It's one thing to throw together a dinner, but to actually create a dish again... It could break a heart.

So I wrote it all out until I could taste the ingredients in my mind, and then I hid it in an old recipe box I found *in the pantry. It's a sort of latke focaccia bound by thyme. Maybe it's enough just to dream it. It's not like the world will miss something that was never created.*

Besides, the May Day doesn't need two chefs. The whole town is in love with Scarlet's menu—for good reason—and business has doubled since word got around that we're restoring the hotel. The world will never know the difference if that recipe never sees the light of day.

But it felt good to almost dream again.

Goodnight Star

LOST AND FOUND, WEDNESDAY EDITION

LOST: Lisa Gail's lighthouse wind chimes disappeared last night. Gail said she has forgiven the thief because maybe somebody needed those bells more than she did.

18

About Roots

From: Harlem Solvang <torturedsol@zoomail.com>
To: Disco Kennedy <lostblue@prairienet.com>

Mom says they need me to work at the May Day every day when I get back. I guess business has gone crazy since the whole town heard we saved the hotel. She said when everybody found out we put the house on the line to buy it, all the people who'd refused to go to the May Day changed their minds.

Well, not all of them changed their minds.

Dad hired two new waitresses, and they still can't keep up, especially if we keep delivering leftovers. Mom said he should just hire a delivery driver, but I like taking the leftovers to South End. I think Dad feels the same way. You should come with us sometime.

From: Disco Kennedy <lostblue@prairienet.com>
To: Harlem Solvang <torturedsol@zoomail.com>

Not coming to the May Day to watch your dad cry in the soup. Come by the house when you're home. And another thing: tell Lindsay to stop emailing; I'm not joining any cooking club.

From: Sid Solvang <brooklyncalling@zoomail.com>
To: Abbey Solvang <abbeyroadyogi@omwardbound.org>

Scarlet says you're worried. I'm fine. Totally fine. I don't know why you're worried. I have a diner to run and a hotel to open and no time to feel anything but busy.

I was thinking, if building birdhouses can heal sadness, imagine what building a hotel could do! Busyness is the answer to all our problems. So I put myself to work. The foundation on the Hallelujah is done, and all the heavy lifting was handled. What's left is the kind of work I can handle on my own. So, over the Christmas break, I've thrown myself into the restoration. I tore the boards off the windows so I can see Emporia Road while I work. The funny thing is once those windows were open, Emporia Road could see me too.

Two days before Christmas, as I was sanding away, I looked up, and there was Ford Hollis with his sons, doing some last-minute shopping at the emporium two doors down. Next thing I knew, Ford invited half his friends over to help. Christmas Eve, I figured I'd have the place to myself, but twice as many people turned up. We took Christmas off, but the day after, so many volunteers came by to help, I was hard-pressed to find jobs for everyone.

The biggest surprise was Scarlet's sister Tanya came by when she heard we needed help. She said, "If you mention to my sisters I was here, I'll deny it. They'll think I've gone soft."

Reverend Arlo brought a truck full of volunteers. I figured they were from his church, but it turns out they were the same folks we've been delivering food to on the south side. Arlo said Raina Freeman called offering to help. She said if someone could pick them up, there were a lot of folks on South End who owed the Solvang family a hand.

We're so far ahead of schedule, we're moving up the opening.

So don't worry about me. And happy New Year!

From: Abbey Solvang <abbeyroadyogi@omwardbound.org>
To: Sid Solvang <brooklyncalling@zoomail.com>

I almost believed you when you said you were fine, until you said *totally*.

Nobody who is totally fine says they are totally fine.

Bedford Falls sounds swell, but Kastor's Drugstore wasn't the only abandoned building in the city. Plenty more crack houses in the sea. Don't give up on New York.

From: Sid Solvang <brooklyncalling@zoomail.com>
To: Abbey Solvang <abbeyroadyogi@omwardbound.org>

Swell? I can hear your sarcasm in my eyes.

For the record, it hasn't been all Zuzu's petals here.

Not everyone in Goodnight wants us here, and lately I've noticed a rusted Nova idling near the diner on the darker side of Emporia Road, like it's watching us. I asked Bailey about it. She said I'm a paranoid narcissist and the whole world couldn't care less what I'm up to.

Don't mention it to Harlem. I know how you talk, and I don't want her getting how she gets. She wants to start a cooking club at school. Scarlet's hoping it will get her to stop obsessing about moving back to Brooklyn. I may have scared her only friend away, and the rest of Harlem's social life revolves around the May Day.

Scarlet's worried she's turning into us, God forbid!

From: Sid Solvang <brooklyncalling@zoomail.com>
To: Disco Kennedy <lostblue@prairienet.com>

I hope you don't mind that I asked Harlem to give me your email address so I could check on you. I can't help noticing you haven't been around since the soup incident. I feel like I should explain myself or at least apologize. Apparently I cry over soup now, which I didn't realize until that night. That's a long story I can't go into, since there's a reasonable chance I'll start crying again. I'm sitting at the May Day counter with Bailey over my shoulder, and as I'm sure you know, Bailey does not abide men crying.

What I want to say is please come back. I know it's been busy, but we'll always make room for you. We all miss you, especially Harlem, who'd like me to tell you there's Snickers pie today. We have dirt cake too, but she says you don't believe in dirt cake, and I'm not supposed to ask why. Please come back. The May Day isn't the same without you.

From: Disco Kennedy <lostblue@prairienet.com>
To: Sid Solvang <brooklyncalling@zoomail.com>

I know why you cry in your soup. I know all your secrets now. I googled you last night.

New York Food Magazine

JUNE 2001 ISSUE

Chutzpah Gone South; Culinary Hotshot Strips Sol's of Soul

By: Tobias North, senior food critic

How do you alienate an entire community of loyal patrons who have been your bread and butter for nearly a century?

Ask Chef Sid Solvang.

A faithful fixture on Bedford Avenue for 84 years, Sol's Delicatessen is closing its Brooklyn doors, and it's no mystery what happened.

Want to know what culinary suicide looks like on a plate?

One dish on the menu at Sol's embodies everything that has gone wrong with Solvang's ill-fated revamp of this Midwood establishment.

Remember the hearty pastrami that towered generously over the sturdy, deeply savory rye Sol's Deli was famous for?

Pastrami no more.

Solvang replaced his grandfather's hearty signature pastrami with *smoked pastrami foam on black mustard-pickled cabbage puree with miso-encrusted artisan rye chips.*

It's not that it wasn't good; it's that it was so precious, such a fussy and self-conscious caricature of the original straightforward sandwich, one could almost feel the earth shake as the entire Jewish cemetery around the corner rolled over in their graves. Not to mention that it was so slight on the plate, it was almost an amuse-bouche fraction of the generous pastrami on his grandfather's menu—an unamused-bouche, if you ask this palate.

And what is corned beef tartare? You don't want to know.

Craving a knish? The luscious knish that Sol made famous, Sid made cringe. This knish is having an identity crisis, and it is called the gnocchi knish kebob.

Gefilte fish is now gefilte ceviche.

And what became of Sol's famous latkes?

Try the *pink Yukon latke glass on Himalayan salt.* The sheer potato shards are so slight that even paired with *su vide gehatke leber mousse,* the duo can't find a plate small enough.

Matzo ball soup is now *black winter truffle-infused matzo spheres,* held together with xanthan gum. But neither xanthan gum nor glue can hold this culinary circus together.

Solvang's molecular gastronomy bells, whistles, and foams are lost on the regulars who kept this beloved neighborhood tradition thriving for eight decades.

According to family legend, when Solomon Soloveitchik came to Ellis Island and became Sol Solvang, he came with $23 and a dream of bringing the recipes of the old world to this new one. He borrowed a friend's weathered pushcart and went to work selling pastrami. It didn't take long to save enough to trade that pushcart for a brick-and-mortar deli. In a neighborhood full of homesick and hungry Jewish immigrants, Sol's traditional Eastern-European fare made the deli a favorite gathering spot for new immigrants looking for community and older expatriates longing for a taste of home.

When Sol retired, his son, Max Solvang, took over and grew the business despite economic downturn. By the time Max handed the business to his son, Sid Solvang had already made a name for himself as a rising star of the academy, combining molecular gastronomy with classic French techniques, earning high praise from professors who called him a wonder chef, and he graduated as "the culinary student most likely to take over the world."

He was well on his way, making guest appearances in Manhattan's most prestigious kitchens when he was awarded the coveted Distinguished Chef's Grant for Up-and-Coming Chefs. Rather than open something new in Manhattan, he took the money and ran back to Brooklyn, taking over Sol's for his aging father and investing the grant in the family business.

Behind the mad scientist was wife and fellow ACS classmate, Scarlet Bannister Solvang, a reclusive but accomplished chef in her own right who turned down an offer at Morimoto to follow her husband off this cliff.

For a humble deli that served Jewish comfort food to immigrants, Sol's took for granted decades of transgenerational loyalty, but the loyalists who kept this mom-and-pop establishment steady all these years have moved on.

For a deli once bustling with locals, now-empty booths and ominous stillness are the fallout that happens when a tone-deaf culinary showman is too busy deconstructing matzo balls to remember patrons come to eat, not to watch a chef play with their food.

Not in this neighborhood.

Sol's will open its doors for the last time on Friday, June 22. No reservation necessary.

From: Disco Kennedy <lostblue@prairienet.com>
To: Sid Solvang <brooklyncalling@zoomail.com>

I read what they said about you, but it didn't sound like you at all. What happened?

I can keep a secret. Trust me, I've got secrets that would make the devil blush. On second thought, maybe nothing makes the devil blush because you'd think he's seen everything by now—war and Madonna and such.

My mama says I ask too many questions and that's why they don't let me go to Sunday school anymore. I wrote a song about it called "If the Devil Were Blue." I can't help it if I want to know everything. If that sends me to the Nethers, maybe I don't mind. I don't wanna go to a Heaven where nobody asks questions. That doesn't sound like Heaven to me.

Anyhow, alls I'm saying is I can keep a secret.

From: Sid Solvang <brooklyncalling@zoomail.com>
To: Disco Kennedy <lostblue@prairienet.com>

I hope you never stop asking questions. I don't know about devils, but I can tell you I came to Goodnight with more skeletons than I could keep in a Brooklyn closet. But no secrets.

It's no secret how everything went off the rails. Before I took over Sol's, I could do no wrong. They called me a genius, and I made the mistake of believing them.

It seemed the Michelin stars were all lined up when my father announced his retirement.

The trouble was I thought Sol's was beneath me and I needed to bring it up to my level.

My father hadn't changed the menu in the 42 years since he'd taken over the kitchen for my grandfather, but I had money to burn, so I started changing things. I was sort of drunk on all these techniques I'd picked up. I rewrote the entire menu.

My father warned me I was taking it too far, but I thought I knew better. I told him he was out of touch. I told him to trust me. He did.

He entrusted me with his life's work, and I destroyed it. I became a joke. Regulars stopped coming. Bills piled up. We had to sell Sol's and the house. I broke everything they built.

That's the heartbreak that killed my parents.

Now you know everything. No one here knows what happened, and while I couldn't bring myself to lie about it, I really don't want to look into anyone's eyes and see Brooklyn, so do me a favor and keep it to yourself?

I've kept my hands off the May Day menu. I'll never make that mistake again, but I'll tell you the truth, ever since that day I made you soup, I've been dreaming of empty plates.

Every night another empty plate.

From: Disco Kennedy <lostblue@prairienet.com>
To: Sid Solvang <brooklyncalling@zoomail.com>

They called you a genius? You mean like Einstein? I know as much about cooking as I know about physics, but somehow good soup doesn't seem like it adds up to rocket science.

Around here we call that getting too big for your britches, but I'll give you this: That was the best soup I've ever had, and if you wanna convince me you're a cooking genius, I don't mind coming to dinner. You just gotta promise not to cry.

I don't know why anyone would waste their time cooking anything for someone whose job it is to criticize food when you could cook for someone whose job it is to love it.

JOURNAL ENTRY, SID SOLVANG

I've been thinking about turmeric. Last night I had another one of my plate dreams. I walked toward the plate, and just beyond it was a perfect line of empty white plates floating like stepping stones. The last one turned turmeric orange when I touched it, and turmeric has been on my mind ever since. The way it possesses a potato is a such a delicate fusion of earth and fire, and that got me thinking about root vegetables. About roots.

Disco turned up at my door this morning, asking if I could make her something better than Hamburger Helper. I asked what she had in mind, and she said she had some Pop Rocks she'd like to throw in the deep fryer to see what would happen. I told her she was thinking like a chef.

When she left, I sketched out an idea for how to fry Pop Rocks.

I stashed it in my recipe box. To my surprise the recipes were adding up, so I put one of Pop's old padlocks on it and hid it in the pantry. It's been liberating coming up with dishes I don't plan on ever plating. No food critics in a recipe box.

Goodnight Star

LOST AND FOUND, SUNDAY EDITION

FOUND: Lime wool mittens were forgotten at bingo Friday night. According to Michelle Tracy, they're too fancy for the lost and found, so they're being held at the front desk.

19

Never Stop If You See a Girl with an Accordion by the Side of the Road

From: Harlem Solvang <torturedsol@zoomail.com>
To: Abbey Solvang <abbeyroadyogi@omwardbound.org>

So I stopped by Disco's house this morning, and her mom answered the door. She said Disco would be home any minute, so I should come inside.

I tried to say no, but she couldn't hear me since her mutant Chihuahuas wouldn't stop barking. So Honey Bee dragged me in and sat me down on her lumpy couch. It was the first time I'd ever been alone with her, and Disco was right, she didn't waste any time.

She was like, "You know the Jews were the chosen ones."

She went into this whole Jewish Jesus thing, and she insisted on taking me to church next Sunday. Disco warned me that would happen if I ever talked to her more than 10 minutes.

But then she told me Disco's story about her uncle giving her that blue guitar is a lie. She said, "There ain't no Uncle Casey, and she's never met the uncles she does have. My brothers sure as heck never touched a guitar, or my daddy would rip the strings right out of it."

Then she blew smoke rings at me and said, "Ever been saved, Harlem?"

When her neighbor came by with a bag of tomatoes, I managed to slip out, but not without a dozen of "Melba's famous heirlooms from the greenest greenhouse in all of Goodnight."

That really happens here. People just show up at the door and hand you tomatoes.

I was on my way to the river to ask Disco why she lied, but I got a bad feeling about it. I turned in the other direction and headed straight for the May Day, where I asked Dad to put me to work, just so I didn't have to think about it.

I wouldn't care where she got that freaking guitar. Why would she make that up?

From: Disco Kennedy <lostblue@prairienet.com>
To: Harlem Solvang <torturedsol@zoomail.com>

Seems like you've been avoiding me since you got home from New York.

Are you gonna tell me what's wrong, or should I expect to see you running away next time I run into you at the Food Barn?

From: Harlem Solvang <torturedsol@zoomail.com>
To: Disco Kennedy <lostblue@prairienet.com>

Your mom said there is no Uncle Casey. She said you were telling stories. Why would you make something like that up? Why would I care? It doesn't make sense.

From: Disco Kennedy <lostblue@prairienet.com>
To: Harlem Solvang <torturedsol@zoomail.com>

Was she drunk? I don't think she'd lie on account of Jesus, but she must've been confused. That guitar didn't fall out of the sky.

I'll tell you the whole story, but I've never told anyone because my very real uncle Casey asked me not to. So keep it to yourself.

Before country music came to my door, my nights were spent alone watching CMT in this old bungalow, covered in Mama's verses of Revelation on yellow Post-its, eating TV dinners. Mama worked three jobs, so Shimmy and Jingle were my only company, and you know those blind Chihuahuas don't love anything.

Sometimes my mama's sisters would break away from the farm and show up at the door.

Just once an uncle turned up.

My mama was working the graveyard shift when a stranger with a blue guitar, a case of root beer, and a hound dog named Ransom swaggered through the door. He turned off the TV and said, "I'm your uncle Casey. I'm here to introduce you to *Real Country Music*."

He started strumming the most beautiful blue twang I'd ever heard come out of a guitar.

"This is a song I wrote about why I quit drinking," he said. "I call it, 'Never Stop If You See a Girl with an Accordion by the Side of the Road.'"

He taught me seven chords that night, and he let me keep the guitar. He stayed long enough to smoke half a pack of Luckys and give me the history of country music.

As he was leaving, he asked if I always opened the door for strangers.

I said yes, and he said, "I could've been a serial killer or a Jehovah's Witness." He laughed in a drinking way and said, "If I were you, I wouldn't tell your mama I came by."

I assured him I don't tell my mama anything.

Before he stepped off the porch, I asked him if he ever knew my father.

He looked me up and down like he was trying to size up how many secrets I could hold in one night. Finally he lit another Lucky Strike and answered through the smoke. "Nobody did."

I asked if he was really dead. He got all fluster bunked and said, "I heard he's in Canada or Alaska. Carter heard Florida. Mighta been Ohio. Nobody knows, so he's probably in Texas."

Then he was gone, midshrug.

I never saw him again. I heard rumors one of my uncles started drinking and wandered off the Kennedy farm. I always wondered if it had something to do with a girl and an accordion by the side of the road, but I knew better than to ask anyone.

Then one day the aunties stopped coming. I ran into my Aunt Eileen at Food Barn, I waved hello, and she took off running, leaving a full grocery cart in the middle of the bakery, like she'd seen a ghost or a spider.

I didn't think too much of it until it happened again with my other aunties and then the cousins. They'd run from me like I had the plague. After a while, I felt like I did have the plague.

Nowadays I don't even know who half of them are, and I have no idea why they run.

But my uncle had a soul full of country music, and I really thought he might turn up for opening night at the May Day. I can't believe I let myself believe such a bridge of sky pie.

I don't know why Mama said there's no Uncle Casey, but if you know anything about her, it's that she can hold a grudge for 107 lives, so it's probably just bad blood between Kennedys.

Anyhow, that's the whole story. You can take it or leave it.

From: Harlem Solvang <torturedsol@zoomail.com>
To: Disco Kennedy <lostblue@prairienet.com>

I can't believe your own family runs away from you. That's fucked up. No wonder you listen to country music and can't get enough glitter.

From: Disco Kennedy <lostblue@prairienet.com>
To: Harlem Solvang <torturedsol@zoomail.com>

So you'll meet me at the Moses?

From: Harlem Solvang <torturedsol@zoomail.com>
To: Disco Kennedy <lostblue@prairienet.com>

Can't. I have to work at the May Day.

By the way, my mom said if we wanna start the cooking club, we can meet at our house.

I've been asking around, and we're up to five out of the eight signatures required to be recognized by Goodnight High as an official club.

Wanna be the sixth?

Almost forgot, my dad asked if we can get more of those tomatoes Melba gave me the other day. You got her email address? He won't shut up about those tomatoes.

20

Dream Drunk

From: Sid Solvang <brooklyncalling@zoomail.com>

To: Melba Deerborn <MelbaMayDeerborn@prairienet.com>

Dear Ms. Deerborn,

I've heard about your tomatoes since the day we pulled into Goodnight. I was tempted to ask about them that day on the lake, but when we found Pop's old box and you gave me the lowdown on lake flu, it didn't seem like the right time. Everywhere I go, I hear people talking about Melba's tomatoes, but I'd never tried one until last week.

My daughter came by the May Day with the most beautiful heirlooms I've ever seen, and when I sliced one, I couldn't believe it tasted better than it looked.

I took one bite and immediately had a vision of turmeric. That night it came to my dreams. I woke up and sketched a turmeric symphony, waves of crushed coriander seeds, warm fennel cooked into Yukon Gold potatoes, hints of ginger, all in savory orbit of those heirlooms.

I can't stop dreaming about it. I told Scarlet about it, and now she's dreaming too. She wants to put it on the May Day menu.

I hear your Speckled Romans earned quite a reputation at the Cannery Wars, and Tyler tells me his Carolina Gold loses the Tomato Showdown to you every year. I'm surprised to hear you give your tomatoes away. I wonder if you'd be interested in selling some to the May Day?

Kindly,

Sid Solvang

From: Melba Deerborn <MelbaMayDeerborn@prairienet.com>
To: Sid Solvang <brooklyncalling@zoomail.com>

If you've heard about my tomatoes, you should've also heard there's no buttering me up.

If your wife wants my tomatoes on her menu, why doesn't she ask me herself?

From: Sid Solvang <brooklyncalling@zoomail.com>
To: Melba Deerborn <MelbaMayDeerborn@prairienet.com>

Dear Melba,

Scarlet doesn't like to leave the kitchen. It's just her way. She doesn't like dealing with people, and until recently I didn't like dealing with food, but that's changing. After a soup incident I'd rather not go into, I started dreaming of empty plates. Some nights it's a looping conveyor belt of empty white plates. Other nights it's one vast plate with nothing on it. The day I tried your heirloom tomatoes, the dream changed. For the first time, the plate wasn't empty. I dreamed of a new dish shaped around your heirloom tomatoes.

Maybe you didn't know every dish on the May Day menu was

conceived by Scarlet. I guess you could say I lost my way to the kitchen. I used to dream new recipes in my sleep, but the dreams stopped years ago.

I've had no desire to create anything until I met your tomatoes.

From: Melba Deerborn <MelbaMayDeerborn@prairienet.com>
To: Sid Solvang <brooklyncalling@zoomail.com>

Before I hand over my heirlooms, I wanna know what your big idea is.

From: Sid Solvang <brooklyncalling@zoomail.com>
To: Melba Deerborn <MelbaMayDeerborn@prairienet.com>

Here's my vision: I'll call it a tamosa, like an Indian samosa, except Kansas-afied, with tomatoes. I'll create a sun-dried heirloom tomato flour and fry it into a samosa. I know there are tomato samosas out there, but as far as I know, no chef has ever used tomatoes to make the pastry crust around the potato puree inside. I would add tomatoes inside too, but the main attraction would be the delicacy of a fried tomato flour crust. The second I tasted your tomatoes, I could taste the recipe inventing itself like all the colors of Christmas in one bite.

Tell me if that sounds like something you could spare a tomato for.

From: Melba Deerborn <MelbaMayDeerborn@prairienet.com>
To: Reverend Arlo Foster <humbleservant@goodshepherd.com>
CC: Good Shepherd East Side Prayer Team

Can we assemble the prayer team at my house tonight please?

Sid Solvang wants my tomatoes, and he's coming to try to win me over cooking some fancy dish he's dream drunk over. I don't trust anyone from New York. Will you come?

From: Reverend Arlo Foster <humbleservant@goodshepherd.com>
To: Melba Deerborn <MelbaMayDeerborn@prairienet.com>
CC: Good Shepherd East Side Prayer Team

Cheryl and I will be in the neighborhood on a prayer request, so we can drop by for a while.

From: Honey Bee Kennedy <RevelationSevenfold@prairienet.com>
To: Melba Deerborn <MelbaMayDeerborn@prairienet.com>
CC: Good Shepherd East Side Prayer Team

I'll try anything with your tomatoes in it, so I'm in. What's for dinner?

From: Melba Deerborn <MelbaMayDeerborn@prairienet.com>
To: Honey Bee Kennedy <RevelationSevenfold@prairienet.com>
CC: Good Shepherd East Side Prayer Team

Come on and find out.

From: Reverend Arlo Foster <humbleservant@goodshepherd.com>
To: Melba Deerborn <MelbaMayDeerborn@prairienet.com>

I'm sorry Cheryl and I couldn't stay longer this evening. It seems everyone at church needs a house call this week, so it's been late nights and early mornings every day. Of course, the Lord's work isn't work at all, but I wish I could've stuck around long enough to tell you what

I thought about that dish Sid Solvang whipped up. I've never tasted anything like it, and Cheryl agrees. The two of us were hard-pressed to keep a poker face at your kitchen table because what those tomatoes can do was beyond me.

I should've known to expect the best from your tomatoes, but this was something else.

I hope you said yes. Tomatoes like yours were meant to be shared. The May Day—the world—will be a brighter place with that dish in it.

Let me know when it's officially on the May Day menu, and we'll announce it on the church bulletin. It'll make the Good Shepherd proud.

From: Harlem Solvang <torturedsol@zoomail.com>
To: Abbey Solvang <abbeyroadyogi@omwardbound.org>

Dad's gone mad scientist over Melba's tomatoes. Really he just introduced Goodnight to Indian food, and now Melba's getting all the credit for samosas. I overheard Bailey trying to explain to a table full of Melba's friends that samosas are from the nation of India and not the Potawatomi Indian Reservation out in Mayetta, which she said just means you don't have to feel guilty when you eat them because America didn't try to kill everyone in India, like they did here, and then yada, yada, yada, something about *The Wizard of Oz.*

She said, "There's two types of people in the world, folks who feel guilty and folks who are guilty. I can say that free and clear because ain't no mystery what kind of folks I am."

Bailey has a way with words.

Melba's entire church came to try the "tamosas," and once they realized how good they are, they told the whole town, so we're slammed. Now we're busier than ever, so they need me to help cover the counter. Dad's teaching me how to make his tamosas because they can hardly keep up with the demand.

The best part is, thanks to the tamosa triumph, we finally got our eight signatures, and the Goodnight High Cooking Club will have our first meeting tomorrow at my house!

From: Jatori Bates <lilchef88@ksmail.com>
To: Jan Feyen <jf1988@prairienet.com>

Guess where I was last night? Lindsay and I went to Harlem Solvang's house! Turns out the Bannister Victorian is not haunted, the alpacas are not deranged, and she's not half as weird as she looks. She hosted our first official meeting of the cooking club, and when we arrived, she'd made these, like, vegan wonton cups that were better than the real deal. The girl can cook!

We're meeting at my house next week. You have to come; we're braving macarons.

PS: Don't mention it to anyone. Lindsay doesn't want it to get back to her mom that she's hanging out with a Solvang. Her parents haven't made up their minds about them since everyone says Sid Solvang is a communist. I'm sure if they ever get around to eating at the May Day, they won't care if Vladimir Lenin is in the kitchen, it's so good!

From: Jules Jamison <livingthedream73@zoomail.com>
To: Sid Solvang <brooklyncalling@zoomail.com>

I don't know what you're doing in the sticks down there, but people are talking about you around here. I heard you're cooking again. I heard it's good. We should catch up. Give me a call.

From: Sid Solvang <brooklyncalling@zoomail.com>

To: Jules Jamison <livingthedream73@zoomail.com>

It was good to hear from you after all this time.

I can't take credit for anything that's gone right. Scarlet is our chef. Everything on that menu is hers with the exception of one appetizer. I've been putzing around in the kitchen on the line, but mostly I stay out of her way.

If Sol's taught me anything, it's not to mess with something that's working. The May Day is working, and the town is finally warming up to us. Holly Wilkes bakes us a bread sculpture every Tuesday to thank us for keeping the May Day going. So far she's made *Nativity in Rye*, *Pumpernickel Last Supper*, and *Resurrection in Sourdough*. This week there's a zucchini bread Eiffel Tower beside the pie safe!

How is New York? For the first time, I went a whole day without missing it yesterday.

I wish you could send me a pizza though. There's a Pizza Hut in the next town, but that's it for pizza. Pizza Hut, Jules. That's all they have, and you have to drive to another town to get it.

If I had my groove back, I'd put a pizza on the May Day menu, but I can't be a chef again, not even to give this town a pizza worthy of it.

At least we're starting to save a little money so we can finally make our way home.

Sometimes it feels like nothing outside New York is real and any minute I'll wake up to the sound of sirens and pigeons on the fire escape, I'll have pizza for breakfast and talk about the weird dream I had that there was a world outside New York and I was lost in it for a while.

Can you believe I miss the sound of pigeons and sirens?

Here it's so still, you can hear the crickets. You could probably hear the thoughts of crickets if you listened close enough. It's dawn right now. Harlem is sleeping in, Scarlet's baking, and it's so quiet, you can actually hear the bread rising and the weight of cold against the windows. The air is so clean, I realize I didn't actually ever taste real air before I got here.

Of course, I'll trade air, crickets, and anything that's mine in Kansas for one more Sicilian slice of Luigi's pizza before I die.

From: Jules Jamison <livingthedream73@zoomail.com>
To: Sid Solvang <brooklyncalling@zoomail.com>

You ARE dreaming, but it's nothing that a little money can't wake up.

I've got a lead, but it's too soon to tell. Don't worry, we'll find you a ticket back before Luigi retires and moves to Florida. Save your money and try not to go out of business. We'll get you out of there yet. I'll see if I can FedEx you a slice in the meantime.

From: Skeeter Bannister<highwater@shotmail.com>
To: Sid Solvang <brooklyncalling@zoomail.com>

I'm not one to beat around the bush, especially when that bush is my dinner.

Everybody knows I hate tomatoes. I wouldn't try Melba's even when her heirlooms made the front page of the *Moses Register*, but that wife of yours tricked me into trying your new appetizer, and all I can say is them tamosa deals are the best thing I've ever tasted, hands down.

I couldn't help noticing your way with potatoes.

You've probably heard about my Purple Viking potatoes. They're as good as you've heard. I told Harlem I might be willing to spare some for a new dish, but Harlem says them tamosas are the end of the line and that was a one-time deal because you're scared of kitchens.

Maybe you oughta get over yourself before you miss out on my Vikings. Why don't I bring a sack Sunday, and we'll see if you're scared of them?

JOURNAL ENTRY, SID SOLVANG, MONDAY

Last night Skeeter brought potatoes to the potluck. It seems that last dream of empty plates called these Purple Vikings to them. This morning a phantom scent of dashi woke me out of a dead sleep. I tried to go back to bed, but the dashi turned to miso reaching for roots: sweet potatoes, Red Cored Chantenay carrots, and the heart of it—Skeeter's Vikings, like those crazy potatoes were dreaming themselves into a new flavor, light as the salt of sea air.

I thought, what if it starts with air? Yes! Air is the first ingredient.

I got so excited, I jumped out of bed and wrote three pages. Scarlet was stirring, so I stashed it in the recipe box and hid it behind the stale matzo, where nobody will find it.

Goodnight Star

LEAD STORY, SUNDAY EDITION

Crime Wave Sweeps Goodnight

Do you know where your chimes are? Dozens of wind bells were stolen from Meridian Road on Saturday. It's unclear if it was vandals or thieves since chime remnants were scattered across the street.

Maddie Verne discovered what was left of her Corinthian bells tangled in string around her gate after waking to the sound of her bloodhounds barking furiously at dawn.

GPD Chief Lane Vincent said this was not the first incident.

The same neighborhood lost three wind chimes last week, and several garden gnomes were knocked over leading local law enforcement to question motives.

"I wouldn't get too riled up," Vincent said. "If you asked me, I'd say it was kids, because surely nobody would bother with wind chimes but madmen or teenagers."

Council Member Clifton Ridge warned citizens not to jump to any conclusions.

"When folks steal in this town, it's usually because they're hungry or drunk," Ridge said. "It's not like there's a black market for porch bells, and you certainly can't eat wind chimes."

21

If the Devil Were Blue

Goodnight Star

FEATURE, SUNDAY EDITION

The Hallelujah is open for business

Need a room? Good luck finding a vacancy on Emporia Road. The Hallelujah Hotel is booked solid for the next month, and the reservations keep coming.

When the city council began a campaign to save the hotel from the wrecking ball last year, the town rallied to support the renovations required to get the building up to code. Now, a year later, business is bustling.

Hotel owners Sid and Scarlet Solvang said if business keeps up like this, they may have to consider expanding to the vacant storefront next door, which has been sitting empty since Myrtle's Antiques closed.

"When I asked Scarlet if she wanted to save the Hallelujah, she just had one question," Sid said. "She asked if it had a kitchen.'"

It had a kitchen.

It took months to get that kitchen up to code, and now that it's ready the Solvangs said they hope to add dining services once they can hire more staff.

Scarlet said they underestimated how much business would pick up at the May Day as a result of hotel traffic. Both businesses are accepting applications, and they're so short-staffed, she encouraged anyone to apply, with or without experience.

"The phone's ringing off the hook," she said. "There's a steady flow of travelers, but we've found most of our guests are the grown children and grandchildren of locals who used to stay on sleeper couches. Now they're staying at the Hallelujah."

The Solvangs had to take out a substantial loan to buy the hotel, but as word spread that the family took on so much debt, their sacrifice was rewarded with a showering of public support.

Goodnight Historical Preservation Society President Melody Hahn said the organization's ranks were split over the future of the landmark, but seeing the family's commitment changed some minds. Hahn said, "No matter how you cut it, that Hallelujah wasn't bought—it was saved."

JOURNAL ENTRY, SID SOLVANG, SUNDAY

People say it was the Hallelujah that turned us around, but it wasn't the hotel.

Ever since word got out about how good Melba's tamosas are, strangers started showing up at our door, offering crates of rutabaga and arugula from their gardens.

Melba's tomatoes changed everything. In the beginning we had to drive farm to farm, knocking on doors. Now we've got so much wheat, we had to buy a bigger mill, and between Scarlet's marbled rye and Bailey's biscuits, we sell so much, we've started prepackaging it and people are taking it home.

Since Rita manages the school program, we don't deal with farms as much as we did, but I still buy from them when they call. I can always find a use for what they've got, except the bread sculptures. I'm not sure what to do with those. Holly Wilkes brought us a new one, so now we've got a six-foot Estonian Kringle bread Elvis in the middle of the May Day.

If that doesn't say things are looking up, I don't know what does.

From: Lainie Hummingbird <HummingbirdMed@fourcorners.com>
To: Sid Solvang <brooklyncalling@zoomail.com>

Dear Sid,

I finally finished the translations of the documents you found. I'm sorry it took so long. You wouldn't believe what a painstaking process it was making sense of Pop's notes. Your father-in-law's handwriting was a trial in itself, never mind two dead languages in between. I didn't know Pop well, but after translating 200 pages of his soul, I feel like I know him as well as I know my own German shepherds.

I want you to know I tore up the check you gave me because I've been following the stories in the paper about what you've done to save the Hallelujah Hotel, and I can't find the words to thank you for what you've done for this town.

You know, Eisenhower stayed there after he was president. It's a true story. My father was a bellhop back when there was such a thing, and he carried the president's bags himself. My father was not one to exaggerate. If he says he carried Eisenhower's bags, he carried Eisenhower's bags. I can't imagine Goodnight without the Hallelujah, and our town is in your debt for keeping them from tearing it down, so I won't take a penny from your family. I'm glad to have some service to offer you.

As far as these documents you found, it's a big deal, Sid. It's gonna flip this town upside down, but there's no way around it. It's too sensitive to discuss at the diner. Can I bring them by the house so we can talk about it as soon as possible?

Blessings,

Lainie Hummingbird

From: Sid Solvang <brooklyncalling@zoomail.com>
To: Lainie Hummingbird <HummingbirdMed@fourcorners.com>

Why don't you come by the house tonight, and we'll talk?

From: Skeeter Bannister<highwater@shotmail.com>
To: Scarlet Bannister Solvang <mystifried@zoomail.com>

I hear the hotel's doing pretty well and your old man ain't half bad for a boss.

The cousins are thinking of driving up from Mulvane to check it out. Maybe you could pull the leaf out on your Sunday table and set a few extra places. You up for company?

From: Scarlet Bannister Solvang <mystifried@zoomail.com>
To:.Skeeter Bannister<highwater@shotmail.com>
CC: Tanya Ann Bannister <holyroller316@prairienet.com>,
Jolene Salina Bannister Cole <JC4JC@prairienet.com>

Brace yourselves.

Skeeter, before you invite the least forgiving end of the family to Sunday dinner, I have to warn you, Sid found the "corpora," and it might as well be a body, because if people find out about it, we're kind of dead.

Sid seems to have made up his mind that we owe it the light of day, but I'm not sure we could weather it. People are only just starting to trust us. I told Sid we should sleep on it and consult a real lawyer that isn't some disgruntled cousin of his because once we go public with this, there's a good chance we'll get run out of town. It took so long to prove ourselves. What if we lose everything again?

On the other hand, Sid's right: if we don't do something, more people may get hurt.

I've attached a few translations so you can see what I'm talking about.

From: Skeeter Bannister <highwater@shotmail.com>
To: Scarlet Bannister Solvang <mystifried@zoomail.com>
CC: Tanya Ann Bannister <holyroller316@prairienet.com>,
Jolene Salina Bannister Cole <JC4JC@prairienet.com>

I'll tell you what you're gonna do… NOTHING! You can't afford to do something. If you go public, it'll ruin the whole family. People always thought Daddy was off his rocker, and if folks find out about this, they won't believe any of it for a second. They'll just think he was a crazy old man going after the factory next door because he didn't like the smell of the lake.

You've gotta think of all of us, Scarlet. Not just your family that can run away to New York when the whole town turns against us. I mean the whole family. I'm talking about generations of Bannisters across Kansas you ain't given the time of day in 20 years. The fallout will hit them too.

You're right, they're gonna run you out of town, and you'll lose everything, but they won't just go after you. You're gonna take us all down with you, and for what? GATC can pay off the government and sue us for slander until nobody has two nickels to rub together.

From: Tanya Ann Bannister <holyroller316@prairienet.com>
To: Scarlet Bannister Solvang <mystifried@zoomail.com>
CC: Skeeter Bannister <highwater@shotmail.com>, Jolene Salina Bannister Cole <JC4JC@prairienet.com>

Skeeter's right. You come forward with this, nobody will believe you. Even if they did believe you, ain't nobody gonna do nothing anyway. Factories can get away with anything.

Nobody wants to know their dirty laundry because they need the jobs too bad. Where else are they gonna make a living in this town?

Want my advice? Keep it to yourself. Burn Daddy's hobbit scribbles, and count your money at the Hallelujah. You can't afford to rock this boat.

From: Skeeter Bannister <highwater@shotmail.com>
To: Sid Solvang <brooklyncalling@zoomail.com>

This is between you and me, because I can tell we're the levelheaded ones in this family.

I tried to talk some sense into your wife, but I couldn't get nowhere on account that she's stubborn as all get-out, so I'm coming to you. I've heard you're a sensible man.

Here are the facts: You can't afford more enemies in this town. Half of Goodnight already hates Scarlet for leaving, and the other half hates her for coming back. And, of course, they blame you for stealing her and then showing up out of nowhere and buying the May Day AND the Hallelujah. Some folks—I ain't saying who—think you pulled something over on us, because you found a way to make a living in a town where nobody saw a living to be made.

We can't blame you for trying, but we can't not blame you neither.

You're between a rock and a hard place, and that hard place is Goodnight American Tires. Believe me when I tell you, you don't wanna get on their bad side. If you ripple that lake, we're all doomed, and this town will never forgive you, no matter what they tell Jesus.

If you go forward with this, it'll ruin you. It'll ruin the family. It'll ruin this town and maybe America. Find a rug. Pick up a broom, and sweep this thing where the sun don't shine.

This town don't need another civil war.

From: Lainie Hummingbird <HummingbirdMed@fourcorners.com>
To: Sid Solvang <brooklyncalling@zoomail.com>

Sid.

You've got to come forward with these documents. We're burning daylight here! Give them to the *Star*. People need to know the truth.

Blessings,

Lainie.

Handwritten note found in a pocket Bible left in the Solvangs' mailbox, Sunday

I think Skeeter and Tanya are wrong about Daddy's hobbit papers. Folks have a right to know what's what. Even if it's bad for us, what's right is right.

Jolene

From: Harlem Solvang <torturedsol@zoomail.com>
To: Disco Kennedy <lostblue@prairienet.com>

Sorry I didn't call. It was really late by the time I got back from Jatori's house. You've gotta come to our next meeting. I made bergamot marmalade macarons, and when I brought them home, Mom said they're so good, she's gonna add them to the dessert menu at the May Day!

It was the first time I'd seen her smile since we got Lainie's translations. Dad wants to turn them over to the *Star*, but she keeps talking him out of it. She thinks her sisters will never speak to her again if it goes public. They're so stressed out.

Do you think we should say something to him? I mean, it practically belongs to us, since we're the only ones who were looking for it.

From: Disco Kennedy <lostblue@prairienet.com>
To: Sid Solvang <brooklyncalling@zoomail.com>

I heard about the drama over Lainie's translations. I also heard you were thinking of keeping it to yourself. I'm sure you've got your reasons, but there's something maybe you didn't think of, so here it is, straight as bourbon.

There are children swimming in Goodnight Lake because they were told by the tire factory there's nothing wrong with that water and nobody else is telling them different.

If I know you at all, you won't sleep with that on your soul.

FedEx from Sid to his cousin Leah, a lawyer at Cohen and Berg, Esq. Hoboken, NJ

Dear Leah,

Enclosed are copies of the documents I mentioned on the phone. There's no question this is the ominous "veritable treasury of corpora" Travis referred to vaguely throughout his will.

You'll notice detailed notes in the margins of several documents are written in Travis's signature code, two layers of dead languages. I've included the translations.

If these documents mean what I think they mean, there's a lot to talk about. Some are just records documenting Travis's illness. One is a list of neighbors with land bordering Goodnight Lake. Travis combined veterinary records detailing illnesses of his alpacas chronologically, which is why I suspect he was building a case.

I appreciate your willingness to take a look at what we've found. Everyone in this town has some connection to each other even if they don't know it, and more often than not, that connection is the factory, so you can imagine how hard it would be to keep this quiet if I approached a lawyer here. Besides that, all the lawyers are in Moses, and I've been told I can't go there because of the Civil War. That's a real thing here.

From: Sid Solvang <brooklyncalling@zoomail.com>
To: Disco Kennedy <lostblue@prairienet.com>

You're right. I sent copies to the only lawyer I trust. I'm waiting to hear back, but in the meantime, I'm not sure how to break the news to this town without taking the May Day down. There's a good chance Goodnight won't believe any of it, and they may never forgive me.

I don't think I've slept a night since I got Lainie's translation.

From: Disco Kennedy <lostblue@prairienet.com>
To: Sid Solvang <brooklyncalling@zoomail.com>

You've got a lot to lose. But I don't. Don't lose any more sleep. I'll handle it.

LOST AND FOUND, FRIDAY EDITION

LOST: A set of Liberty Bell–themed wind chimes have gone missing from the porch of the Hunter family on Derby Road. According to the family, the chimes were a commemorative souvenir from a Daughters of the Revolution reunion.

"Clearly this is an attack on America," said Duncan Hunter. "I don't think there's any other way to look at this act of terrorism against our patriot bells."

GPD does not suspect terrorism, but if you have information about the missing bells, please contact the station.

22

Where the Sun Don't Shine

Goodnight Star

LEAD STORY, TUESDAY EDITION

Something in the water at Goodnight Lake

A mysterious box was discovered on the land that belonged to the late Travis "Pop" Bannister and what was inside that box is rattling Goodnight.

Contrary to claims by Goodnight American Tire Company that water from Goodnight Lake is safe, hundreds of documents contained in Bannister's box suggest otherwise.

The box included copies of his neighbors' medical records, Bannister's own records detailing what was described as an "abstract cancer," and veterinary records documenting an alarming trend of animals born with birth defects on farms that border the lake. Also included were handwritten results of water tests Bannister commissioned from an independent company.

The documents were given to the *Star* by Disco Kennedy, who said she found the box while hiking. "I was walking alone when I happened upon it, and I could tell right off I was led there by the ghost of Pop Bannister himself to tell the truth about Goodnight American."

Bannister wasn't the first to raise questions about the environmental impact of GATC.

The factory first came under fire several years ago when neighbors whose land bordered the lake complained about a discoloration in the water. Shortly after, farmers reported a loss of livestock and other wildlife in the area.

Bannister's land was the nearest to the factory, and other farmers speculated that his proximity explains why he was the only human casualty of the lake flu. According to his records, a dozen other farmers and their families were treated for similar symptoms.

City officials have formed a task force to investigate.

Council Member Ford Hollis said, "These records raise concerning questions about the water quality in our lake, and we won't stop until we find the truth."

The company issued a statement assuring neighbors that they are in compliance with EPA standards, but the EPA has launched their own investigation.

GATC Spokesman Jefferson Winfield couldn't be found for comment, but Mayor Carol Shultz warned the public not to jump to any conclusions.

"Goodnight American has always been a good neighbor. They've invested in Goodnight, from supporting our schools to building playgrounds. Let's not forget that."

The council will meet behind closed doors tonight to discuss the issue and to consider a public forum, but Kennedy said task forces and public forums take too long.

"If this town read what I read about Goodnight American, they'd be picketing in the parking lot," said Kennedy. "Somebody's gotta stand up to them before we lose another farmer."

From: Honey Bee Kennedy <RevelationSevenfold@prairienet.com>
To: Reverend Arlo Foster <humbleservant@goodshepherd.com>

Lord have mercy. Tell me you've seen the paper.

Is Disco a teenager, or is she the Antichrist? I really couldn't tell you.

I've gotta show my face at work in an hour, and I expect they'll throw me out the window. They're short laundry workers, but they can't be desperate enough to keep me after this. Nine years of applications to get that job! I proved myself to Tuesday and back, and now what?

From: Reverend Arlo Foster <humbleservant@goodshepherd.com>
To: Honey Bee Kennedy <RevelationSevenfold@prairienet.com>

This may seem out of left field, but hear me out. I think you oughta be proud of Disco. Not too many folks in this town would be brave enough to do what she did.

From: Sid Solvang <brooklyncalling@zoomail.com>
To: Disco Kennedy <lostblue@prairienet.com>

Where are you? There's a rumor you were chased out of Goodnight High this morning.

Harlem has been looking everywhere for you. Scarlet's been calling everyone. I can't believe what you did. I would've talked you out of it if I'd known what you were up to.

I'm waiting to hear from my lawyer if she thinks we have a case, but either way I'm coming clean in tomorrow's paper. There's no way I'm letting this town blame you for this.

Come to the May Day. Bring your Pop Rocks. I'll deep-fry anything you want.

JOURNAL ENTRY, SID SOLVANG: POP ROCKS AND EXISTENTIAL DREAD? WEDNESDAY

I went to bed wondering what could be bitter enough to balance such a thing as Pop Rocks. That led to another empty-plate dream, which led to waking with the taste of umeboshi plum paste almost on the tips of my fingers, which led to this recipe nebula.

What is the taste of irony? A fusion that shouldn't be good, but somehow the favors are so polarized, they find a sort of gravitational lock. Pickled daikon? Ginger? Yuzu?

Note to self: create a dish that represents existential dread using nori.

Maybe Japanese flavors are too clean. Pickled cranberries? Gravy with a midlife crisis?

What is the taste of existential dread? It should be Russian. Is Russian too obvious?

From: Leah Cohen <LCohenEsq@CCB.com>
To: Sid Solvang <brooklyncalling@zoomail.com>

Dear Sid,

My partners and I have reviewed the documents you sent from

your father-in-law's farm, and we believe you have a significant case. We would be honored to represent it.

There is so much evidence in this file; it is rare to start a case with such headway. We believe it has the potential for a class action lawsuit and treble damages. We would like to approach neighbors and workers for prelitigation discovery as soon as possible. It's easy enough to get a list of GATC workers, but maybe you could get me a list of neighbors, and in the meantime, stay away from that lake.

Sid, between us, this case could be landmark, not to mention a jackpot. It's a significant litigatory intersection of corporate accountability, environmental responsibility, and labor law.

Best,

Leah

From: Sid Solvang <brooklyncalling@zoomail.com>
To: Leah Cohen <LCohenEsq@CCB.com>

I've attached lists of GATC workers and neighbors whose lands border Goodnight Lake. A couple of members of the city council are very invested in this case. I've given them your contact information, so you can expect to hear from them.

I can't thank you enough for taking this on.

From: Honey Bee Kennedy <RevelationSevenfold@prairienet.com>
To: Reverend Arlo Foster <humbleservant@goodshepherd.com>

My supervisor said I'd better thank the Lord for gall bladders because if it weren't for Helen's gall bladder trouble, they'd fire me on the spot after what Disco said about GATC.

Jim said the only reason I still have a job is they can't find anyone to replace me on account of the a rumor that laundry workers get sick more than the rest of the factory. She asked if I believe the yarn Disco's spinning. I told him my gall bladder ain't afraid of lake flu or anything else and I think the whole town's smoking turnip feathers. So I've got a second chance.

Now all I need is a muzzle for that girl.

Letter in a bottle of Heaven Hill, caught by a beaver

Dear Uncle Casey,

As you can see from this empty 80 proof bourbon, I've turned to the life of crime.

Word spread about the "subversive implications" of what I said in the *Star*, so instead of running away from me, now folks run up to me to call me a traitor.

It's not all bad news. After my homeroom chased me out of Goodnight High, Harlem and I were invited to the notorious Cypress tunnels, and we found stories underground.

Three Jasons, two Brians, and some guy with no front teeth who might've been like, 25 or 50, offered us a ride to Cypress Park. Next thing I knew, I was drinking Everclear by flashlight in what sure seemed like a sewage tunnel, although it didn't smell that bad, so Harlem said it couldn't be, and the more we drank, the better it smelled.

Turns out a bunch of them used to work for—guess who—Goodnight American Tires!

The more they drank, the more they had to say about it, and the more I drank, the more I had to say about what they had to say. One Jason was laid off because he was an assistant to a guy who tried to make tires out of trees or something. I don't know, by that time I had whiskey ears. Long story short, I'm working on a letter to the *Goodnight Star*, but don't worry, I'm still writing songs. I finished a new one called "Meet Me at the Bottom of the Everclear and Bring All Your Jasons."

LETTERS FROM GOODNIGHTERS, WEDNESDAY EDITION

Dear Goodnighters,

I need to set the record straight. Disco Kennedy is not responsible for going public with Pop Bannister's evidence against the Goodnight American Tire Company.

Disco claimed it was her discovery to protect me, but I can't let her take the blame. From now on you can direct your judgment my way. I found the records. I gave them to the *Goodnight Star* because I thought the town has a right to know it's not the lake making the factory sick, but the factory that's making the lake sick. Please leave innocent teenagers out of this.

Sid Solvang

Goodnight Star

LETTERS FROM GOODNIGHTERS, THURSDAY EDITION

Dear Goodnighters,

Why is this newspaper determined to run Goodnight American out of this town?

Are we to believe Travis Bannister went around collecting the veterinary records of sick goats while he was dying of cancer? There's something fishy about all this.

Friends, don't let the outsiders pull the wool over your eyes. There are strangers among us who are selling us a bill. Next thing you know, they'll be trying to tell us there's something wrong with tap water.

The bottom line is Goodnight cannot afford to lose this factory.

A line has been drawn on Goodnight Road, and here it is: You want to stand with the tire factory that has kept Goodnight on the map, fed our grandparents, our parents, and our children?

Or do you want to stand with outsiders who are too good for tap water? Maybe they don't need Goodnight American, but we do.

The New Patriot Alliance will meet tomorrow at 7:00 p.m. at the New Tabernacle Church to discuss this travesty and make a plan to take back our town. Bring a hot dish.

The New Patriot Alliance

From: Bailey Nation <hellrazor@shotmail.com>
To: Tallayla Parks <onedayatatime@stillscountycorrections.org>

I think I may be out of a job soon. They're coming after my boss, and they're coming hard. Them dimwitted starch-mouthed fiddlers are blaming Sid for stirring controversy at the factory. There's a rumor going around they're gonna call for a boycott. Do you know what that is? I looked it up in the dictionary, and it means folks will stop coming to the May Day. Those vampires are gonna keep slinging smack on Sid until they've turned the whole town against him.

Just between us, I don't think the May Day can take it.

From: Leah Cohen <LCohenEsq@CCB.com>
To: Sid Solvang <brooklyncalling@zoomail.com>

Something seems to be spooking that town of yours. We're having difficulty gathering parties for collective representation. We need 40 plaintiffs to sign on. Bannister's records indicate hundreds of potential victims, but very few are willing to talk to an attorney at all.

They're so distrustful of lawyers, only the 12 neighbors who lost the most livestock have signed on. None of the workers from GATC will cooperate. Everyone is afraid to lose their job.

We may have to proceed without the workers.

JOURNAL ENTRY, SID SOLVANG, MONDAY

Scarlet's sisters came to dinner last night and ragged us out for letting the Star get its hands on what they call Pop's hobbit papers. Scarlet said it's a miracle they came at all.

The tension between the Bannister sisters has an angry, fermented binding. Note to self: Invent a dish to capture the Bannister tension. Something with mushrooms. Angry mushrooms.

At the end of the night, they left their casserole dishes behind. Scarlet says that means they'll be back next Sunday unless things take a turn, but what's the worst that could happen between now and Sunday?

PART 3

A Very Blue Heart

23

Between Now and Sunday

Flyer stapled to streetlamps, phone poles, and bulletin boards of Goodnight, Friday.

WHO'S TRYING TO TAKE DOWN GOODNIGHT AMERICAN TIRE COMPANY?

There are forces in this town trying to run commerce right out of Goodnight.

You want to keep your job, keep our flags in the air and our soldiers on the ground?

Don't spend your hard-earned cash at businesses that destroy America.

Boycott the May Day Diner!

Stop the outsiders from destroying Goodnight!

We are your neighbors. We are Kansans.
We are real Americans.

Join the New Patriot Alliance before it's too late!

www.npalliance.org

From: Harlem Solvang <torturedsol@zoomail.com>
To: Abbey Solvang <abbeyroadyogi@omwardbound.org>

Dad is tripping about this whole New Patriot crusade. Their signs are everywhere. Mom says it's nothing and the kind of people who'd boycott us weren't giving us any business to begin with, but I think Dad's looking for the fire escape.

It doesn't help that Disco keeps writing letters to the newspaper taking shots at the factory. All day she gets shade for it at school, so then she hitches a ride to Cypress Park, drinks her weight in Everclear, and writes another letter to the *Goodnight Star*.

Dad begged her to stop putting herself in harm's way, but she said, "I'm the only one in this town who can tell the truth on Monday and be just as hated on Tuesday as I was on Sunday, so what difference does it make?"

The diner's slow, but Mom and Dad are so busy with the hotel, they asked me to work more hours. I don't mind. There's something about the May Day kitchen that makes everything outside it disappear. I can see why Mom never wants to leave the kitchen. It reminds me of being underwater, like that time we went scuba diving in the reef, how everything above the surface blurred, taking all the sound out of the world. The sun comes up, the jukebox goes on, and I can close the curtain and forget everything but the next ingredient.

Disco called ranting about the factory, but all I could think of was risotto.

Dad says I have a soul for cooking and maybe I should go to the academy when we move back. I asked him when exactly that will be. He was like, "We've gotta see this town through the drama at the factory, and then I promise we'll make our way back to Brooklyn."

SID SOLVANG, RECIPE BOX NOTES, #67

A dish that represents dissonance. If the mission of every dish is to find balance, what if you created a dish with dissonant flavors? Isn't that what spices are for? And a salad isn't in harmony; it's a collision of competing flavors so polarized that in not blending, somehow the acrimony is balanced, without losing definition. Mixed greens?

What could greens do that they've never done before?

From: <editor@goodnightstar.com>
To: Sid Solvang <brooklyncalling@zoomail.com>

Dear Mr. Solvang,

I've received word from an EPA insider that the allegations in your father-in-law's documents have been substantiated, and it's an iceberg of *Titanic* proportions. It will be a headline in the morning's paper. The story features shocking details of GATC's deception.

There's a rumor a number of workers are planning something big tomorrow, some kind of protest. I don't expect it to be a lot of workers, and the backlash against them will be considerable. Our town is in your debt (whether they know it or not) for being willing to speak a truth nobody wanted to hear. GATC is in a heap of trouble, and I have reason to believe the NPA and others who are unwavering in their support of the factory blame you. I believe we're in the same boat, and I wanted to give you a running start for the tornado on our horizon.

Your humble servant of the press

From: Sid Solvang <brooklyncalling@zoomail.com>
To: <editor@goodnightstar.com>

Dear Editor,

Thanks for the warning. As far as this patriot crusade, I feel an increasing sense that I'm being watched, and it's unsettling. Assuming business doesn't take too hard a hit over it, maybe we can save enough to go back to New York before it gets too ugly. Nevertheless, I can't say it hasn't gotten under my skin, so I appreciate the support.

My greater concern is for Disco. Since she started speaking out against the factory, she's made herself a target. I asked her to stop writing letters to the paper, but she seems to think she's the only one who can tell the truth. The other trouble is I think that truth may be drunk.

After the first letter she wrote to the *Star*, her classmates chased her out of Goodnight High, and it seems she found her way to the tunnels under Cypress Park. You probably know more about what goes on in that park than I do. I'm getting the impression she's been drinking ever since, and it's not doing her social life any favors. Can you discourage her from writing her letters or stop publishing them before these neopatriots chase her out of town?

Kindly,

Sid

From: <editor@goodnightstar.com>
To: Sid Solvang <brooklyncalling@zoomail.com>

It's too late for tomorrow. The ink is set for her latest soapbox, but it's a good one.

I'm of a mind that when a rebel finds a truth worth fighting for, it's worth the price of ink.

SID SOLVANG, RECIPE BOX NOTES, #77?

What is the taste of truth?

Create a dish that captures the essence of truth. What flavors tell the story of the space where a truth known becomes a truth spoken? Citrus—lime? Some kind of acid...

Onions! Onions tell the truth. Or are onions the truth unsaid? The dish has to be something clean, served on a bed of shredded daikon, but what's in the center? What's missing?

From: Scarlet Bannister Solvang <mystifried@zoomail.com>
To: Jules Jamison <livingthedream73@zoomail.com>

Last night I saw Sid hide something in the pantry, so after he fell asleep, I went down to see what it was. He had the guilty side-eye of a cheating man, so I was expecting the worst.

The only thing that seemed out of place was a recipe box that belonged to my mother. It had the look of something that doesn't want to be seen, so I opened it, and it was crammed to the brim with notes. I unfolded one, and when I realized what he was hiding, I felt as betrayed as if it were another woman's number written on that paper and not a recipe for tempura.

There must have been a hundred recipes in there!

Sid's been letting me carry the whole weight of the May Day menu while he's been sitting on an arsenal of new recipes. Roasted shishito ravioli! I was so furious, I was going to wake him to demand answers, but then I started reading his notes, and for all the genius in that box, there was twice as much doubt. Manicotti fried matzo brei?

I might've said something anyway, but when I got to the top of the stairs, there was Sid, walking the floors again. He said he couldn't sleep because something was coming, something big—too big, and what if it was all a mistake? I asked him what in the world he was talking about. He said he couldn't tell me and I'd find out in the morning anyway.

Whatever it is, it can't be worse than lying to your wife. Do you think it'll push him over the edge if I say something about his covert recipe box?

24

The Taste of Truth

Goodnight Star

LEAD STORY, THURSDAY EDITION

Hundreds of workers trade assembly line for picket line; GATC faces first strike in 50 years

More than 400 workers walked out of Goodnight American Tire Company Monday morning as news spread that the Environmental Protection Agency (EPA) issued dozens of citations for widespread health and safety violations at the factory.

Federal regulators confirmed the validity of internal memos leaked last week issuing some $750,000 in fines. According to the agency, there are more to come as inspections continue at the embattled factory.

"This is not the last word," EPA Spokesperson Simon Errol said. "What our team found appears to be only the tip of an iceberg that gets deeper the closer we look."

Leading up to the walkout, productivity had been at a virtual standstill for days as a team of EPA and OSHA inspectors made their way through the plant.

According to Goodnight Council Member Ford Hollis, the council is forming a new task force to address the scandal. "We're working closely with the Kansas Department of Agriculture to get to the bottom of this," Hollis said. "I don't blame the workers for walking out. GATC has betrayed the public trust, and there is no reason to believe they wouldn't cut corners again, given the spirit of these internal memos. They demonstrate an utter disregard for the welfare of the workers who made them what they are today."

Not everyone has been on board with the inquiry. Mayor Carol Shultz and Council Member Wilson Moreland issued statements in support of the factory.

"These allegations don't ring true to my book, and you know what book I'm talking about. This has got 'Big Government' written all over it," Moreland said. "I'll believe it when I see it, and I don't see anything but a good old-fashioned American company trying to make a living in a day and age where government is heck-bent on regulating us all to death."

More than half the workers at GATC refused to join the rank and file on the picket line, and the council has been as split as the factory over the controversy unfolding there.

"I see no reason to doubt GATC's word," Shultz said. "They've done right by us for half a century, and no worker ever walked out on the company before."

While GATC has no history of work stoppages, it has had a history of labor strife.

"Let's be clear about one thing, GATC hasn't avoided a strike for half a century because they were doing something right," said Terrence Reed, one of the workers who walked out.

Reed was an organizer in the last failed attempt to unionize in 1995.

"The only reason this company managed to elude a strike this long is because it's spent millions on propaganda, lobbyists, and union-busting schemes to keep organized labor out."

As strikers picketed outside the factory, Distribution Manager Boone Kelmsworth addressed workers who remained on the plant floor, warning them that GATC was prepared to offer replacement employees $12 an hour, about 30 percent less than striking workers.

"Management has an open door. It's a shame a handful of workers felt they couldn't come to us with their concerns and instead chose to walk out on their responsibilities during our busy season," Kelmsworth said. "It's bad timing is what it is."

Hollis said, "There's never a good time for a strike, but there's never a good time for cancer either, and that's where we're headed if GATC doesn't clean up its act now."

Reed speculated if the company hadn't crushed attempts to form a union, they'd be looking at twice as many picketing workers.

In the 50 years since the factory came to Goodnight, the company has thwarted multiple attempts to unionize. According to company legend, organizers with United Rubber Workers were run out of town with pitchforks in the 1970s. United Steelworkers of America made more ground in the early 1990s following a string of injuries at the plant. The company's promise of increased wages and more stringent safety standards won over the rank and file, and the workers voted unanimously to reject unionization.

In addition to EPA citations, OSHA issued penalties on

Wednesday, including some $300,000 in fines, and ordered the tire manufacturer to turn over more documents.

"What is most troubling is the lengths this company went to in order to deceive regulators, when they could have just as easily put that effort into fixing the problem," Errol said.

According to a statement released by Nancy Wood, the new GATC spokesperson, the tire maker is complying with state and federal regulators, and they expect to have the plant running at capacity again by the end of the week, with or without those on the picket line.

LETTERS FROM GOODNIGHTERS, WEDNESDAY EDITION

Dear Goodnight,

When 400 workers walk out on the job, do you know what I see? I see 400 jobs for hire. I see jobs for deserving folks who aren't afraid to roll up their sleeves. I'm sure those laid-off workers we lost last year would be glad to take their jobs back. I wouldn't be surprised to see it happen. There's nothing to stop GATC from firing every last one of those no-good slackers on the picket line. To those who can't be bothered to show up, clock in, and earn their keep, I say good riddance. You can take your communist values back to Russia.

Virginia Easton of Northwind Road

Note passed from Disco to Harlem, Wednesday

Did you see the paper this morning? This town's off its

rocker and fresh out of marbles. I'm working on a new letter to the *Star*, and I need a drink. Wanna come?

Note passed from Harlem to Disco, one hour later

I have to get to the May Day straight after school. Dad's so caught up in the strike, he asked me to work more hours. I don't mind; if I could get away with it, I'd quit school and just cook all day. Anyway, they need me. Lately the May Day is Strike Support Central.

A bunch of regulars stopped coming when they heard about it, but a whole new bunch of regulars we'd never seen before have started coming around to support the strike.

Benner's Dairy Farm donated so much cheese to feed the strikers, Mom's teaching me how to make enough rye ciabatta to fix 459 submarine sandwiches for the picket line tomorrow.

They're letting me skip school to help hand it out!

Dad says this strike could go on a while. More workers join every day. I guess I don't have to ask if your mom will join the strike, but it's a funny thought. You think she'd ever do it?

Note passed from Disco to Harlem, third period

Mama wouldn't join a picket line even if lake flu made her sprout a radioactive third boob on her head. She told me to cool it on my letters to the *Star* before she gets fired, but she must've figured out this strike is job security for the future boob heads scabbing at Goodnight American, because if she wanted to stop me, she could.

Want some help tomorrow?

Note passed from Harlem to Disco, fourth period

Yes, but Dad's worried about you being seen helping us with the strike.

Note passed from Disco to Harlem, fifth period

You should be more worried about being seen with me. I'll meet you there.

From: Harlem Solvang <torturedsol@zoomail.com>
To: Disco Kennedy <lostblue@prairienet.com>

Did you really get grounded for going to the picket line last night? Dad thought he heard your mom yell something about it as she dragged you into the Buick. I tried to call seven times today, but she threatened to send an exorcist to the house if I called one more time.

Can you get away? Come to the diner and let us feed you. I'll make you something blue.

From: Harlem Solvang <torturedsol@zoomail.com>
To: Abbey Solvang <abbeyroadyogi@omwardbound.org>

I invented a casserole! Dad said I could try it out at the May Day, and people actually liked it. Mom put it on the list of blue-light specials, and she called it Blue Harlem Casserole because it looked so blue. I made it with purple potatoes, blue carrots, and blue corn on blue Thai butterfly pea flower tea rice. Ever heard of blue rice?

Dad lets me experiment in the May Day kitchen when it's slow, so I made the blue casserole for Disco. She always says she wishes the whole world were the color of her guitar. It got me thinking about what it would be like to have a whole dish that was nothing but blue. Bailey said I should call it Vegan Smurf Pie, but Mom said people hate Smurfs almost as much as they hate vegans, so no Smurfs. She said not to tell anybody it was vegan.

Disco never came, but some chefs from my cooking club came by, and they loved it!

Mitch Minor, my favorite farmer, said it's the best casserole he's had in a lifetime of casseroles. Blue is his wife's favorite color, so he asked if Mom would give him the recipe. When I told him it was my recipe, he couldn't believe it. He said I'm destined to be a chef like Mom. I told him Dad is a chef too, and he said, "That settles it. It's in your blood. You have no choice."

That sort of made me happy, but I don't know why it would. It seems sad to be trapped in one fate, especially one that keeps you stuck in the kitchen all the time, like Mom. But it just made me so happy how much Mitch loved my casserole. I think it might've been the happiest feeling I've ever had. I can't wait to come up with something new.

It's hard to come up with any idea Mom or Dad hasn't thought of. By the way, did you know Dad dreams of recipes? He wakes up scribbling ideas in his little journal, and then he rips them out, locks them in his recipe box, and never actually makes them! So lame.

Note from Mitch Minor to the May Day, Wednesday

Dear Mr. and Mrs. Solvang,

You must be very proud of your daughter. She's a good kid and a good cook. That blue casserole is something else. Besides making a charming casserole, she is Kansas kind.

Your friend,
Mitch Minor

Goodnight Star

LOST AND FOUND, SUNDAY EDITION

FOUND: The Hobbes family's calico, Spoon, is home again. Thanks to Goodnight's esteemed mail carrier, Carter Bell, who found the kitten in a mailbox on Emporia Road.

LOST: Jackie Fraser's K-State Wildcats-themed wind chimes have gone missing. She suspects the culprit was a Jayhawk and would appreciate any witnesses to come forward.

25

Yodel Against the Machine

Note passed from Harlem to Disco, Thursday

I've been elected vice president of our cooking club! I mean, we only have eight members and five of them still sleep with a night-light, so it wasn't hard to rise through the ranks. Jatori tasted my blue casserole and nominated me. Of course, Jatori has to be president because she's the only one who can make Baked Alaska, a dish that gives me nightmares.

You can't make fun of me since I hear you're selling out. Dad says you're auditioning for the National Anthem solo on football night.

Is that true? And why did I have to hear about it from my dad? When's the audition?

I know you'll get it. Nobody sings like you.

Note passed from Disco to Harlem, second period

The audition is tonight. You can't come—it'll make me too

nervous. Not that I'm not nervous. Even my haters say I'm gonna get it. I heard the choir director tell the volleyball coach she didn't know why they were even going through the hassle of auditions because nobody can sing like that chatty blue tornado of a delinquent youth!

I'm finally gonna do something right.

Note left in Disco's locker from Harlem, Friday

What the hell happened last night?

Note left in Harlem's locker from Disco, an hour later

I NEED TO TALK TO YOU.

Note left in Disco's locker from Harlem an hour later

I've got cooking club today. Why don't you come? We can talk there.

Note passed from Disco to Harlem, seventh period

Never mind. I'll be down at Cypress Park with a backpack full of stolen Heaven Hill I found hidden in my mama's pantry. I have an idea.

From: Honey Bee Kennedy <RevelationSevenfold@prairienet.com>
To: Reverend Arlo Foster <humbleservant@goodshepherd.com>

I think we need to gather our prayer team or at least start another prayer chain for Disco.

Maybe you heard Disco didn't get picked to sing the anthem at the game tonight.

I tried to tell her all those lunatic letters she was sending to the paper were gonna come back to bite her, but she didn't believe me.

Well, she took it pretty hard. She took it harder when they chose Summer Pottstock.

Of course, you know her daddy is our landlord, and he makes a sport out of raising rents, but there's more history than that. The Pottstocks donate their old clothes to the Goodwill on Emporia Road. Disco turned up at school in one of Summer's old dresses with no idea what kind of firing squad that dress had in store for her. Summer started writing her name on her tags in permanent ink to make sure everyone could see it, and all the girls gave Disco a terrible time.

So you can imagine how she took it when she showed up at the audition to sing the anthem in front of those same girls last night and the principal flat-out refused to let her audition.

When she told me what had happened, I dragged her straight back there to demand an explanation, and do you know what he said?

"Disco can't represent our school, because she *doesn't* represent our school."

I asked what he meant, and he hollered for the world to hear, "We put up with that Jezebel long enough, but now that she's gone after our factory, she's gone too far. As far as I'm concerned, you're either with Goodnight American or you're against America!"

I gave him a piece of my mind right there in the middle of that gymnasium, and I backed up my what-for with four Biblical references so he was clear whose dark side he was on.

But, Arlo, the look on her face.

Maybe I shouldn't have pitched my soapbox with half the school watching, but someone had to call the devil red.

As we left, Disco unhinged a nether-worldly smile and said, "I have an idea."

You know whiskey never spoke more hazardous words than *I have an idea.*

The game's tonight, and I've got a bad feeling about it.

Can we gather the prayer team? I think this is a bigger deal than Maggie's tonsils, and Lord knows we all dropped our yarn and went running over that travesty.

From: Reverend Arlo Foster <humbleservant@goodshepherd.com>
To: Honey Bee Kennedy <RevelationSevenfold@prairienet.com>

Half the prayer team has choir rehearsal, and the other half can't make it on account of drama at City Hall, but you can count on me and Cheryl. She made her hamburger casserole, so we'll bring dinner. We've gotta drop by Millie Carter's house. Poor thing's in bed with the flu. Bill's on the road again, and her kids are crawling up the ceiling, so if we're running late, that's why. Maybe you could send a prayer Millie's way. This flu's a bad one.

From: Honey Bee Kennedy <RevelationSevenfold@prairienet.com>
To: Reverend Arlo Foster <humbleservant@goodshepherd.com>

Hold your horses. I'm coming with you. I've got a Tater Tot casserole I can wrap up for the kids and Melba's mean green tomato soup for Millie.

What kind of flu are we talking about? The kind you catch from lakes?

POLICE REPORT FILED BY GOODNIGHT POLICE DEPARTMENT CLERK JAN BRAXTON

Witness 1 Report: Lori Taylor—Faculty Prairie Spirit Cheerleading Adviser

The crime occurred just before the game. The Prairie Dogs were praying, and our Prairie Spirit girls were stretching. That's what we always do before a game. I noticed right away, something was off. There seemed to be something awry with the sound system—come to find out it was hijacked. Someone had handcuffed the sound guy to the radiator. I was pounding on the door to the little sound room, but it was locked. Our school is bare-bones when it comes to budgeting, so we only have one sound guy. I've told them for years we need a better system, but they always say the same thing: "This isn't Moses."

So it probably wasn't hard for Disco to do what she did.

Witness 2 Report: Summer Pottstock—JV Cheer Captain

I was the first person to see her. I look up from my pom-poms, and there she is. It's that glitter-bomb loser, Disco Kennedy. Next thing you know, here comes Disco climbing up the scoreboard with a microphone. She's always hated me because her mom rents a house from my dad and makes her wear all the clothes we donate to Goodwill. So there's your motive.

Most of the crowd didn't even notice until we stood to salute the American flag.

That's when it happened.

Witness 3 Report: Wesley Mills—Goodnight High Principal

We rose at the start of the game, as we always do, expecting to hear the anthem, sacred as football itself, but instead of hearing America, what we heard was an abomination. What we heard was Disco Kennedy belting out the angriest, drunkest rendition of "You're Looking at Country" the world has ever heard.

That was only the beginning.

Then she started in on our tire factory. Disco unleashed a tree-hugging fury against Goodnight American worse than anything I ever heard on *COPS*. She must've hollered every combination of profanity from Satan's bank before anybody could stop her. She yelled, "Lake assassins! Alpaca murderers! Lying, no-good grandpa killers!" And then she yodeled.

Of course, we have no security at the school. No operation in Stills County bothers with security guards anywhere but Walmart, so it took some scrambling for the football team itself to drag her down from the scoreboard. When the police arrived, she was still yodeling as they carried her off to the county drunk tank to wait for her mother.

Witness 4 Report: Booking Officer Chris Kendrick

I told the mother, the girl didn't stop from the second she walked in yelling, "Down with alpaca murderers!" until they dragged her out of the holding cell howling "Folsom Prison Blues."

"Better singing than talking," the mother said, and she apologized. "You just never know what's gonna come out of that girl's mouth. There ain't enough soap in the world."

I told her it's a shame because she's got a pretty voice for a potty mouth.

That's what we were all thinking.

I've got a feeling that's not the last we've heard from Disco Kennedy.

From: Honey Bee Kennedy <RevelationSevenfold@prairienet.com>
To: Reverend Arlo Foster <humbleservant@goodshepherd.com>

I guess you heard what happened, and I'm as fit to be tied as the school over it.

So the life of crime begins.

When I picked her up at the station, it was a somber scene, but Disco wouldn't have known it. The officer said, "That child didn't shut up from the mug shot to the fingerprints. She only took a break from ranting to sing and then went right back to raging against the factory."

On the ride home, she sang Hank Williams's entire 1949 Opry show, word for blessed word, until I thought I'd drive off a cliff if Kansas would give me one. But, of course, it wouldn't.

Is the Lord testing me?

Melba gave me a brochure from some kind of evangelical rehabilitation lockdown out in Western Kansas called Prairie Forge. It was a pretty brochure, and they say they can cure anything. Remember Melba's niece Tammy, the one who talked so much, she even talked to horses and wouldn't wear a dress? Well, they cured that right up, and Melba said now the girl wears dresses and don't ever talk to horses nor anything else, she's so quiet and obedient.

Do you think maybe they could help Disco? Now that I've got health insurance from the factory, we could actually get her in there, but I just don't know. It seems a place like that might not know what to do with a girl like Disco. What do you think?

From: Reverend Arlo Foster <humbleservant@goodshepherd.com>

To: Honey Bee Kennedy <RevelationSevenfold@prairienet.com>

The second I heard, I put in a request to our prayer ministry. So the big guns are praying on it even as we speak. Don't forget Hazel Wells is our new prayer captain, so take heart. If praying could talk the earth into turning the other way, it'd be her prayer that would do it.

I haven't heard of this Christian rehab you mentioned, but I wouldn't give up on Disco just yet. I see a heart that means well behind all that glitter.

www.PrairieChat.org Live Chat Room, Sunday

MELBA: Better do something about that kid of yours. That girl's going nowhere fast.

HONEY BEE: It's too late. She's already nowhere.

MELBA: I didn't want to say nothing, but I could tell something was south the first time I smelled that patchouli oil drifting into your kitchen. That's Satan if I ever smelled Satan.

HONEY BEE: Do you think she's on drugs?

MELBA: Of course. All the kids are. She's probably dangerous. If I were you, I'd lock your bedroom door when you go to sleep.

HONEY BEE: None of my doors lock.

MELBA: Mine either. I never had to lock a door before, but I never had no teenagers living under my roof. Maybe you should call somebody to get you some locks so you can sleep.

HONEY BEE: I don't know.

MELBA: You heard about them boys that killed their parents? Shot 'em in cold blood right in their own bed. The dog too.

HONEY BEE: I didn't know they shot the dog.

MELBA: Oh yes, a little Pekingese thing, wasn't even no threat.

HONEY BEE: That's just awful.

MELBA: It happens.

HONEY BEE: I guess it can't hurt to put a lock on my door.

MELBA: Call the church. They'll send somebody down.

Message from Honey Bee to Reverend Arlo taken by his wife at 9:00 a.m. sharp

Please call me right away. I need a God-fearing locksmith, a dead bolt, and a prayer.

From: Sid Solvang <brooklyncalling@zoomail.com>
To: Disco Kennedy <lostblue@prairienet.com>

Disco.

Harlem told me what happened, not to mention I heard it from every angle at the diner. In some versions you sprouted wings and flew to the scoreboard. In other versions you sprouted fangs and hung by your boots. In all the Disco mythology, you were either singing Loretta Lynn or you became Loretta Lynn, and in every version, you were hammered out of your mind.

I'm sorry they wouldn't let you sing at the game.

I had a feeling this town would be too small for you, but I'm afraid we've made it so much worse, getting you swept into this drama with the factory.

I can't promise high school will get better, but I can promise it ends, and on a rare reunion that you travel back, you may discover some of the hellions who hurt you most drank themselves to death before they made it to 35 or died in fiery accidents on the very night a beautiful stranger taught you how to eat with chopsticks and you stayed up till dawn listening to Miles Davis until you thought your whole body was made of jazz.

They say feelings aren't fatal, but I don't believe it. I've lost friends to the inconsolable void where I've misplaced myself more times than I can count. It might surprise you to know most chefs aren't right in the head, and I know you've listened to enough Hank Williams to understand musicians aren't exactly the portrait of mental health. Chefs and artists are among the most likely to die by suicide. I find that encouraging. Maybe *validating* is a better word.

There are weirdos dying of alienation across this earth, and I can't help thinking, if New York were big enough to take us all in, to keep us together in one place, maybe we wouldn't lose so many to that fatally delicate line between art and madness.

At this moment I'm writing from the May Day, where the tables are full and the register is singing. Business is steady, and we're well on our way back to Brooklyn. If you can find a way to get through it and your mother is willing, I promise we'll take you with us when we go back.

Meet me at the May Day tomorrow, and we can talk about it.

From: Disco Kennedy <lostblue@prairienet.com>
To: Sid Solvang <brooklyncalling@zoomail.com>

Can't go to the May Day tomorrow. I'm going to the picket line. Wanna come?

Handwritten letter in an empty bottle of Dad's Root Beer last seen drifting on the Moses

Dear Uncle Casey,

You might've noticed it's been a while since I threw a bottle your way. I haven't had time for rivers on account of my new mission. Maybe you've heard. I thought I was doing some good in the world, but I've been told I make the workers look bad with my whiskey letters to the *Star*.

Yesterday one of the tire workers thanked me, but he said maybe I could consider taking a break from drinking. He said if I put the plug in the jug, I'm welcome to join them on the picket line. As you can tell by this root beer, I took his advice.

So I gave all my bourbon to Bailey, and tomorrow I'm headed to Goodnight Road.

LOST AND FOUND, TUESDAY EDITION

FOUND: A coat of many colors somebody's mother went to some trouble to stitch was found in the parking lot of Wonder. It's homespun, so there's no tag.

LOST: Two more sets of chimes have gone missing from Clifton

Street. Bobby Lee's Picasso-themed chimes and Tori Brigg's barnyard-bamboo bells disappeared in the night.

"It's a shame no bell is safe in this town anymore," said Briggs.

26

Stone Soup

From: Honey Bee Kennedy <RevelationSevenfold@prairienet.com>
To: Reverend Arlo Foster <humbleservant@goodshepherd.com>

You said the Lord don't test us, but that can't possibly be true. As if I don't have enough mayhem in my prayer jar over Disco, now this GATC strike has reached the laundry room.

They said a strike wouldn't affect our department, and we could opt out, but word around the factory is that the lake flu isn't just in the lake—it's inside the factory!

The place is crawling with frowning folks from the government carrying clipboards, asking a million questions, and asking to test our blood. There's a rumor if we talk to them, we can lose our jobs, but my supervisor, Jim, came in drunk off his gourd and admitted they hired me because the last sucker to have my job caught the lake flu. He swears she caught it from fishing, but he insisted the whole department get tested.

Arlo, the government took my blood! I don't know when we'll hear back, but in the meantime, I don't like thinking at this very moment they could be cloning every last one of us.

Jim said he doesn't care if they fire him, that if his test comes back all Chernobyl, he's joining the strike, but I can't do that. If I lose this job, how am I gonna pay for nursing school so I don't have to work in a laundry room until the end of days?

Half the factory's gone one way, the other half's the other way, and I've gotta pick a side.

If I go one way, I keep my job and my ride to nursing school, but there's a chance we'll all die of lake flu before I ever get that far. So I've gotta choose between unemployment and uncertainty on the side of the workers or money and cancer on the side of the bosses?

Tell me straight, Reverend: Whose side is Jesus on?

From: Reverend Arlo Foster <humbleservant@goodshepherd.com>
To: Honey Bee Kennedy <RevelationSevenfold@prairienet.com>

The way it looks from my window, the question is, what side are you on?

From: Abbey Solvang <abbeyroadyogi@omwardbound.org>
To: Sid Solvang <brooklyncalling@zoomail.com>

Your little town was on the national news! I only caught the tail end of the story, but I swear I saw you, only it couldn't have been you, because the dude I saw was hanging off the back of a farm truck wearing overalls. It looked like you were in a mob of, like, Teamsters and church people. What the hell is going on in Goodnight, Kansas?

From: Sid Solvang <brooklyncalling@zoomail.com>
To: Abbey Solvang <abbeyroadyogi@omwardbound.org>

You wouldn't believe it. When word spread about the *Star* article, about half the town was convinced Goodnight American was responsible for killing Pop. I don't know who the other half believes poisoned the lake, but they passed the newspaper around the factory, and an hour later, hundreds more workers walked out.

I heard it would be a cold day for a picket line, so I wanted to see what I could do to help. Disco mentioned she was walking to the factory today, so I let Harlem skip school to go with me.

Don't judge me for corrupting minors. Disco said the strike sobered her up and that she gave up drinking for the workers.

She said, "If I can cut class for Southern Comfort, I can cut class for Midwestern justice."

Harlem said she's just happy Disco stopped yodeling.

We pulled up, and there were hundreds of workers and supporters lining the ditches of Goodnight Road, even though it was well below freezing. We found Disco right away because she had the loudest mouth, and of course, she was the only one to wear glitter to a picket line.

I asked if she was worried her mom might see her, but she said, "The laundry room has no windows, praise Jesus."

Someone yelled, "Go back to work, you lazy bums," from a passing truck.

Turns out they were yelling at a huddle of ministers who'd come to support the strike. That set the whole picket line off praying. When the "amens" had run their course, we approached the workers and ministers to ask if we could bring them lunch. They said no thank you, which I've learned Kansans almost always say at least three times before accepting something free.

To my surprise, Harlem seemed to know half of them from the diner, and she said, "Cut the bull guys, we're bringing lunch. What do you want?"

"*Anything*, I don't know—we're freezing. Something hot. Can you make us soup?"

"Can he make a soup?" Disco made a face that cornered me. "He can make a soup."

"We'll bring you something," I said.

Disco turned to me with her bullet of a soul and said, "You're gonna make soup."

"We don't want you to go to any trouble," one worker said. "Whatever you've got."

"We'll be back with soup," Disco promised. "Stay hungry."

"Always," said the worker.

There was something about the way he said *always*, something about that bitter wind and just being there with Harlem's heart and Disco's certainty. There was something about the way the trucks passed us, some waving and hollering, "Jesus is on your side," and some yelling, "Burn in Hell, you lazy commies!"

All the while we could see management looking down from the windows above us.

We drove back to the May Day and went to work.

I can't really explain it, but I really just wanted to make them soup—the best soup. It wasn't like we didn't already have soup at the May Day that I could've wrapped up for them. Scarlet's killer potato soup was fresh and, of course, killer, and Tyler's bacon corn chowder was fresher, but I wanted to make it myself. And I wanted to make it from scratch.

"You want to grab a chopping board?" I asked Harlem.

She smiled and started gathering ingredients. She and Disco chopped veggies. Bailey and Tyler rolled up their sleeves, and we all went to it.

Mitch Minor had just brought us a barrel of red onions the night before, so we started with those. I added Skeeter's Irish potatoes, the Winnickers' wild carrots, Jonathan Andrew's celery, and of course, Melba's greenhouse tomatoes. There was savoy cabbage from the Micheners, barley from the Coldwells, and a handful of Scarlet's herbs.

As we added Lainie Hummingbird's leeks, Disco said, "There's something in this soup from every corner of Goodnight."

"Dad!" Harlem said. "It's stone soup!"

She was right. Do you remember that story, Abbey? Dad used to tell it sometimes when we'd help make soup for the deli. Maybe you were too young to remember.

Anyway, we packed cups and spoons and took Tyler's Ford down to Goodnight Road, where we served those workers right out of the bed of that truck.

They liked it so much, they keep calling the diner to ask when we'll get it on the menu.

From: Abbey Solvang <abbeyroadyogi@omwardbound.org>
To: Sid Solvang <brooklyncalling@zoomail.com>

Of course, I remember stone soup! That's the first time I've heard you say something nice about Dad in years. You sound good. Better than you've been in a long time. Maybe too good. Did you get brainwashed by the corn? Please tell me you're not staying in Kansas.

From: Sid Solvang <brooklyncalling@zoomail.com>
To: Abbey Solvang <abbeyroadyogi@omwardbound.org>

Not to worry, we'll come back once I can make things right for the factory workers, but I started this, and I can't leave them hanging out to dry.

We'll be home sooner than later if business at the hotel keeps up.

Maybe the cornfields did brainwash me, but my brain might've needed a little washing.

I'm going to turn in. One of the workers brought us a bag of root veggies from her greenhouse. The carrots are so fresh, I'm thinking I'll get up early and throw something together.

From: Scarlet Bannister Solvang <mystifried@zoomail.com>
To: Jules Jamison <livingthedream73@zoomail.com>

Did you say something to Sid? Something's gotten into him, and I couldn't tell you what. For two years I couldn't get him into the May Day kitchen, and now I can't get him out. Not that I want to. This is the most I've seen him since we moved here. Since Sol's closed, we've been on different sides of the moon, and now we are literally sharing a chopping board.

I've been begging him to put more dishes on the menu since the day we signed our souls over to Emporia Road, and you would've thought I asked him to sacrifice a birdhouse the way he would shut down. But he and Harlem came back from the picket line and went straight to the kitchen, raving about the new stone soup. They were on fire to get it on the menu. That soup has been selling out so fast, people actually call to find out if we have any left.

I figured that was the end of it, but remember Sid's secret recipe box?

This morning I woke at dawn because I heard something bustling downstairs. I figured the alpacas had gotten into something, so I came running. When I opened the door, all those recipes from that box were hanging on clotheslines across the kitchen, looking like the scribbled math of rapture. Every burner was lit, pots were simmering, the scent of it was a rhapsody of savory colors, and there was Sid in some kind of dervish trance, conducting it all, whirling across the linoleum in house slippers singing "Strangers in the Night."

When I asked him what he was doing, he twirled me around, dipped me, and said, "Scarlet, we're going to need to buy an oven with more burners."

He said he'd been dreaming of dishes all night until he couldn't sleep anymore.

I don't know what's gotten into him. Something changed that day he took soup to the picket line. Now Sid wants to put a pizza on the menu. He's ranting about "a pizza worthy of Goodnight." He said, "This town deserves real pizza."

I guess word traveled because we're getting calls asking if Sid's pizza is ready yet. I think it's ready, but Sid says, "The sauce is still finding its way, and it's just not *there* yet."

He hasn't talked like this in years.

It's nothing less than a miracle to see him cooking like he used to, and what he's making is good. Really good! And not a moment too soon. With the town at war and Harlem's college years looming, we're running out of reasons to stay.

From: Jules Jamison <livingthedream73@zoomail.com>
To: Scarlet Bannister Solvang <mystifried@zoomail.com>

Would you believe I heard about that soup? I wouldn't believe anyone could get so excited about a soup if I'd never tried Sid's food before. But I know what the man can do with a bowl of hot water. What does surprise me is how some foodie from around here came upon your little nowhere truck stop and got a taste of that soup. They wrote about it on the internet and, cut to 24 hours later, all of Brooklyn has heard about it. They're calling it the No Flyover Soup.

As much as I'd love to take credit, I didn't say anything to Sid. I don't know what got into him nor why he got over his little phobia of kitchens so suddenly.

I don't know if you know this, but apparently Sid has a fan page someone set up after Sol's went down, and he's collected quite a cult following of molecular gastronomy fanatics, foodies, and anti-foodies. I guess people have been looking for him, and when the rumor got out that he was cooking again, it was seismic.

Tell Sid to get on that pizza in a hurry because he has groupies who are probably making their way to Missouri as we speak.

From: Scarlet Bannister Solvang <mystifried@zoomail.com>
To: Jules Jamison <livingthedream73@zoomail.com>

KANSAS, Jules. We are in KANSAS. NOT MISSOURI. NOT KANSAS CITY, MISSOURI. JUST STRAIGHT KANSAS.

Goodnight, Kansas.

From: Jules Jamison <livingthedream73@zoomail.com>
To: Sid Solvang <brooklyncalling@zoomail.com>

New York is talking about you.

A number of investors from our old circle have begun following you with interest.

If you want my advice, distance yourself from this scandal at the tire factory. New York is watching. I'm talking to a couple of interested parties, but the interest is—how shall we say?—al dente. Everyone seems a little gun-shy after what happened at Sol's. Nobody's ready to jump, but if you can keep up whatever you're doing right, it's only a matter of time.

The culinary tide is changing in Brooklyn. I know you're not a fan of gentrification, but gentrification is a fan of fine dining. The more conceptual, the better. The old Brooklyn that put you out of business is the same Brooklyn being displaced. With gentrification in full swing, now there's more of a market here for experimental trends like the plates that took down Sol's.

You should see the line to get into Oliver Dean's place these days. The waiting list is so long, they're turning people away. If that hack can bank like that, imagine what you can do.

Play your cards right. Stay out of controversy. No doubt there's an offer on the horizon.

From: Bailey Nation <hellrazor@shotmail.com>
To: Sid Solvang <brooklyncalling@zoomail.com>

Hey, boss,

Somebody was looking for you last night.

Did you know you had a groupie? And do you know your groupie walks around in pink loafers? He was pin-striped and sideburned with a goatee, leather bracelets, and a paisley pocket square. If I weren't on probation, I might've slapped him just for looking stupid, but Tallayla says I can't hit nobody until July.

So Pocket Square strutted to the counter, giddy as all get-out, while Disco and I were negotiating the next song on the jukebox. She might actually think she owns that Wurlitzer.

Pocket Square interrupted to say, "This is Chef Sid Solvang's new restaurant, am I right?"

Only he didn't say *restaurant* like you, me, and America, he said it like *raaawzdaraaowwnnnn*.

I swear he said *restaurant* like half his teeth were from France and the other half hated France, but by the end of the sentence, all his teeth were American again.

I said, "I wouldn't call it 'new,' and I wouldn't call it a restaurant."

He gave a look around like he was inspecting for leaks and said, "What do you call it?"

"This is a truck stop," Disco answered in her Ajax voice. "You got a truck?"

He looked confused, so I gave him a menu and told him to seat himself.

He slithered to the farthest booth, and you won't guess what he did next. He ordered half the menu, took a few bites of everything, and split. He didn't even take a doggy bag. He just left a fat stack of very stiff cash on the table and slipped out the door when nobody was looking.

The tip almost made up for his shoes, but not that pocket square.

You've been warned.

From: Sid Solvang <brooklyncalling@zoomail.com>
To: Bailey Nation <hellrazor@shotmail.com>

I hate to break it to you, but there may be more pocket squares.

You know we always planned on going back to New York, so this could be our way home. My old business partner has been talking to potential investors.

God knows we could use the money. This tire controversy is taking a toll.

Don't worry—we'll keep the May Day going one way or another, but the way things have been going, I have a feeling it would be better for business if my name weren't on it.

27

An Empty Bed

Goodnight Star

LEAD STORY

Record winds don't stop striking workers

Despite the windchill from an unexpected cold front, new workers joined the picket line on Monday as fallout continued over allegations Goodnight American Tire Company is responsible for deadly pollution in Goodnight Lake. Striking workers spent the morning passing a bullhorn to air concerns, resulting in a vote to revive efforts to unionize.

As churches passed out doughnuts, workers elected de facto leader Margaret Grace, an organizer of several failed attempts to unionize in the 1990s. Grace said the movement has more momentum now as stakes for workers have never been higher.

"Every day the news spreads and another worker walks out," she said. "We thought the cold front would kill turnout, but we have more support now than ever."

In addition to growing community solidarity, the strike has drawn support from local youth, including Disco Kennedy, who found the documents Grace called "the first domino."

"There's a country song that speaks to how Goodnight American has treated this town, and I didn't wear the right shoes to sing it, but I'm gonna sing it anyhow," Kennedy hollered through a bullhorn and then serenaded workers with Patty Loveless's "Blame It on Your Heart."

Several local churches have formed a coalition to raise money and awareness.

"We wouldn't be able to stay this strong without so much community support," said Grace. "One by one churches are getting behind the cause, and of course, we couldn't do it without the May Day. The Solvangs have brought lunch to the picket line every day this week."

The May Day has started a strike-support fund. Donations can be left in the six-foot tire-shaped bread statue between the gumballs and the maps.

From: Disco Kennedy <lostblue@prairienet.com>
To: Harlem Solvang <torturedsol@zoomail.com>

I've gotta get out of here. Wanna meet me at Cypress Park after school?

From: Harlem Solvang <torturedsol@zoomail.com>
To: Disco Kennedy <lostblue@prairienet.com>

Can't. I'll be at the May Day.

From: Disco Kennedy <lostblue@prairienet.com>
To: Harlem Solvang <torturedsol@zoomail.com>

I thought you were off today?

From: Harlem Solvang <torturedsol@zoomail.com>
To: Disco Kennedy <lostblue@prairienet.com>

I just felt like going. It's Rita and Clive's anniversary, so I thought I'd whip something up.

You're not going to the factory? Dad says he'll take lunch to the workers every day until this thing is over if you wanna help him again.

And why do you wanna go to the tunnels anyway? I thought you quit drinking?

From: Disco Kennedy <lostblue@prairienet.com>
To: Harlem Solvang <torturedsol@zoomail.com>

I quit the quitting because I got in a terrible fight with my mama. She saw my name in the paper this morning. When she put together that I skipped algebra for the picket line again, I got the what-for and a half. She went on about troublemakers at the factory ruining everything and how she'll never join the strike because it's all a communist conspiracy.

So I told her maybe she should get her rifle and sign up for the New Patriots.

I said she was gutless and that if she had any guts, she'd join the picket line. I know I shouldn't have said it, but it was true.

Mama slapped me so Baptist hard, it knocked me off my feet and onto the kitchen floor.

She just left to go to work. I'm not going to school with her handprint across my face.

I'm leaving. I don't care how cold it is. I'm stealing her whiskey, and I'm finding a Jason to take me to the tunnels. Wanna meet me there?

From: Honey Bee Kennedy <RevelationSevenfold@prairienet.com>
To: Melba Deerborn <MelbaMayDeerborn@prairienet.com>

Remember that Bible treatment place you told me about? The hour has come. My boss said if I wanna keep my job, I'd better do something and do it fast.

No sooner did I cross ways with Disco this morning over her skipping school to join the Communist Party, than the second I walked into work, HR sent for me!

I had a bad feeling when I stepped into that windowless basement office and there were two of the bosses, Rob and Marcy. They started going on about how they valued my work ethic and it would be a shame to lose me.

Rob asked if I read the original article in the paper, when Disco suggested the ghost of Travis Bannister led her to this alleged evidence. He wanted to know if I thought that was something a sane individual would say.

Marcy said, "Nobody's blaming you for your daughter's mental health crisis. We're just concerned, and we want to share all the options. Drinking and cutting school is one thing, but spinning conspiracy theories that threaten livelihoods is another, and Disco crossed the line."

My mind was spinning when he asked if I was aware of the company's generous health plan, and he pulled out the Sears catalog of nuthouses. They wanted to send her to the Stills County Psychiatric

Hospital, but when I mentioned I'd heard about a Christian rehabilitation out in Western Kansas, they said, "Even better."

Marcy said, "Well, that's that."

Rob picked up the phone and started dialing. Before I knew which way was up, he was hanging up the phone, chirping, "Good news! There's an empty bed at Prairie Forge, and it's got her name on it."

They're giving me the day off tomorrow to drive her down there.

Got any bourbon?

From: Melba Deerborn <MelbaMayDeerborn@prairienet.com>
To: Honey Bee Kennedy <RevelationSevenfold@prairienet.com>

It's about time. I'm all out of bourbon, but I can come by if you wanna pray it out.

From: Honey Bee Kennedy <RevelationSevenfold@prairienet.com>
To: Reverend Arlo Foster <humbleservant@goodshepherd.com>

There ain't enough chapters in the Bible to make me right today. Jesus is gonna have to write another chapter. I signed Disco into Prairie Forge. I'm done for. I called in sick. Tell the prayer team not to bother bringing Bibles unless they're bringing whiskey.

OBSERVATION REPORT ON DISCO KENNEDY. PRAIRIE FORGE, MONDAY

Reported by Marilyn Powell, intake nurse

Where to start with Disco Kennedy?

This glitter-drenched misanthrope has an incendiary charm and most unladylike understanding of the world. Beyond swaggering through the halls of Prairie Forge raging against Goodnight American Tires, she's inclined to sudden outbursts of country music, compulsive chatter, and profound cynicism. It took the pleas, warnings, and finally, threats of three nurses to stop her singing. When the singing stopped, the conspiracy talk started, and it hasn't stopped.

She believes her school and the factory are *in on it*, insists strangers run from her, and says secret maps are hidden in barns. Most alarming, she claims the tire factory is killing people and she's determined to stop them, *by any means necessary, even yodeling.*

Based on our preliminary observation of Ms. Kennedy and the availability of beds at Prairie Forge, I suggest the most aggressive treatment at our disposal. There is no shortage of empty beds, and Ms. Kennedy's mother, as an employee of Goodnight American, has a premium insurance plan to accommodate long-term residency. Ms. Kennedy has proven fundamentally unstable and vulnerable to the charms of Satan.

I recommend the maximum long-term residential treatment not to exceed 36 months.

From: Honey Bee Kennedy <RevelationSevenfold@prairienet.com>
To: Sid Solvang <brooklyncalling@zoomail.com>

Maybe it's the whiskey talking, or maybe it's because I just drove to Western Kansas and back, staring at my Jesus bobblehead for ten hours, but the road ahead seems clear as Tuesday and narrow as an unpraised string on King Saul's harp.

I checked Disco into Prairie Forge to get cured of her troubles, and when she gets out, God knows when, I'd thank you to keep your daughter away from her.

I'm not blaming Harlem for the yellow jackets in the outhouse, but I think we can agree the two of them add up to Armageddon when they get together.

JOURNAL ENTRY OF SID SOLVANG, TUESDAY

Is there anything they won't blame on us? Disco's locked up and Honey Bee blames Harlem. She hasn't noticed Harlem is a straight-A student on the gifted track with the highest scores at Goodnight High and Disco's drinking her way to the bottom of Cypress Park.

It's one less reason to stay, as if we needed another reason to leave. Bailey says not to hold my breath because bad news comes in threes, but bad luck travels in nines. I've lost count.

Mail Bag 3, Prairie Forge, B Wing, Wednesday

DISCO! WHAT THE ****?????

I can't believe your mom actually went through with it! She wasn't even gonna tell me!

My dad broke the news you're in Prairie Forge, and I was so angry, I made risotto.

He says your mom wants our family to stay away from you, but of course, Bailey got your address, so at least we can write. She and Dad are conspiring to get you out. Even my mom is making phone calls! We'll find a way. Is it true you have to wear a bonnet there?

Mail Bag 3 Prairie Forge, B Wing, Wednesday

Dear Disco,

Your mother told us you're at Prairie Forge, and I had to tell you how sorry I am. I feel I failed you. I never should've let you get caught up in this drama at the factory. I think it put a target on your back, and that's my fault.

Bailey offered to break into Prairie Forge to rescue you, but her probation officer talked her into making a Snickers pie instead. We'll overnight it. Let us know what we can do for you.

They say GATC is headhunting scabs in Moses, and it's not looking good for anyone associated with the strike. That won't stop me, but it should stop you. I don't want you getting into any more trouble. It doesn't look like anything will break this impasse.

Sid

Letter attached to a package mailed to the PO Box of the *Goodnight Star*, Thursday

Dear Editor,

Since the first reports of so-called lake flu began to surface, I've been trying to drink away my conscience, but there's not enough Maker's Mark in the world to do the job. I've barely slept since the death of Travis Bannister. I'm through covering the tracks of a company whose executives seem to be sleeping fine despite the blood on their hands.

I've worked at Goodnight American for 20 years. In that time I've witnessed the breaking of both man's law and God's law. The paper trail that Travis Bannister started is just the tip of the iceberg because those records only account for what's going on outside the factory.

What's in this box exposes what's going on inside the factory.

The truth must be shared, no matter the price. I'm coming clean.

It won't take long for them to put together who I am, so I'm leaving Goodnight. Don't attempt to track me down. This is only the beginning.

Anonymous at GATC

28

Maker's Mark

Goodnight Star

LEAD STORY, MONDAY EDITION

Internal memos reveal GATC deceived regulators about health risks

Hundreds of incriminating internal memos were leaked exclusively to the *Goodnight Star* this week from a whistleblower at Goodnight American Tire Company.

The memos detailed scores of violations of Environmental Protection Agency (EPA) standards and attempts by GATC management to cover up these infractions and their impact on air and water quality in Goodnight, specifically Goodnight Lake.

These records, which were authenticated, contradicted analysis turned over to the EPA. The memos exposed dozens of exchanges authorizing falsified emissions records, doctored environmental reports, and misappropriation of funds—essentially hush money to keep sick workers from acknowledging their illnesses publicly.

The memos implicated 27 managers, including personnel going up to the highest ranks at GATC, suggesting the manufacturer was in violation of regulations known as the National Emissions Standards for Hazardous Air Pollutants (NESHAP).

The EPA has identified tire production as a major source of Hazardous Air Pollutants (HAP). The agency enforces strict guidelines for manufacturers, especially workers' exposure to toluene and hexane. These pollutants have been linked to chronic and acute health disorders.

In addition to revealing GATC was exposing hundreds of workers on the plant floor to hazardous levels, the documents revealed a cover-up of EPA violations in the handling of industrial waste.

Initial reports read, "Rubber tire leachates in the aquatic environment indicate concerning levels of environmental degradation," but the findings appeared altered in inspectors' reports.

EPA Spokesperson Simon Errol said, "We're taking these allegations very seriously, and this investigation could have profound implications. We urge residents to avoid the lake and to be wary of well water near the factory until we determine how severe the contamination is."

Companies are required by the EPA to provide analysis of chemicals within water and sediment, analysis of contaminants within organisms, and analysis of the biological effects of these compounds on plants, animals, microbes, and organelles. The whistleblower turned over duplicates of each of these reports. Without exception, all of them appear altered.

The communications implicated three tiers of management complicit in misleading safety inspectors on the potential risks to workers and neighboring farms.

GATC Spokesperson Nancy Wood turned in her resignation without comment, and management did not return phone calls. The company issued a statement: "We are cooperating with federal regulators, but we can assure the public no wrongdoing has occurred."

The communications are being reviewed by several state and federal agencies, including OSHA, the Occupational Safety and Health Administration.

"The level of deception is staggering," OSHA Spokesperson Emma Lauren said. "Federal agencies are coordinating with the state to launch a broader investigation. We're just getting started."

To date, OSHA issued 23 citations for health and safety hazards and placed the manufacturer on its Severe Violator Enforcement Program.

The whistleblower promised there is more to come.

Tuesday Headlines:

Wichita Eagle: Corruption at Kansas factory goes all the way to the top

---

Kansas City Star: Whistleblower says Kansas factory knew risk to workers

---

The Guardian: "They've poisoned us for decades"; US tire workers on Cancer Lake

---

New York Times: Big trouble in little Goodnight, Kansas

Lawrence Journal-World: Stills County town divided over fate of Goodnight American

---

Agence France-Presse: Workers unite to stop corruption, pollution at tire factory

---

Beijing Daily Press: (Translated) Beautiful small-town farm death makes Kansas rebels

---

USA Today: Goodnight American Tire Company faces toxic-water scandal

From: Honey Bee Kennedy <RevelationSevenfold@prairienet.com>
To: Reverend Arlo Foster <humbleservant@goodshepherd.com>

Not a minute after I clocked in for work this morning, I was swept into a stampede of laundry ladies storming out to join the picket line. I couldn't swim against that current if I wanted to, but here's the funny thing: I didn't want to.

Did you read the paper? Turns out those bigwig tire phonies knew all along they were poisoning the whole town. The *Star* printed emails from the bosses, and it said, clear as day, they knew right well they were making more lake flu than tires. They said even if they were caught, it would be cheaper to pay off the sick ones and fines than to fix the trouble.

In one of the emails, they made fun of what suckers the workers were for not putting two and two together. My supervisor read the paper to our whole department. She was so steaming mad when she realized her nosebleeds may well be lake flu, she said if we knew what was good for us, we'd follow her right out that door and onto the picket line.

Arlo, we did!

Every last laundry worker threw down their apron and marched out to the picket line.

Can you believe Disco was right? I was so worried about losing my job, I let those scoundrels at GATC convince me she was crazy. I mean, of course, that scalawag is playing three decks with glitter in her eyes, but she was telling the truth! I called Prairie Forge, but I couldn't get through, so I left a message to see about getting her out, seeing's how everything she said about GATC was true. I suppose she'll expect an apology, so I'd better start baking. Then again, a little church boot camp never hurt nobody.

I'm still waiting to hear back from her counselor, so there's a chance I'll be driving to Prairie Forge tomorrow. Otherwise, I'm going back to the picket line in the morning.

I never thought I'd hear myself utter such a thing in a million years!

From: Reverend Arlo Foster <humbleservant@goodshepherd.com>
To: Honey Bee Kennedy <RevelationSevenfold@prairienet.com>

It's so heartening to witness what's happening at the factory. It's a long time coming.

Goodnight's been at the mercy of GATC far too long.

As for Disco, I've heard some things about that Christian rehab, and none of it sounds very Christian to me. The sooner you bring her home, the better.

If the Buick is still acting up, you're welcome to take my truck to Prairie Forge.

From: Honey Bee Kennedy <RevelationSevenfold@prairienet.com>
To: Reverend Arlo Foster <humbleservant@goodshepherd.com>

I'm way ahead of you. I've been on the phone with everyone under the sun.

I got a call from someone who was locked up at Prairie Forge once upon a time. I can't say who, so don't tempt me to gossip by asking. I took such an earful, I called the Forge and told them I was hitting the road tonight. The nurse said they can keep her so long as she's a threat to herself or society. They say she's both! I called the sheriff to see if I could report her kidnapped, but he said they can't fight a psychiatric hold.

I told him we'll see about that. The Buick's dead, but I found a ride. Start praying…

From: Harlem Solvang <torturedsol@zoomail.com>
To: Disco Kennedy <lostblue@prairienet.com>

I don't know if they let you check your email at prairie prison, but if you get this message, pack your bags!

So I'm working after school when your mom comes charging into the May Day, in pink curlers and that yellow flea market kimono you hate so much. She's ranting that Prairie Forge won't let you out, which got Dad ranting, Mom pacing, and Bailey was all, "That's it, we're stealing a mission bus and driving through the gates of Jesus's nuthouse."

My mom's like, "I don't think that'll be necessary," but your mom's like, "It sure is necessary 'cause the Buick won't make it any farther than Hillsboro."

And Dad's like, "Take our truck—On second thought, I'll drive."

But my mom throws her coat on over her apron and practically runs him over to get to the door, and she's like, "No, I'll drive. I'm coming with you, Honey Bee!"

And your mom's like, "Gimme a second to grab my dashboard Jesus."

Bailey wanted to go, but she's on probation, so she sent about a thousand biscuits instead.

Disco, at this very moment, our moms are westbound across Kansas in our ugliest but most reliable truck, one in curlers and a kimono, the other in a May Day apron, two blind Chihuahuas and a thousand biscuits between them, Jesus bobblehead on the dashboard!

So say goodbye to Prairie Forge, the mothers are coming for you!

INCIDENT REPORT, PRAIRIE FORGE, TUESDAY, 4:32 A.M.

Filed by D. Pope, Crisis Management Team Leader

Violet Ellinsky, Third Shift Supervisor: It started with the thumping. *Flumping* might be a better word for it. Something was belting the window. I figured it was hail, but it wasn't hail. It was biscuits! Those troublemakers must've had a hundred biscuits, and they were pitching them like Satan's Yankees. I wanted to call the sheriff, but the intake nurse said to hold off on account of one of them had a King James Bible.

Unfortunately they'd already woken half the Forge.

Lee Spencer, Third Shift Security Officer: It was an ambush. Two hysterical women. One barged through the gate in a kimono no less, curlers flying, waving a Bible, shouting scripture with a Baptist velocity that'd give Tammy Faye a run. The other one was wearing an apron, hollering, "Remember me? I'm back! Remember me?"

I tried to stop them, but I thought they had some kind of weapon. I felt something hit me in the eye. Before I could make heads or tails of it, I was struck again. And again. Biscuits. You wouldn't think a biscuit could stop a man, but when I got a look at the attackers, what was I gonna do, Tase a couple of wound-up mothers whose only weapons were biscuits?

While I weighed the options, they slipped around me and straight to B Wing. Apron Lady seemed to know exactly where she was going. She hit the fire alarm, which unlocked all the doors. Next thing I knew, girls in pajamas were running in every direction.

We all knew there could be only one girl causing that much trouble.

Charity Slater, Prayer Manager, B Wing: Since the moment that yodeling communist arrived, none of us have had a moment's peace, but tonight was a new low. There's just no room in Heaven for that mouth. The strings will fall off the harps! There will be no angels left. No matter how many times we made her recite Leviticus, she'd just go back to rambling about evil tires and injustice, singing, *"Socialism ain't no sin, 'cause Jesus ain't no capitalist."*

And now her mother tries to bust her out! We might've tried harder to stop her, but the truth is, Satan won. We're spent. Jesus forgive us for giving up on that spaghetti-wire soul.

D. Pope, Crisis Management Team Leader: It's been a long night for all of us in B Wing, and the sooner we can put this chapter to bed, the better off we'll be. Though we planned for long-term treatment of Ms. Kennedy, my understanding from her file is that even before this unfortunate event, her care team requested her discharge, not for her mental health, but for theirs.

In addition to the intrusion witnessed tonight, the phone hasn't stopped ringing. We've received virtually nonstop calls of varying degrees of sobriety and sanity. It started with a call from a minister of Ms. Kennedy's church threatening to bring down the law if we don't release her. Since then I can't tell if the whole town is calling or if it's just the same unstable waitress calling over and over again. All I know is the team has had enough.

In light of tonight's events and the sheer exhaustion of our staff, I've authorized the discharge of Decapolis Galilee Kennedy effective immediately.

From: Disco Kennedy <lostblue@prairienet.com>
To: Harlem Solvang <torturedsol@zoomail.com>

They tried to strip the glitter off me, but they couldn't do it!

It's nice knowing that after our bones return to dust, our glitter will still be here. I'm working on a song about it I'm calling "Nothing Lasts Forever but Glitter and Trauma." It's about what happened at Prairie Forge. But that's a whole different book.

I'll say this much: When I was locked in the isolation station, the Forge changed my mind about something. The world got very clear when I was the only one in it. There's only one place for someone like me. That's why I can't go with you to New York anymore. I'm sorry.

By the way, what in the world did your mom say to my mom?

It's been night and day since I got home. She tiptoes around me, baking shepherd's pies, offering to let me stay home from school until I'm *good and ready*.

Does that sound like Honey Bee Kennedy?

Maybe it's this whistleblower changing minds all over town. Mama said Melba told her that Cheryl told Melba that Arlo told Cheryl he couldn't say how he knew, but there's another leak coming. I asked if I could skip school to go with her to the picket line tomorrow.

She said yes!

From: Harlem Solvang <torturedsol@zoomail.com>

To: Disco Kennedy <lostblue@prairienet.com>

I can't believe you're the one they locked up when this whole town's gone crazy. Wanna hear the strangest thing? Promise you won't tell my dad because I know his heart is set, but I don't wanna go back to New York anymore.

I'll meet you at the factory after school so you can talk some sense into me.

Welcome home, by the way!

29

Red Hands

Goodnight Star

LEAD STORY, THURSDAY EDITION

GATC "caught red-handed": More workers walk out of embattled factory on heels of new leak

The tide turned on Goodnight American Tire Company Wednesday morning as copies of more scathing internal memos circulated across the plant floor. By noon some 300 more workers had abandoned their posts to join the picket line, including many supervisors.

GATC Operations Manager Gil Brenner said lower management had been kept in the dark about scores of health and safety violations that have been surfacing from a whistleblower.

"Nobody told us we were chin-deep in lake flu every time we stepped through those factory doors," Brenner said. "I'm not afraid to call them out. They turned their backs on their own workers, they betrayed our trust, and they put our whole town in harm's way."

The documents revealed GATC demoted engineers who proposed the adoption of innovative green technology, leading to the resignations of five developers.

Now an engineer in the Netherlands, Holden Chase was one of them.

"It was clean, it was cost-effective, and we had a solid plan," Chase said. "All Goodnight American had to do was say yes, and we could've taken the lead in green tire technology."

Clergy and civic leaders joined the rank and file to protest outside the factory.

Council Member Ford Hollis told the cheering crowd, "I'll stand side by side with workers until this factory does right by labor and right by our town."

GATC did not respond to phone calls and issued no further statements.

Hollis said a class action lawsuit against GATC is gathering momentum as reluctant workers like Brennan sign on.

"We trusted them, and they sent us to our deaths, all the while cutting our wages and rewarding themselves with raises." Brennan addressed the rank and file through a bullhorn. "The way I see it, GATC's got blood on their hands, and they've been caught red-handed."

From: Bailey Nation <hellrazor@shotmail.com>

To: Tallayla Parks <onedayatatime@stillscountycorrections.org>

They're storming the factory tomorrow to raise some hell, even though it's colder than penguin balls outside. Don't you know, Sid's paying us to cater the little revolution for free.

He said sometimes they arrest folks for feeding workers on a picket line, so he said maybe I shouldn't go on account of how I've almost graduated from my probation. It's one thing to get arrested for a DUI, but I don't wanna go to jail for handing out Frito pie to tire techs.

You think they'd arrest me for that?

From: Tallayla Parks <onedayatatime@stillscountycorrections.org>
To: Bailey Nation <hellrazor@shotmail.com>

They sure would arrest you in Moses, but not in Goodnight. And not tomorrow. The sheriff's brother came down with lake flu. He works at the factory, so nobody's getting arrested tomorrow. I heard the cops are gonna join the workers. I don't know if it's true because I heard it at the Blue Felony, and you know you can't believe anything you hear in a country bar after midnight. Don't judge me. I just went for the music.

Maybe I'll stop by the factory tomorrow. I think the whole town's gonna be there.

From: Honey Bee Kennedy <RevelationSevenfold@prairienet.com>
To: Reverend Arlo Foster <humbleservant@goodshepherd.com>

I never thought I'd see the day, and Lord knows the day never thought it would see me!

Maybe you heard I've gone communist. I carried a sign! I half expected a bolt of Heaven's lightning to strike me dead, but it didn't. I lived to tell the tale, and Lord, is it a story!

I woke up to Disco waving the *Star* over my bed, begging to go with me to the protest.

When I read the paper, I couldn't say no.

I don't know if you saw the front page this morning, but if you didn't, it seems that whistleblower is at it again. This time, the leak was so bad that when word spread, the rest of the factory walked out. Someone got ahold of the memos and made copies for everyone at GATC.

They say the whole factory's signing on to that lake flu lawsuit now. Even some of our supervisors are on board.

By the time Disco and I arrived, there must've been a thousand people raising heck out there. The strikers blocked the entrance to GATC so no truck could get in, but we didn't really need to because when the Teamsters heard what was going on at the factory, they joined us!

What happened next was beyond me. I still can't believe it. The whole town started pulling up. Every which way, trucks kept coming, pouring out of nowhere until all of Goodnight Road was jammed with folks raising heck against the factory.

Folks I'd never seen before showed up to support us. If I came from a weeping house, I might've shed 77 tears, thinking of the jobs where I worked myself to the bone for nothing, treated like dirt under the shoes of Satan's third cousin, but there was nobody to speak for me, and now here's the whole town leaning out their Chevys, hollering, "Keep your head up, y'all!"

We stayed all day. When the sun went down, we went to the May Day and made signs to go back tomorrow. I heard a heap of ministers are coming. Any chance you'll be there?

From: Reverend Arlo Foster <humbleservant@goodshepherd.com>
To: Honey Bee Kennedy <RevelationSevenfold@prairienet.com>

You might be surprised to know I was there too. It's no surprise to me I didn't see you because there were so many of us. I didn't follow the rest of you to the May Day because I had my hands full with commitments, but I promise I'll meet you on Goodnight Road tomorrow. Not only is the whole church going to be there, the whole town is!

Cheryl is bringing about a million sloppy joes to hand out. I'll save one for you.

From: Leah Cohen <LCohenEsq@CCB.com>
To: Sid Solvang <brooklyncalling@zoomail.com>

Nobody's picking up the phone. Maybe you're out celebrating? I'm going into meetings now, so we'll have to catch up tonight. In the meantime, I'm assuming you've heard the news, but in case you haven't, let me make your day. They caved! GATC caved harder than anyone expected. I've never seen a class action suit settled so fast, and I think the workers will find the numbers healing—to say the least.

Between picket lines and bad press, once we got our hands on the latest memos, it was over. What really sealed the deal was when they saw how many workers opted in this week.

They folded like origami. All told, the final number to sign on was 997 workers!

It didn't hurt that GATC stocks have been plummeting in the wake of all the bad press.

Your little community paper is the least of their worries now.

The best news is soon you'll be able to look out your window and see the cleanup of Goodnight Lake in full effect.

Congratulations! I think all of Goodnight will be sleeping better very soon.

From: Sid Solvang <brooklyncalling@zoomail.com>
To: Goodnight Strike Support <GSS@mayday.com>, <GATCworkersfund@mayday.com>, Christian Coalition for Labor <ccl@prairienet.com>, Interfaith Labor Coalition <ilc@ilc.org>

We have an important announcement. Meet us on Goodnight Road at 9:00 a.m. tomorrow.

In solidarity,
Sid Solvang

Letter in an empty bottle of root beer last seen drifting down the Moses, Friday

Dear Uncle Casey,

First off, Mama's lost her marbles. She let me skip school to go with her to the picket line again. She said she had a feeling about it. Everybody else must've had the same feeling because I swear the whole town was there, waving signs, stomping, and chanting.

Reverend Arlo and his wife brought sloppy joes and a video camera because he said, "Goodnight American workers aren't making tires anymore—they're making history!"

Sid and Ford stood on the back of Pop's old truck, hollering through a bullhorn louder than anyone needs to holler with a bullhorn.

Ford hushed the protest, and Sid said they had an announcement.

Once the crowd settled, Sid tried to speak, but he couldn't finish the sentence before he fell into one of those laughing spells like you get in church when you're trying to be serious, only once you start, you can't stop. There was no stopping it, so Ford took the bullhorn.

"What Solvang's trying to say is congratulations, y'all! We won! We won the lawsuit against Goodnight American!" He got the words out just before he caught the laughing fit too.

"We won!" Sid finally mustered, his fist flying high enough to punch a cloud.

That crowd went crazy, cheering so wildly, you could see the shifty little eyes of management spying out the factory windows to see what was going down. You've never heard such a racket! It was louder than that time the Good Shepherd Choir found the communion wine while they were stuck in the cellar all night waiting for a storm to pass.

One manager dared to poke his head out a window, and one of the strikers unleashed a fireball of profanity so intricate, Teamsters blushed and Melba covered her ears.

But the rest of us sinners cheered like there was no tomorrow.

All the while Sid kept laughing until Ford passed him

the bullhorn, and we all chanted, "The workers, united, will never be defeated!"

I'd bet my guitar I saw a tear well in Mama's eye, not that she'd ever let it fall. Reverend Arlo, on the other hand, was crying his eyes out so revival style, Melba had to hold him up!

30

The End of Goodnight Road

Goodnight Star

LEAD STORY, FRIDAY EDITION

GATC closed for good, CEO claims Kansas "unfriendly to business"

Workers were left reeling Thursday morning, following the announcement that Goodnight American Tire Company is permanently closing its doors, leaving more than 1,000 workers out of a job.

The news came one day after a settlement was reached in the massive class action lawsuit against the company for widespread health and safety violations and an illegal cover-up.

As workers returned to work for the first time since their victory was announced, they found a locked door and an abandoned factory. Windows were boarded. A notice on the door informed the stunned crowd that GATC was leaving and wouldn't be back.

In a press release, GATC's new spokesperson, Carl Reimer, wrote,

"GATC is leaving Goodnight to pursue interests in friendlier, more competitive markets."

By that, GATC means China. CEO Stephen Lyons confirmed the company accepted a tentative offer in China. "It's been a good run here, but this town can't compete in the world market. Too often, workers' greed comes between commerce and progress, and once that slippery slope starts, it's a dead end."

Workers celebrated a short victory over the class action settlement that exceeded expectations by a long shot. As Dennis Redding, a senior tire tech, put it, "It feels like GATC is punishing us by leaving. Once those settlement checks run out, what are we going to do?"

Lyons said the settlement didn't influence the decision to leave. "With mounting pressure from regulations, deepening recession, and strained labor relations, our hands were tied."

GATC released a public statement that Goodnight was "no longer friendly to business," though Kansas is tied with Ohio for the lowest minimum wage in the nation, below $5.15 an hour. In contrast, GATC executives implicated in the scandal averaged $118 an hour. Top executives took home some $700,000 annually.

"We've got a business to run," Lyons said. "If this town can't appreciate the jobs we're providing, we have no choice but to find a market that can."

Lyons blamed "a perfect storm of regulation red tape, workers' demands, and environmentalism run riot for making Goodnight a pressure cooker hostile to profit."

A longtime worker who spoke to the *Star* on the condition of anonymity said, "It doesn't make sense. Federal regulations have been loosening since Reagan, and we had every reason to believe those standards would only become more relaxed given the climate in Washington."

As former employees wait for settlement checks, local churches have offered support. Volunteers are available for prayer or to walk workers through applications for federal assistance.

Workers can be escorted by a security team to gather personal effects by appointment.

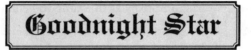

LETTERS FROM GOODNIGHTERS, SATURDAY EDITION

Who Killed Goodnight American?

Dear Goodnight,

I'm reeling from the news that our towns' largest employer is shutting its doors. GATC has been the pillar of our community for 50 years. It brought jobs, glory, and revenue that paved half the roads in this town. Who will pay for the roads now? Who will sponsor the America Festival?

I think we all know who killed Goodnight American.

Cordially,

Virginia Easton, New Patriot Alliance cofounder

From: Abbey Solvang <abbeyroadyogi@omwardbound.org>

To: Sid Solvang <brooklyncalling@zoomail.com>

Why aren't you returning my calls?

Leah told me the good news about the lawsuit, but Harlem says you won't come out of the barn. She thinks you've gone off the deep end. She says you've been hiding in a barn with alpacas while wearing Dad's old praying schmatas. Scarlet says you slept there last night.

According to MapQuest, I can be there in 19 hours if I leave now.

My new girlfriend has one of those old-school campers. We can fit the whole family in it and bring you back to Brooklyn, if you don't mind that it's pink and says *Fuck Golf* all over it. I could bring Luigi's. Say the word. Tomorrow at this time you could be eating a cold Sicilian.

From: Sid Solvang <brooklyncalling@zoomail.com>
To: Abbey Solvang <abbeyroadyogi@omwardbound.org>

You don't want to come here. There is no *here* anymore.

Bailey might've been right about bad luck traveling in nines.

I didn't think it could get worse than the factory closing, but when I got to the May Day yesterday, the whole diner was in one of its polite Midwestern frenzies. I couldn't ask what was wrong, because I got the feeling whatever it was, it was my fault.

Bailey and Tyler stood by the register, looking over a map of Kansas stretched across the counter. Regulars had left their booths to hover over the map with the same frenetic—what was it, resignation? People seemed to have lost their seams and margins the way they do when something has gone very wrong, some shared loss, and it filled the room.

"Look, boss," Bailey said with a tone I'd never heard in her voice before, a funeral's voice. "We got the new maps—those state maps we ordered."

I guess I shrugged, because I only vaguely remembered we had to restock the maps, and it had been a while since we ordered them.

They were being reprinted, so there was some kind of delay. I couldn't imagine why a map would steal all the gravity out of the May Day.

I asked what was wrong.

"The map," Bailey said. "We ain't on it."

"What do you mean?" I asked.

"Look!" She pointed to the eastern edge of Kansas, where jagged hairline rivers crossed the fragile ghosts of borders.

I looked at the soft italic ink that whispered the names of the smallest towns, faint as apologies, but when I looked down at our little paper fraction of the Earth, we were gone.

There was no Goodnight, Kansas.

There was Moses above and the river through it. There was the Missouri border, black as dried blood, but no Goodnight.

If the May Day took it hard, the rest of the town took it harder.

Everywhere I went all day, I felt like the whole town had seen the map. Everyone knew, and they knew it was my fault. Every time I think I'm getting somewhere, it turns to curveballs, crapshoots and 'paca beans.

They were right about me. I didn't just kill the factory.

I killed Goodnight, Kansas.

From: Abbey Solvang <abbeyroadyogi@omwardbound.org>
To: Sid Solvang <brooklyncalling@zoomail.com>

Dude, just like, logistically, I don't think it's possible the map people could've reprinted all the maps that fast nor that they would just erase a town because it stopped making tires. Seriously, those maps were probably printed months ago. It's not like the factory called the map people to tell them it was over and they all came running to redraw Kansas.

So what if Goodnight isn't there? Sciatica Falls is on a map, and what the fuck is that town for? You can't blame yourself; there's no way it had anything to do with what happened.

And another thing: not to be all grammar police, but you said *we*. *We* were gone.

Have you forgotten New York is your *we*? You're in a town that doesn't even exist. Come back. It's time. Sell everything and come home!

What are you waiting for?

LETTERS FROM GOODNIGHTERS, SUNDAY EDITION

Honey Bee Kennedy

Call me *trouble*. Call me *unfriendly*. I don't care. GATC can't shut us up [any]more. I'm here to tell you what I learned on the picket line. GATC said Kansas is unfriendly to business for asking for a dollar more. That's after a 7-year wage freeze. Rents went up every one of those years. Price of gas, milk, and my Thousand Island dressing [has] gone up. AND the cost of tires [has] gone up! But not our wages.

Our CEO called us greedy. He said the workers asked for too much.

That man's face is on the cover of *American Fortune Magazine*, bragging on how much money he's making and how much money the company's making. Turns out, while he was calling us greedy for asking for a dollar more, his salary went up every year. Not by a dollar an hour! In the article, they said Stephen Lyons makes $18 million a year. Last year he gave himself a 37 percent raise. In case you're wondering, that's more than a dollar an hour.

If Lyons [doesn't] show up for work, the tires keep coming, but when the workers walked out, not a single tire came off that line. All the best-paid folks were left in that factory, but not one of them could turn out a tire. None of them ever worked a day on the floor of a tire factory.

I don't know about you, but that [doesn't] sit right with me. Makes me feel unfriendly.

Not unfriendly to honest work, if you're hiring.

Abilene "Honey Bee" Kennedy

JOURNAL ENTRY, SID SOLVANG, MONDAY

Maybe it's the Manischewitz wine talking, but I think I'm on to something. I've been camped out in the barn with the alpacas, surrounded by birdhouses and drinking my way through the Seder wine while I reread weeks of the Goodnight Star over and over, trying to figure out where it all went wrong.

Scarlet came to check on me because Harlem told her I found my father's prayer shawl and yarmulke, and she saw me praying in the barn, something she'd never seen before.

They took one look at me in that old tallit and Taco in Dad's yarmulke, and Scarlet said, "I'm glad to see you're finally letting yourself grieve."

She nodded like she was congratulating me, and Harlem said she'd make me a grief-themed dish for dinner.

Later she served me an omelet so good, it could save the

world. Then Scarlet brought me a pillow and blanket and said, "Try not to get the alpacas drunk on Jewish Easter wine."

I tried to remind her Passover is not Easter, but she laughed like she thought I was joking, and Harlem rolled her eyes and said, "I thought 'Passover' was just Hebrew for 'Easter bunny'?"

If my mother weren't already dead, that would've killed her.

They went to bed, and I kept drinking until I found something that turned the lights on.

It was a letter in the Star from—of all people—Honey Bee Kennedy. She wrote something that shook me sober.

With all those overpaid, undertaxed managers milling inside GATC, when the last of the workers walked out, not a single tire came out of the factory. The best-paid staff were all there with everything a man could need to build a tire, but not one of them could do it.

It got me thinking. Or mulling.

From: Sid Solvang <brooklyncalling@zoomail.com>
To: Council Member Ford Hollis <FHollis@goodnight.gov>

I don't suppose you could tell me what conditions are like inside GATC? Word at the diner is the factory was left as is. Gil said they just locked the doors and fled. Any truth to that?

From: Council Member Ford Hollis <FHollis@goodnight.gov>
To: Sid Solvang <brooklyncalling@zoomail.com>

That's the story. Why do you ask?

From: Sid Solvang <brooklyncalling@zoomail.com>
To: Council Member Ford Hollis <FHollis@goodnight.gov>

Let me get this straight: So Goodnight American is gone, but the entire factory is exactly as it was? I mean, they left all the equipment, everything still intact?

From: Council Member Ford Hollis <FHollis@goodnight.gov>
To: Sid Solvang <brooklyncalling@zoomail.com>

Everything but the files are still in place. Any shred of paper the government didn't seize is gone or in disarray on the floor, but not a slab of rubber has been touched. Those *Enrons* were so busy trying to burn the trail behind them, they didn't move so much as a paper clip.

We went in with every kind of federal agent you've ever heard of and some you've never heard of. The EPA, FBI, SEC, FTC, IRS, NLRB, NHTSA. And of course, OSHA was all over it. Even Fish and Wildlife was there. There was so much yellow and red tape, so many agents scampering around, it looked like a government convention.

Why do you ask?

From: Sid Solvang <brooklyncalling@zoomail.com>
To: Council Member Ford Hollis <FHollis@goodnight.gov>

I have an idea.

31

View from the Roses

From: Virginia Easton <veaston@prairienet.com>
To: Mayor Carol Shultz <mayor@goodnight.gov>

I'm not one to be spreading hedge talk, but the view from my roses is talking. I can't help it if my lot sits so high on Northwind Road, my rose garden looks down on my neighbors.

That Solvang is up to something.

He's been sleeping in his barn dressed like a fiddler on the roof. Those lunatic alpacas come and go, but I don't think Solvang has stepped out of the barn since the factory closed.

Last night I saw a member of our very own city council go into that barn, and his car was still parked outside when I finally fell asleep at dawn while keeping watch from my picture window. When I went to church, there was another car parked outside, and when I came back, I saw our mailman—on his day off—go in, and he didn't come out for an hour.

Something doesn't sit right. As mayor, I thought you should know.

From: Mayor Carol Shultz <mayor@goodnight.gov>
To: Virginia Easton <veaston@prairienet.com>

Dear Ms. Easton,

It's always a delight to hear from our constituents.

After what happened this week, I'm confident any council member tying their horse to the wagon that chased GATC to China will receive their reckoning on election day, which is right around the corner. I have faith it will all wash out at the ballot box.

I sleep better knowing folks such as yourself are keeping watch, but rest assured there's no coming back from what they did to lose our tire factory.

Best regards,

Mayor Carol Shultz

From: Harlem Solvang <torturedsol@zoomail.com>

To: Abbey Solvang <abbeyroadyogi@omwardbound.org>

Have you spoken to Dad? I don't know what's gotten into him besides a lot of crappy wine, or possibly Cuervo, but he's hiding in the barn again. This time he's not alone.

Dad made friends with this council dude who's so obsessed with Christmas trees, he actually smells like one, and they were out there drinking with the alpacas all night.

Around Midnight I heard "Round Midnight" on vinyl drifting from the barn windows followed by "Kind of Blue," followed by a thrashing of actual trumpets—drunk trumpets. As you know, Dad doesn't play the trumpet. Mom was at the hotel, so I went to check on them.

When I opened the barn door, there was Dad still in Grandpa's praying clothes with his arm around Ford, who had an American flag wrapped around him, and they were singing the "Star-Spangled Banner" for an audience of alpacas.

It looked like Kinko's on acid because there were files scattered everywhere.

I asked what they were doing, and Dad answered with the voice of tequila that they had a plan to save Goodnight, Kansas, maybe even the world. Ford said Dad is a genius, and Dad said Ford is a mensch, and Ford said, "Thank you," and they went back to singing.

Since then, Ford practically moved into the barn, along with the mailman and the minister from Disco's church. Strangers come and go, schlepping milk crates full of papers.

It's not just our house that's gone crazy. Everyone's so torn up about GATC closing, the town's in a daze.

The worst part is my cooking club didn't show up last night because their parents blame Dad for the factory closing. Mom said the May Day has been a graveyard, and we had a bunch of cancellations at the hotel. Tyler says we should sell everything before it gets any worse, but Bailey says it's too late.

LETTERS FROM GOODNIGHTERS, THURSDAY EDITION

Dear Goodnight,

What if it isn't doomed?

There are a lot of checks coming to Goodnight from the settlement with GATC. Maybe with your share, you could buy a truck or put a down payment on a house, but at the end of the day, once that check is spent, that's it, and you're still out of a job.

But I had an idea. Maybe you didn't know that when GATC

moved to China, it virtually abandoned the factory as is. They just shut off the lights and locked the door. It's cheaper for the company to start over in China than to ship the existing infrastructure to the other side of the world. What that means is the factory is just sitting there exactly how it was when you left, waiting for someone who can afford to buy it.

Call me crazy, but what if all the workers put their settlement money together and bought the factory? Management didn't keep the company going all those years—the workers did.

I'm talking about a co-op. There's a tire factory in Mexico that did it, and it's working.

The way I see it, if there are no bosses, there are no bosses to pay. The majority of profits never went to the workers. What if the workers decided how much they should get paid? Imagine how much money the workers could take home without the burden of paying the suits at the top.

Did you know the CEO of GATC made 530 times the wage of his average worker? That factory ran without that CEO ever setting foot on the factory floor. No one needs a CEO to produce a tire. If being a boss has taught me anything, it's that a company can't function without its workers, but it can function fine without a boss. If none of the workers show up one day, the whole place shuts down. If management doesn't show up to work, nobody even notices.

I had my accountant do some calculations, and based on the current cost to buy the plant and the amount employees are receiving in settlement payoffs, what we found is that we only need 587 of GATC's nonmanagement workforce, a little more than half the workers, to be able to buy the factory as is. That means if there are more than half the workers willing to buy into ownership, there will be settlement money left, *and* you get to keep your job. Only, this time, you're working for yourself as part owner of the company.

GATC is working with the EPA to clean up the lake. As a co-op, you can keep it clean.

Unlike stakeholders, what happens to the factory has no bearing on my life. Like I said, it's just an idea, but I've watched GATC workers losing sleep, losing jobs, and packing their 18-year-olds up to leave this town in search of work. It seems to me maybe there's a better way.

I think this town knows how to make a tire. What do you think?

Kindly,

Sid Solvang

LETTERS TO GOODNIGHTERS, MONDAY EDITION

Dear Goodnight,

I grew up in South End and worked my way up at GATC to lead the engineering team in developing greener tire technology. When my team presented our plan, we were essentially told we had no future at Goodnight American. Some opposition was based on existing contracts and investment ties; some was philosophical.

The question isn't, why are companies getting away with distorting environmental reports? The real question is, why are we regulating toxic chemicals that could be banned? Our technologies and our imaginations are not so limited as our willingness to change. From manufacturing to tire emissions, we have to face the verdict that trusting corporations to regulate themselves and allowing corporations' "experts" to infiltrate the regulating agencies that govern them has been a disastrous experiment. Is anyone really surprised by this?

That would be like appointing a Monsanto lawyer to run the FDA!

The EPA promoted the Rubber Tire Manufacturing NESHAP last year, but we've known these chemicals were a problem since the 1950s and began tracking tire-related cancers among workers in the 1970s. That means regulations are failing, not just because they're not enforced, as in the example of GATC, but because those regulations even when enforced aren't enough to protect public health. Workers are only the first hit. If these chemicals are making them sick, we have to assume the same chemicals will have devastating impacts elsewhere, from road runoff to local water sources.

Those profiting from lax corporate and manufacturing regulations that harm workers would have you believe the solution to toxic conditions for American workers is to export those toxic conditions to workers in less regulated countries. The regulatory forces whose job it is to protect the safety of American workers are allowing those companies essentially to export cancer. It's not enough to applaud government agencies for finally stepping in; it begs a deeper, more menacing question—if these chemicals have been identified as dangerous for decades, why are we allowing them in any form?

I left when I was recruited by a company specializing in sustainable technology in the Netherlands, but if I had job to come back to, I'd move home in a heartbeat.

You may be surprised to know I still subscribe to the *Goodnight Star*. My parents still live in Goodnight, and I'm always a little homesick. Of course, by the time the paper gets to the Netherlands, I'm behind the times, but I like to keep up with Emporia Road.

When I saw the proposal for GATC to go co-op, I thought this could be my chance to come home. If GATC goes co-op and you're hiring, I'm in.

Holden Chase, former tire-development engineer, GATC

Goodnight Star

LEAD STORY, TUESDAY EDITION

Co-op proposal picks up steam

A town hall meeting has been scheduled for public input following an outpouring of calls to City Hall in response to Sid Solvang's suggestion that former Goodnight American tire workers pool their class action settlement checks to buy the plant.

According to City Hall's switchboard supervisor, Cindy Webber, they received hundreds of calls from former GATC workers inquiring about a potential co-op.

The forum will include presentations from public officials and former GATC supervisors to discuss the logistics of what it would take to get the factory running again.

The public forum has been scheduled for the last Saturday of the month at 6:00 p.m. Speakers will be limited to three minutes, and all are welcome to speak their piece.

From: Jules Jamison <livingthedream73@zoomail.com>
To: Sid Solvang <brooklyncalling@zoomail.com>

I hope you're sitting down and within reach of some worthy champagne.

Remember that investor I mentioned? So Tristan Deveraux is the hipster restaurateur behind pickled-okra ice cream. He made his name financing Phoodie's Sci-Scream, a chain of liquid-nitrogen ice cream trucks taking over the East Coast, and now he's starting to invest in brick and mortar. He was the money behind Oliver Dean's Ein Sof Grille, and it's made such a killing, he's hunting for more.

True story, last night we were having drinks there, and we heard someone say, "Oliver Dean's secret ingredient is Sid Solvang."

It wasn't lost on Tristan.

Check out his blog, *Have Nitrogen, Will Travel.* It's not just that this guy has a soft spot for molecular gastronomy and money to burn. Remember that third party I mentioned in the pipeline? It's his family. They have a huge vineyard—more like a wine empire in Sonoma—and they want to partner with a new chef. Tristan has a thing for soul food, and he's looking for a chef who can marry down-home with modernist techniques like yours. I told him all about you.

Brooklyn is changing. There's a new spot selling pizza foam, and people are actually buying it. I can't say the notion of molecular pizza foam doesn't make even me want to move to Naples and never look back, but I'm telling you the culinary tide is changing.

We had quite an interesting conversation about it. Tristan will be in touch.

You're welcome.

From: Tristan Deveraux <NitroGenius@TristanDeveraux.com>
To: Sid Solvang <brooklyncalling@zoomail.com>

I've been following your career with interest since I first heard your name at the academy. I was a few years behind you, and you were somewhat of a legend there.

By the time I got a chance to check out Sol's, the writing was on the wall. I sat at the empty counter, and the place was so abandoned, I could hear the florescent lights buzz.

But the plates told a different story.

From the first bite, I embarked on what could only be described as a spiritual experience.

Those gnocchi knish kebobs slayed me. Your Ashkenazi caviar was a scream—an American scream on a plate. My palate was mystified.

Brooklyn wasn't ready for you in 1999, but they're ready now. New blood is taking over. They're hustling one-bite zucchini cupcakes for $5 because they can.

Your culinary fashion was over the palates of the masses. It's couture. Like me.

But the world is catching up with us. The market is catching up.

I've secured a killer location, and we have investors contingent on finding the right chef. I've narrowed my search to a short list of candidates. The terms are beyond generous, but I have ask, if you're interested, are you open to relocating to New York?

Ciao,

Tristan Deveraux

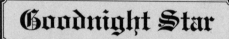

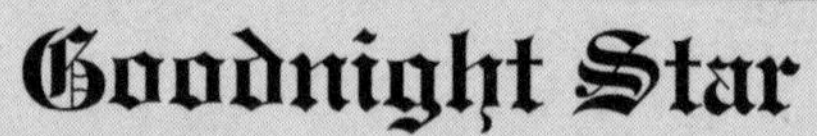

LOST AND FOUND, THURSDAY EDITION

LOST: The Minor farm is short three goats since Monday. Sherwood,

Thurgood, and Clive disappeared in the night, but Mitch Minor blames himself.

"I meant to get around to mending our gates, but my arthritis has been so bad, I couldn't get to it before they slipped out. They're sables, black as gunpowder, so it's not easy to see them at night, especially with my night vision these days, and my wife's eyes are worse than mine. So please keep your eyes open for them."

PART 4

An American Scream

32

Truth or Dare

From: Aspen Pottstock <aspen@pottstockenterprises.com>
To: Sid Solvang <brooklyncalling@zoomail.com>

Dear Mr. Solvang,

There's talk around town you might be looking to sell the diner. I'd be a player if the deal included sale of the hotel. Why don't I drop by the diner this afternoon, and we can talk it over.

Aspen Pottstock

From: Harlem Solvang <torturedsol@zoomail.com>
To: Abbey Solvang <abbeyroadyogi@omwardbound.org>

The whole town has lost its glue.

The settlement checks from Goodnight American are rolling in, so there are drunk people everywhere! Dad says it's because nobody has work, and everybody's scared. He says anxiety with nowhere to go and a fat check is a good way to get a whole town drunk, but he has an idea that maybe could help people out. He always has an idea.

Did he tell you some hipster wants to hire him to run a restaurant back in Brooklyn? I think he's made up his mind. Mom tried to talk him out of it at first until she found out how much money he could make, including moving expenses, and that put her on the fence. Now Aspen Pottstock has started slithering around the May Day, offering crazy money to buy it and the Hallelujah so we can leave Goodnight free and clear, like he's doing us a favor!

I don't know... Maybe he would be doing us a favor.

The New Patriots started a petition to fire the editor of the *Star* because they say it's half the *Star*'s fault the factory shut down. Guess whose fault the other half is?

Ours, of course.

The crazy thing is I don't want to sell the diner anymore. Selling the May Day would be selling a piece of my soul. I can't imagine not walking into that pink neon haze every day, through the sizzle of fryers in the buzz of the kitchen rush, which stops at the window bell, where Tyler yells, "Order up: Blue Harlem Special," and Bailey carries my plate away.

Yes, I said *soul*. Don't get all excited expecting me to take up yoga now. It's not a spirit thing; it's an art thing. And don't worry, the church people didn't get to me.

I don't believe in God; I just believe in cooking.

From: Aspen Pottstock <aspen@pottstockenterprises.com>
To: Sid Solvang <brooklyncalling@zoomail.com>

Dear Mr. Solvang,

I'm fresh from my lawyer's office. You'll find my offer to buy the May Day and the Hallelujah attached. The offer is generous given the market, but I value your vision, and I appreciate the elbow grease that went into getting these businesses viable again.

I admit my plans for a Super 8 and a Burger King franchise were a failure of imagination meant to be fiscally conservative in an unpredictable market. Of course, they would've been a tremendously lucrative success for a failure of imagination, but no one could argue you must've done something right because it looks like it's been hand over fist even with an enemy like the Patriot Alliance out for your blood.

Despite your reputation for being a man of charity, everybody knows you've been searching for a way out of this town since you got here, and now you've got it. Take your time looking over my offer. When you're ready to discuss it further, I'd love to have you up to the Moses Country Club for a round of golf.

Best regards,

Aspen Pottstock

From: Skeeter Bannister <highwater@shotmail.com>
To: Scarlet Bannister Solvang <mystifried@zoomail.com>

Talk around town is you're leaving.

I heard somebody gave you an offer you can't refuse.

I'm just gonna lay it on the table: I don't want you to go back to New York. I know I said you should take the money and run a time or two, but I was just blowing smoke.

Maybe I had some things wrong that might explain why Dad was crosswise with the rest of us. Daddy had been complaining for years about feeling sick, and he kept blaming the tire factory, telling us they were up to something, but none of us believed him. He swore something came over him every time he fished in the lake. We thought he was losing his marbles. Even when the alpacas started dying, we didn't believe it was the lake.

I told Daddy, "Half our friends work for GATC, so don't you think they'd know if something was going down?"

But they didn't know. Or maybe nobody wanted to believe the only thing paying their bills might be selling us a river of cancer.

Anyhow, what I really mean to say is that your kid is decent, and your husband ain't half bad. I don't think any of us expected him to do right by the May Day like he did.

Alls I'm saying is maybe you should stay.

I'm sorry we didn't exactly roll out the red carpet when you came home, but I'm asking you to stay. Don't go back to New York. You belong here with your family.

From: Scarlet Bannister Solvang <mystifried@zoomail.com>
To: Skeeter Bannister <highwater@shotmail.com>

I'm sorry you were hurt when I left. For the record, I didn't run away so much as I was sent away. I figured y'all knew. I thought the whole town knew. It's why I didn't come back.

It's ancient history now, and I make a point of not talking about it because I make a point of not thinking about it. Why dig up dead horses when there's bread to be baked?

As far as leaving, I'm afraid that ship sailed. Even if I want to stay, Sid's too close to finally getting everything he worked so hard for. I couldn't ask him to give that up, and we promised Harlem we'd move back to Brooklyn as soon as we could afford it.

Maybe it's for the best because between that patriot mob and the glitter girl getting locked up, it doesn't seem like this town has changed enough for people who are...different.

From: Skeeter Bannister <highwater@shotmail.com>
To: Scarlet Bannister Solvang <mystifried@zoomail.com>

Maybe you're not so different. Tanya's husband's afflicted with a fear of sesame seeds so terminal, he can't walk into a bakery. Jolene's gotta count her peas before she can eat them. Cousin Sam's taken up eating paper—to the tune of a whole *TV Guide* at a time. I'm suffering from a mean case of pickled lady bits, and my hot flashes got so bad, I slapped a cow yesterday.

What does *different* even mean anymore?

And what do you mean, you were sent away?

JOURNAL ENTRY, SID SOLVANG, SATURDAY

Harlem stayed late at the May Day, so it was just me, three alpacas, and a sink full of dirty dishes tonight. The dishwasher was acting up again, so I put on a little Thelonious and went to work washing by hand. I was three spoons and one colander in when Scarlet came home.

She offered to help, so we stood in the kitchen washing dishes. I couldn't remember the last time we had been alone in the same room. I meant to tell her about Pottstock's offer, but it slipped my mind. Even though the offer had taken my breath away, my mind had been on the upcoming co-op hearing.

When it finally occurred to me to mention it, Scarlet

said, "So Skeeter sent an email saying she wants us to stay here."

I hesitated because Scarlet and her sisters speak in land mines and brushfires.

Cautiously, I said, "That's...funny."

"Yep. It's funny," she said with an expression that said it wasn't funny.

I asked how the May Day was going, since I'd been tied up at the Hallelujah all week. She said it was a good night. Mitch Minor's grandchildren were in town for a family reunion, so they all came by asking for cotton candy pie, which apparently Harlem had promised them. Carter Bell had breakfast there and came back for dinner, since his wife went to visit her mother and he can't cook anything but toast. Raina Freeman won a thousand dollars in lotto scratchers and said she was going to spend it all at the May Day to thank us for getting her through the year.

"Bless her heart," Scarlet said, letting out a sigh that seemed to belong to Kansas.

"When did you start saying 'bless your heart'?" I asked.

"I don't know when I stopped saying it."

As I washed and she dried, she told me who was watching their cholesterol, who sat where and what they ordered, though I could've guessed.

I told her washing dishes on a Saturday night reminded me of our first apartment in Brooklyn. We'd just graduated from culinary school, and I'd leave a formidable trail of dirty pots and pans trying new dishes. She'd wash and I'd dry, and she never complained, no matter how Frankensteinian the molecular-gastronomy experiments got.

To pass the time, we'd play truth or dare, but we gave it up after a while because I always chose nothing but truth, and she always chose nothing but dare.

"It's been a long time. Wanna play truth or dare?" I asked.

"You know I'm gonna dare you to kiss an alpaca."

"That's why I always pick truth."

"Is that why?"

"I thought the purpose of truth or dare was to have an excuse to tell all your secrets," I said, which inspired a sigh that could give an F5 a run for its money.

Scarlet frowned, scowled, huffed, and laid down her dish towel.

When I was thoroughly confused, she said, "Truth. They locked me up in the loony bin for four months when I was 17. There you go. There's your truth."

I asked who locked her up.

Her chin turned pure Bannister, and she said, "That's enough. Now you can kiss Vertigo, and we'll be even."

"I guess that's how you win truth or dare." I laughed.

But the more I thought about it, the more it simmered. We were almost out of dishes, and I got the feeling once the last dish was in the cupboard, the conversation would be out of reach, like that moment, that kitchen, was the only place in eternity where this conversation could exist. Maybe that's why I couldn't back down. I said, "You've gotta tell me who locked you up and why they did it and why you didn't tell me."

She held a blue dish towel against the last bowl like she

understood what it was worth. "You might've noticed it's not too hard to get locked up around here."

"You don't have to answer all my questions," I said. "Would you give me one?"

"Pop," she said. "Pop had me locked up."

The physics that governed that moment in the kitchen seemed to belong to a different universe, one without water, dish towels, or time—a universe composed only of one conversation, a boundless verse. Then again, maybe it's not so different. Why would the Greeks call it a uni-verse in the first place? One unified verse. "Verse" means metrics—how we measure—but it also means poetry. And what does it mean that the act of measuring and poetry share the same word? One verse, not a measurement of the constant sum, but a measurement of the constant interaction, the metrics between things, between us. I could see the conversation on a plate, a dish to represent all invisible things. Something steamed or blackened. Something released.

"The veteran debt?" I asked.

"The veteran debt," she answered.

"I don't understand how your sisters didn't know."

"He told them I ran away," she said. "They had no reason not to believe him."

"That's why you drove across Western Kansas to get Disco."

"That's why I drove across Western Kansas for Disco." Scarlet stacked the last bowl in the cupboard. I expected one of her sighs. Instead, she nodded in an atmosphere I've come to know as Kansas and said, "Wanna see what's on TV?"

We made popcorn and fell asleep watching Seinfeld reruns with the alpacas.

Even on Pop's lumpy water mill-patterned velour couch that hasn't moved since the Eisenhower administration, it was the best I'd slept in months.

For the record, no alpacas were kissed.

Scarlet never asked about Pottstock's offer, though she must've known it came, and I never asked what people were saying about the co-op, though I knew she must've heard something.

It could wait.

33

The Only Things Left Were the Bells

From: Disco Kennedy <lostblue@prairienet.com>
To: Sid Solvang <brooklyncalling@zoomail.com>

SID.

If you think Aspen Pottstock is fit to run the May Day, you're shopping bridges from the devil and somebody should probably slap you. Ask anyone. Ask Bailey. Of course, if anyone's gonna slap you, it'll be her.

Let me tell you something about Pottstock: He's been our landlord since the Big Bang, which I'm sure he'd buy too, if science would sell it to him. No matter what's happening in this town or in the world, he raises rent every January 1, seven days after Christmas.

So we never had one good Christmas. My mama always had *the bad nerves* because she knew the rent was going up. That house of a thousand drafts was always cold, and every December when I said anything about Christmas, she'd say, "Do you want Christmas, or do you want heat? I'll let you decide."

I was 5 years old the first time she asked me, and I was just old enough to understand the gravity of Christmas, so I said, "I want Christmas. I don't care if I freeze to death."

She asked if I was sure, and I said yes. We got a Christmas tree, and I got a stocking full of Jolly Ranchers and Pixy Stix and Jesus whatnot and a pink dollhouse with little furniture and a roof that sparkled with silver glitter. It was the prettiest thing I'd ever seen in my whole life.

And then we almost froze to death that winter because we couldn't pay the electric bill. By Easter the dogs had chewed up half the dollhouse furniture anyway.

The next year, when she asked if I wanted Christmas or heat, I answered heat that year and every year until she stopped asking. Some winters the heat went out anyway, and Pottstock wouldn't answer his phone. He says he can't get reception when he's skiing in Vail.

One Christmas the heat was out, and it was so cold, my mama caught pneumonia. Pottstock wouldn't pick up the phone, so we stayed on Reverend Arlo's sofa bed because the cold was too much even for my mama. She missed so much work, we couldn't pay rent, and when we told him why, do you think he cut us a break? Do you think that stopped him from raising the rent January 1? Melba said we could sue him, but he claimed dog hair broke it and so it was our fault. Mama was so busy taking extra hours to make up for missing work, I didn't see her for a month. Pottstock finally fixed the furnace, but as you well know, it breaks if you look at it wrong. Mama's been saving to move to a better house, but that man owns the whole south side.

That's not the only thing.

You can't go. You're one of us now. I thought you knew that.

Disco

From: Bailey Nation <hellrazor@shotmail.com>
To: Sid Solvang <brooklyncalling@zoomail.com>

SIDNEY SOLVANG.

Where are you hiding, boss?

Listen up and listen good.

Disco asked me to give you my two cents on Aspen Pottstock. I can give you two dollars, which I'd give you to your face if anybody knew where you're hiding. If I'd known you were scheming to sell what was left of this town to the devil, I'd have tracked you down earlier.

If you turn over the May Day to Pottstock, it's like giving all your keys to the Russian doll of lies selling a Russian dollhouse of cards. Pottstock ain't a liar like the Oz man behind the curtain; he's more like if the man behind the curtain had another guy behind a curtain and that guy was a lawyer who paid for law school but stuck being a meter maid because his billionaire parents were mad at him for spending all their money on child prostitutes from Bosnia.

If you think that man will do right by the May Day, you're dreaming in French subtitles.

Wake up, Solvang!

From: Sid Solvang <brooklyncalling@zoomail.com>
To: Bailey Nation <hellrazor@shotmail.com>

I guess you didn't read the paper this morning, or you'd know why I'm hiding.

On the front page, in the boldest ink, the editor announced, "The *Goodnight Star* unequivocally endorses Sid Solvang's proposal to convert our tire factory into a worker's co-op."

Apparently the editor asked permission from their editorial team to take a public position on the issue, and the vote was unanimous.

Not everyone is happy about it.

Ford called to warn me there have been some vague threats around City Hall, and he's concerned. He suggested we stay at the Hallelujah until the public forum. I told him we can't take the alpacas to the hotel, so he insisted on putting us up at his Christmas-tree farm. We'll just stay for a few nights until things calm down.

You'll be happy to know I told Tyler you're in charge of the May Day until we get back.

Don't be too proud of yourself—we left Honey Bee Kennedy running the hotel.

I'm sure this will blow over in a couple of days, but if it doesn't, we may not have a choice about selling the diner.

Two days later, a flyer stapled to every streetlamp and bulletin board on Emporia Road

TAKE BACK THE PRESS!

Tired of the communist conspiracy that killed Goodnight American?

Sign the petition to remove the heathen behind the ink curtain.

Bring a hot dish and meet us in Eisenhower Park to gather signatures.

Bring your newspapers, and we will burn them in protest!

BURN THE GOODNIGHT STAR!

Eisenhower Park, Tuesday 5:00 p.m.

Sponsored by the New Patriot Alliance

Goodnight Star

LETTERS FROM GOODNIGHTERS, FRIDAY EDITION

Dear Neighbors,

I come out to my tractor, and what do I find? An invitation to a burning of the printed word. Trespassers left a flyer on my tractor that was hellfire, war fever, and damnation. I've had enough of folks trying to turn good folks against other good folks who've done nothing but good for the roads and bells and the suppers of this town.

I prayed on it and slept on it and prayed on it again, and my conscience won't leave me any peace if I don't say what needs to be said.

This New Patriot Alliance has gone too far.

They are not patriots. They are not allies. There is nothing new nor Christian about the kind of fight they're picking.

You can thank the Solvangs for that. You can thank Pop Bannister. You can thank this whistleblower, never mind who. Most of all, you can thank our *Goodnight Star* for telling the truth, knowing full well what kind of trouble the truth would stir up.

So, NO, I will not be burning newspapers on our streets.

NO, I will not be attacking my fellow neighbors, who have done nothing but bake us pie, feed our poorest families, and mend our church bells.

And YES, I will be at the town forum prepared to vote my conscience on the future of Goodnight American. I've seen a lot of sheep pay good money to buy the wool over their eyes, but I didn't think Goodnight was that kind of town.

My mother used to say everything has a way of coming out in the wash, but that's only true if somebody puts it in the wash.

Mitch Minor

EDITOR'S BULLHORN, SUNDAY EDITION

A petition is being passed behind church doors calling for my resignation as editor of this humble rag. I have received many letters of support for making public the scandal at GATC and for standing up for Sid Solvang, but I have also been called a "youth-corrupting communist who worships Satan."

I've been criticized for falling short as a journalist. No editor of the *Goodnight Star* has ever had a degree in journalism. That's no accident. Our newspaper wasn't started by journalists. It was started by farmers who shared a contempt for the propaganda that was being spun by the *Moses Register*.

Before the founding of the *Goodnight Star*, we relied on the *Register* for all our news. Corruption plagued the *Register* because the editors could be influenced to reinterpret the most definitive truths with land deals, tax breaks, and even free pie.

When the *Goodnight Star* started, the founders didn't embrace anonymity for novelty nor superstition—they embraced it to preserve the integrity of a truly democratic press. The founders recognized a position of such power could be too easily influenced, so the editor went underground, where the editors have stayed for a century and a half.

This was never to protect the editor. It was to protect the truth.

From: Virginia Easton <veaston@prairienet.com>
To: Erik Ruston Bounty Services <eruston@texasbountyplus.com>

Dear Mr. Ruston,

You come highly recommended from our common friend at the Moses Golf Club for your discretion. This is a sensitive matter, legally gray maybe. It needs to be handled delicately, which is why I'm paying the difference to hire out of state. I should be clear that we just want to apprehend the subject, not to harm anyone. We are all Christians here. Let's be clear on that.

The alliance has raised enough money for the down payment on your services. We can pay more when the subject is delivered, with a bonus if you can manage to deliver him to the Goodnight Town Hall this Saturday, during the public forum regarding the tire factory. I'm enclosing the leaflet with the location, time, and other details, along with any information that might help you to identify and locate him. I'll address the forum when they open for public comment, and I'd like to time it just right to expose this heathen when the spotlight is brightest.

Do not contact me directly. I trust the information I've provided is more than enough to find this criminal and bring him to justice.

Virginia Easton

Goodnight Star

LOST AND FOUND, TUESDAY EDITION

FOUND: Mitch Minor's latest missing sable goats—Clive, Thurgood, and Sherwood—were found grazing by the side of his very own barn, but the real story is what they were grazing on.

It wasn't shoes nor shrubs.

They were chewing on wind chimes.

"When we realized it was our goats eating our chimes all along, we took a good look around the shed, and we found bells from the floorboards to the rafters. They'd eaten all the wind catchers and the strings, but they left no trace of bamboo or even driftwood. The only thing left were the bells."

Minor extends deepest apologies for the goat vandals.

"We're replacing the wood fence with steel to address this public threat to wind chimes. In the meantime, you can pick up your lost bells at the farm."

34

The Back Doors of Emporia Road

From: Council Member Ford Hollis <FHollis@goodnight.gov>
To: Sid Solvang <brooklyncalling@zoomail.com>

Don't come through the front door. You'll never get through. It's already packed.

The council has a private passage into the town hall. It's from Prohibition days, so it's discreet. I'll meet you there so you don't have to endure the wrath of the New Patriots. The protest is small, but they're blocking the entrance. You have to walk through the saddest scent of burning ink from a bunch of dimwits lighting newspapers on fire in the middle of Emporia Road.

They've been there all day.

Don't let them scare you away. The majority of this town is behind your co-op idea. The more the council talks it over, the more it seems possible to make the transition from the old GATC to a worker-owned model. The whole town's buzzing over this.

Take the alley. I'll save you a seat.

From: Sid Solvang <brooklyncalling@zoomail.com>
To: Council Member Ford Hollis <FHollis@goodnight.gov>

I can't make it tonight. Something came up, and I have a meeting at the May Day.

Unrelated, I received another letter from the whistleblower. Since the forum is tonight, I didn't open it. I sent Carter straight over to deliver it by hand. He should be there any minute.

As far as the co-op, you know everything I know. I turned all my research over to the committee. No one needs me getting in the way at the forum, but I'm truly sorry to miss it.

From: Council Member Ford Hollis <FHollis@goodnight.gov>
To: Sid Solvang <brooklyncalling@zoomail.com>

I heard you had company coming and that it had something to do with leaving. Word around town is you found yourself a way back to New York. I guess I was hoping it was just a rumor.

Nobody can blame you for looking for a way out of this town. I can see why folks like you wouldn't want to stick around. If I had anywhere else in the world to go, I might consider leaving myself, but like most farmers here, I find there's no leaving. Our roots are too deep.

I suppose as long as there's a Christmas, folks will keep coming for Christmas trees, so my family will scrape by one way or the other.

Don't burden yourself thinking you owe this town anything, Sid. You've done more than enough, and it's Goodnight that is in your debt, not the other way around.

A lot of folks gave up on this town. Without you, the Hallelujah would be nothing but dust in the gutters of Emporia Road, and our May Day would be a Burger King.

My phone's ringing off the hook with folks asking how they can get in on this co-op idea.

There's no doubt once the rest of them see the numbers in bold print tonight, we'll sign on more than enough former workers to pull this off. It's a shame you'll miss it, but I wish you luck with your meeting.

Carter just walked in. I can't imagine there's anything left for a whistleblower to whistle.

From: Sid Solvang <brooklyncalling@zoomail.com>
To: Jules Jamison <livingthedream73@zoomail.com>

I couldn't do it.

I apologize for putting you out. I know it couldn't have been easy greasing the wheels behind the Tristan Deveraux Empire, but I just couldn't go through with it. Unfortunately, I didn't know that until the very moment I was sitting across the May Day booth from Tristan. It was like sitting across a table from New York, from everything I thought I wanted.

It was at that moment that I realized the May Day is everything I didn't know I wanted.

That booth is the dream, but I didn't see it until my old dream was sitting across from me, snapping his fingers at a waitress he looked right through, not seeing a person who could save someone's life. When Bailey tried to take his order, he missed it. Maybe I missed it until that moment. But she saw it. Bailey gave me the sly eye and said, "You know, boss, there's two kinds of eyes in the world: eyes that look through you and eyes that see through you."

She brought us the new pizza bowl, the one-serving pizza pie I just added to the menu.

He called it "operatic, a pizza with a 7-octave range to set the culinary zeitgeist on fire." And he said, "They were wrong about you. You were never P. T. Barnum—you were Tesla."

That would've really meant something to me before, but now it felt flimsy.

"I went by Sol's before it closed," he said. "I thought your pastrami foam was…platinum, utterly fascinating. The austerity was brave. It was also misunderstood. You were ahead of your time, but we caught up."

He said, "My culinary hero is Chef Hubert Keller, not because his cuisine is killer, though it is. It's not even because his technique is stellar. It's because he had the culinary balls to put a $5,000 hamburger on his menu. You know what I think when I see a $5,000 burger? I think why not a $6,000 burger? Why not $10,000? If people are willing to pay it, why not give it to them? Most people don't know what they want until you tell them what they want anyway.

"I've made my empire convincing people they want things that don't make sense to them. Maybe molecular is a circus act, but when it's done right, it's couture—people will pay anything for it. That's where I think you went wrong at Sol's. You could've asked for more. You should've asked for more. You charged pastrami prices, so diners expected pastrami. If you charge $100 for it, they'll taste $100. They may convince themselves it's good just so they don't feel like a sucker for spending that much. And your pastrami foam was *that* good."

"It really wasn't," I told him. "People came to Sol's because they were hungry, but they left hungry. I was so caught up in the artificial wizardry, I forgot food service is about service. It's about feeding people, not blowing their minds with chemistry histrionics. Maybe molecular gastronomy is more about art than food. It's certainly not food for hungry people. You can't eat art. The reviews were right."

"You're being too modest," he said. "Your food *is* art. To a refined palate, it's nothing less than music, and I want a 7-octave chef for a 7-octave menu. I believe you're the guy."

"I'm not the guy," I said, before I could reason with myself. "Maybe I was that guy before, but not anymore. I'm sorry."

Tonight, sitting in that booth, knowing my whole town was gathered in our town hall across the road without me, I could finally see where I belong and where I don't.

So I wanted to tell you, before you heard it somewhere else, why I left Tristan Deveraux, imperialist restaurateur, offering everything in the world I thought I wanted, sitting alone at a booth at the May Day.

35

Minutes from the Watershed

CHAMBER CLERK MINUTES, GOODNIGHT TOWN HALL PUBLIC FORUM ON THE FUTURE OF GATC

PUBLIC FORUM ON FUTURE OF
GOODNIGHT AMERICAN TIRE CO.

Transcribed by Sandy Fielding, KSR. No. 1192357

Opening remarks by COUNCIL MEMBER FORD HOLLIS:

As chair of the Goodnight American Oversight Committee, and on behalf of our council, I welcome all of you to this public forum. Our committee organized this meeting as a first step in our special agenda to address the future of Goodnight's displaced workers. You won't be hearing from our mayor nor council because this is your forum, not ours. This is an informal stage to hear from the public. I'll keep it short because I know there's a lot of ground to cover and we want to hear from you. Let me remind you to try to keep comments under two minutes.

We'll start with a statement from a former GATC worker, and then we'll open the floor.

STATEMENT READ BY GIL BRENNER, GATC OPERATIONS MANAGER:

My name is Gil Brenner. I am—or was—manager of operations at Goodnight American for nine years. Before that I worked on the floor, as a technician. First, I'd like to go on record that I'm a lifelong Republican from a family of Republicans gone back to Lincoln. Let me be clear about that, as I do not appreciate folks asking my aging mother why I've gone communist. I'm a tried and true loyalist of the Grand Old Party, but I also know what it's like to support a family on minimum wage. This is the difference between a manager who comes up through the ranks like me and the ones who come in as management, having never gone home with oil stains and a paycheck that won't cover the rent. I don't see any of those managers here today.

If folks think the idea of workers sharing the profits of their own work is a bad deal, maybe they don't understand just how much money our bosses have been making off our work.

Until the second production stopped, GATC was selling more tires than ever, charging *more* for tires than ever, while paying workers roughly the same wages they paid 30 years ago.

I've put the numbers into a handout. It should be making its way around, although I didn't make nearly enough copies. I didn't imagine this many folks would show up.

The paper going around details GATC profits, the fraction of profits workers take home, and the much larger margin our bosses have been taking to the golf course while the rest of us cough up our lungs on the floor, because GATC didn't see fit to clean the air we breathe.

If it sounds like communism that we don't want our people breathing poison, passed up for raises while our bosses get bonuses and lay off workers by claiming there's a recession despite record profits, you can call it what you will, but I call it bad math.

As a middleman between management and workers, I saw how the folks who worked least exploited the folks who worked hardest, all to raise a bottom line that never benefited the workers. The price tag on the factory is $11 million. Everyone in this room knows as well as I do, our settlement checks add up to more than that.

FREDDIE SUMNER, NEW PATRIOT ALLIANCE:

What you're asking for is socialism!

GIL BRENNER, GATC OPERATIONS MANAGER:

What we're asking for is democracy. Every worker has equal ownership, equal vote.

When voters vote, it's democracy, so why is it when workers vote, it's socialism? I don't care what you call it. I'm a wool-dyed, straight-talking Republican, and this is not the half-baked crackpot pipe dream some folks are making it out to be.

(APPLAUSE AND CHEERING)

MAYOR CAROL SHULTZ:

Order! Order! Mr. Brenner, when most folks hear the word *co-op*, they think of tree-hugging hippies who make their own soap and eat birdseed. If we wanted to live like that, we'd move to Lawrence. Goodnight is not that kind of town.

GIL BRENNER, GATC OPERATIONS MANAGER:

As Solvang said, if the word *co-op* scares folks away, the job market'll scare them back.

MAYOR CAROL SHULTZ:

I find it hard to believe seasoned company men are taking advice from a cook who knows nothing about running a factory and has no skin in this game.

SID SOLVANG:

Mayor, I'd like to say a word, to set the record straight.

MAYOR CAROL SHULTZ:

Order! You'll have to wait.

GIL BRENNER, GATC OPERATIONS MANAGER:

I'll yield what's left of my time to Mr. Solvang.

(CHEERING)

SID SOLVANG:

Call me *Sid*. (APPLAUSE) These workers aren't just customers; they're neighbors. Our children go to school together. Our taxes pave each other's roads. There's nobody in this town who doesn't have skin in this game. When any family struggles, there's a ripple effect. We can't afford to lose the factory, and we don't have to if we work together. That's it. I'll yield the floor.

FORMER GATC LAUNDRY WORKER PATSY STARKS:

I don't need two minutes to say what I've gotta say. A co-op is better than nothing, which is what we've got now. This town's been to heck and back. The way it looks from the unemployment line, we've got nothing to lose.

COUNCIL MEMBER FORD HOLLIS:

Just out of curiosity, maybe we could have an informal show of hands, how many folks like the idea of a co-op?

(APPLAUSE AND LOUDER CHEERING)

MAYOR CAROL SHULTZ:

This is not protocol for a formal vote. This is only a forum for public discussion. Order!

CHANTING:

Vote! Vote! Vote! Vote!

COUNCIL MEMBER FORD HOLLIS:

It doesn't have to be a vote. Consider it an opinion poll. Who favors investing at least part of our class action settlements to buy the bones of GATC and create a worker-owned co-op?

(MORE THAN 95 PERCENT OF THE AUDIENCE RAISES THEIR HANDS, CHEERING WILDLY.)

MAYOR CAROL SHULTZ:

Councilman, you're out of order.

CHANTING:

Co-op! Co-op! Co-op!

COUNCIL MEMBER CLIFTON RIDGE:

If we can have some order, we'll continue with public comment.

VIRGINIA EASTON, COFOUNDER, NEW PATRIOT ALLIANCE:

On behalf of the New Patriot Alliance, we citizens of Goodnight are here to present a petition for the resignation of the editor of the *Goodnight Star* for the following transgressions:

1. For slandering the good name of Goodnight American Tire Company, resulting in its shutdown and move to China.
2. For defending the outsiders who are taking over our local economy.
3. For inciting public outrage and civil disobedience among workers.

The time has come to discuss the fate of commerce in Goodnight as we witness a conspiracy to destroy the free market as we know it. The powers that be, and by that, I mean the *Goodnight Star*, got in cahoots with outsiders bent on destroying the moral fabric of this town—

COUNCIL MEMBER FORD HOLLIS:

I have to interject. Today I received a letter from the whistleblower with a series of exchanges between the CEO and GATC shareholders. These exchanges reveal they'd been planning to move the plant to China long before this scandal surfaced. The new memos suggest GATC has been shopping for a market with the lowest minimum wage and loosest regulations as early as 1998, and they zeroed in on China in January 2002—

VIRGINIA EASTON, COFOUNDER, NEW PATRIOT ALLIANCE:

It's fake! There's no way that's true. You're all brainwashed! We need look no further than the plain English of Romans to see the Bible was very clear on how Jesus felt about communism. This editor is destroying the

God-fearing foundation of this town with his communist agenda, and it's chased GATC off to China, leaving half the town out of work—

COUNCIL MEMBER FORD HOLLIS:

I told you, GATC already had plans to relocate and—

VIRGINIA EASTON, COFOUNDER, NEW PATRIOT ALLIANCE:

This godless swindler is using our paper for the work of Satan. Today I'm here to present a petition. I'll read it:

Never in our history has any editor destroyed commerce, taken up with infidels, and turned this town against itself. For the grievances aforementioned, we, the undersigned citizens of Goodnight, demand immediate removal of the editor in chief of the *Goodnight Star*.

Over the years, this town has gone to the greatest lengths to keep the identity of the editor a secret, supposedly to keep our paper free of corruption, but keeping a secret identity has allowed our editor to corrupt public perception against our factory.

Well, I have a surprise for you. They said it couldn't be done. They said no one could find him, but we did. Our alliance went door to door, church to church, raising money for a bounty hunter—Mr. Ruston—to expose the heathen hiding behind the ink. Any second he'll arrive with the editor of the *Goodnight Star*, and then this editor will be forced to answer for his crimes.

Are you here, Mr. Ruston? There he is. He's just coming—

Letter left in an empty bottle of Dad's Root Beer eastbound on the Moses River

Dear Uncle Casey,

You won't believe what happened at the town hall tonight. Everybody said there was gonna be some kind of showdown. I didn't believe it until I started seeing people burning the *Goodnight Star* right on the street! They actually started a bonfire of newspapers outside City Hall, so we could see it from the May Day windows.

As soon as they opened for public comment, Virginia turned up with her turbo-patriots.

When she got to the microphone, she started rattling off like one of those TV preachers, railing on the *Star*, blaming the editor for destroying the Christian fabric of Goodnight, threatening to expose the godless devil worshipper behind the paper for wrecking the tire factory.

So, anyway, she tells us her little patriot cult hired a bounty hunter to find the editor of the *Star*. A BOUNTY HUNTER! Then she says he's on his way, and he's gonna, like, *out* the editor!

Sure enough, a minute later, there he is—a freaking bounty hunter, wearing camouflage and bulletproof armor at the door, looking like the Terminator!

And guess who he's dragging behind him, handcuffed to his giant Terminator wrist?

REVEREND FREAKING ARLO!!!!!!!

IN HANDCUFFS!!!!

YES, I mean Mama's Reverend Arlo, senior minister of the Good Shepherd, humble servant who apologizes for saying "darn." Reverend Arlo, who has probably never broken a law, a rule, nor a promise, who takes food to poor folks, makes house calls to sick folks, no matter how sick they are, the same reverend I see walking all over town half-frozen because he lends his truck to anyone, anywhere, even if it's 10 below zero. Reverend Arlo, who's so humble, he doesn't even dress up for church. He just steps off his tractor in his overalls, shakes off the prairie dust, and walks onto the pulpit like a rainbow with a Bible so worn out that even Jesus is jealous.

And there is that rainbow Bible of a man, fresh off his tractor in his grass-stained overalls, standing handcuffed to the Terminator in the middle of City Hall with the whole town watching, their jaws on the floor, their brains exploding! I think they must've dragged the poor man off his John Deere because I swear you could smell the farm dirt on his boots from across the room.

You can't imagine what happened next.

You should've seen the look on Virginia's face when she realized the godless heathen she's been crusading against was like, the holiest, most beloved minister in the whole town!

The New Patriots freaked. They were all like, "We didn't know! We swear we didn't know!"

They glared at Virginia, and she was like, "There's some mistake, for Jesus's sake. Take off those handcuffs—that's a man of God! That's not the editor. It's our minister. There's been a terrible mistake!"

The bounty hunter uncuffed him, but Arlo said, "There's no mistake. I've been the editor of the *Star* for 20 years, but now it's done. Once an editor's identity is exposed, it's over."

That did it—the whole room gasped.

Everyone begged Arlo not to step down, but he said, "The *Star*'s regulations are very clear for good reason. The editor must function with the highest integrity, without being influenced even by his own need for approval. Even with the best of intentions, it's too easy for our objectivity to be compromised by holding a public position. So I hereby resign as editor of the *Goodnight Star*."

So then the whole town goes crazy and starts yelling at Virginia that she ruined everything! Even her little patriot friends turned on her.

She was so shocked and humiliated, she fell to her knees and started crying.

Arlo hushed them. He got down on his knees with her and closed his eyes. "Forgive us our trespasses as we forgive those who trespass against us," he said. "It's time we all lay down our judgment and forgive our debts."

You know that just made everybody love him more.

When the mayor realized it was a minister the New Patriots had been attacking all along, she dropped her opposition to the co-op. So we lost our editor, but we gained a tire co-op.

I've never seen anything like the look on Mama's face when Sid explained to her that being a worker at a co-op means she's about to own a tire factory.

36

Salt of the Earth

From: Honey Bee Kennedy <RevelationSevenfold@prairienet.com>
To: Reverend Arlo Foster <humbleservant@goodshepherd.com>

I, for one, am glad you can put this newspapering behind you so you have more time to devote to the prayer team—and just in time.

Disco is different since she got out of the forge. I think I'd better find her a job. I heard they're shorthanded at the May Day, and those Solvangs aren't half bad for heathens.

The doctors told me to throw Disco's guitar in the trash, but I didn't have the heart.

I wouldn't have made it through those years on my daddy's farm without my old accordion. Of course, I was only allowed to play gospel, but I played that accordion so hard, my father threatened to burn it if I didn't get that thing out of the house! I'd wander the edge of town for hours, playing that accordion like nobody's business. I'll bet you didn't know that, did you?

I never did thank you for what you've done for us and for this town. A better person might bring you a pie, but that's neither here nor there. See you Sunday. Maybe there will be pie.

From: Sid Solvang <brooklyncalling@zoomail.com>

To: Honey Bee Kennedy <RevelationSevenfold@prairienet.com>

Guess who turned up at the May Day counter today?

I'll give you a hint. She was pale, polite, and as dignified as glitter can be.

She said, "I need a job, and it wasn't my mama's idea. She told me to say that."

I said, "She told you to lie?" and she answered yes.

I asked her why she told me the truth. She said, "Mama taught me never to tell a lie, not for anyone, because Jesus tells the truth, even if it kills him, which it pretty much did."

I asked her, "You ever washed a dish?"

"All of them," she answered. "My mama doesn't believe in dishwashers, so I've washed every kind of dish there is in the world except a silver one."

"Well, the May Day doesn't have any silver dishes, so maybe you could handle it," I said. And then I told her, "You know, a lot of people sing when they wash dishes."

She said, "I don't want any kind of special treatment just because you love me so much."

I asked her what made her think I loved her so much, and she said, "You're nicer to me than anyone in this whole town."

I told her I hoped that wasn't true.

I'm sure you know that child leaks country music, and the world is better for it.

I handed Disco a May Day apron, and you would've thought it was the Holy Grail, the way her eyes misted. She seemed to run out of words, which I don't have to tell you is not something the May Day has seen before.

Honey Bee, I want you to know you raised a good kid. There's a reason we never change the songs on the Wurlitzer. It's the same reason the riverside houses leave their back porch lights on when they see Disco coming, and it's why we always set an extra plate, just in case.

One more thing: I've canceled my subscription to the *New York Times*. I thought maybe you and Disco should know that. It's not so much a philosophical decision on my part. I just don't care what's happening in New York anymore. I can't even make myself care.

From: Scarlet Bannister Solvang <mystifried@zoomail.com>
To: Disco Kennedy <lostblue@prairienet.com>

When I called your mother to warn her about Prairie Forge, I think you should know she dropped everything to get you out. She badgered the forge, the police, the governor, and the president. You know—of the United States. All to try to get you out.

I was honored to be part of your rescue.

No one came for me when I was at Prairie Forge. No one knew where I was, except my father. Even my sisters didn't know. The church pressured him to lock me up in "treatment" when I went a little crazy after my mother's death. Now you know a secret nobody knows—why my father left me everything. I think it was his way of making it up to me, but as you must know by now, for some debts, there is no compensation.

I was in Prairie Forge for 127 days. They couldn't cure me because they couldn't figure out what was wrong with me. I was like you—a kind of different without a name.

Those months, the only joy I found was working in the cafeteria. One of the cooks took me under his wing and taught me everything about cooking. I never wanted to leave that kitchen.

I made up my mind that if I ever got out, I'd get as far away from Kansas as cooking school would take me and I'd never come back. Funny thing is, no matter where I was, the only place I ever felt right was in a kitchen.

I owe you an apology for trying to keep you away from Harlem. I was afraid she'd end up like me if she became friends with someone… like me. Now, seeing the little jump in her step when she walks into the kitchen, I realize maybe it's not the worst thing if she turns out like us.

From: Bailey Nation <hellrazor@shotmail.com>
To: Tallayla Parks <onedayatatime@stillscountycorrections.org>

Sid said now that my probation's over, maybe I can manage the May Day. Of course, I'll still be waiting tables since nobody else can do it right.

In other news, Tyler made me a cake, so I decided to marry him.

I clocked in at the May Day on Monday with only half a hangover, and right there on the list of specials, he had written in handwriting about as tidy as Lucifer, *PROBATION GRADUATION CAKE, MUST BE 21*.

I guess word got out about me winning probation.

You remember Tyler? He's the May Day cook who talks like a devil, but cooks like a saint, if saints went around frying things. Sid says, "Sure, I could find people I trust with my life, but who do I trust with my lasagna?"

Tyler, that's who. If he's good enough for Solvang, he's good enough for my kitchen.

We hitched it yesterday at City Hall. Since we've both been married before, we don't need no wedding, but I've got a honeymoon to plan. I've gotta clear Tyler's closet and shine him up, so it don't look like I'm dragging a fishing pole across Caesar's Palace. I've got my work cut out because he's got the fashion sense of a toothache.

Between bossing Tyler and managing the diner, I'm as fixed as a six-top range. Ever since the tire factory—I mean co-op—reopened, we're slammed with business. Folks got money to burn on biscuits now!

From: Tallayla Parks <onedayatatime@stillscountycorrections.org>
To: Bailey Nation <hellrazor@shotmail.com>

You don't have to keep checking in with me. Your probation's over, honey. Once you get your paper and your key chain, you're free. You don't owe me anything. Well, you do actually owe me that Tupperware you borrowed. Please return it when you get a chance.

Also, congratulations on getting hitched, but you don't have to go around marrying every cowboy who bakes you a cake. Just so we're clear.

From: Bailey Nation <hellrazor@shotmail.com>
To: Tallayla Parks <onedayatatime@stillscountycorrections.org>

I figured you'd miss me too much if I didn't keep checking in. It must be hard to get so attached to people like me, hearing every detail of my life and then one day just cutting the cord and sending us off into the sunset or whatnot.

It couldn't hurt to keep checking in a while longer.

And about that cake. It was rum cake—chocolate Tennessee whiskey icing made of Jack Daniel's and fudge. Whiskey. Rum. Fudge. Jack Daniel's Single Barrel 94-proof bourbon.

In a cake. JUST SO WE'RE CLEAR.

From: Harlem Solvang <torturedsol@zoomail.com>

To: Abbey Solvang <abbeyroadyogi@omwardbound.org>

I can't make it to Brooklyn next month after all. My cooking club is up to nine members, and it's kept me so busy, I haven't had time to try out new recipes. So I plan to spend my whole summer break in the May Day kitchen with Dad until I can sear tofu like he can sear steak.

That's not the only reason. Dad added a Harlem's Special to the daily specials. People come around the May Day just to see what I'm gonna come up with next, so I can't let them down. Monday, I made ghost caviar out of ghost peppers. They were so spicy, Bailey was the only one who could eat them.

Dad's teaching me his molecular gastronomy MacGyvery, and I've got gelification down, so now I can make noodles out of pretty much anything. The *Star* is doing a May Day Challenge to come up with the weirdest thing to turn into a noodle. The winner gets a free dinner, so everyone in town is bringing us pretty strange things.

So far, I've made broccotini and leekguini. Disco's idea, the tequila noodle, is my favorite. Dad says we can't put it on the menu because we can't be getting the whole town drunk on spaghetti. It's too bad because I think if you've got a noodle named fusilli, it's asking to be made out of tequila.

Disco and her mom came in for dinner the other day to celebrate because Honey Bee finally got back into nursing school. I made them my Froot Loop caviar. Honey Bee said I'm turning into a mad scientist like Dad, but Bailey told them if anyone raises one ill word against my cooking, we'll turn them into noodles.

Gotta run. I promised Disco I'd go dancing with her tonight

at some hillbilly bar—or behind some hillbilly bar, I don't know—somewhere out in the sticks.

Letter written in glitter ink, last seen floating southbound down the Moses River, Friday

Dear Uncle Casey,

I promised Harlem I'd wait until we finish school, but I made my mind up at Prairie Forge: the second I graduate, I'm headed straight to Nashville. I wrote a song about it called "Blue Dirt Girl in a Red Dirt Town."

I don't mind waiting because Sid put me in charge of the dishwashing, and I get to wear an official blue apron with the words "May Day Diner" stitched in pink cursive. Sid says he doesn't know how he ever ran a kitchen without me. He says every dish begins with an empty plate, so it has to be clean since it's the most important ingredient.

Bailey said, "If you believe that, I've got a bridge to sell you, honey."

I wish she did have a bridge to sell me. I think I'd like to have one.

Harlem and I are headed to the Blue Felony tonight. They've started having live country bands. Of course, they won't let us in, so we dance out back. It's a decent place to two-step. There are so many cracks in those rafters, country music escapes from everywhere, leaking that rusted neon twang and sweet pedal-steel swagger into the sky, like drunk stars.

When you stand between the roadhouse and the wheat fields, you can hear everything.

Maybe I'll see you there one day. I wrote a song about it called "How that Whiskey Sky Was Made." At first I thought it was about you. Halfway through, it seemed like it was really about me. Now that it's done, I think maybe it's about country music, but I couldn't tell you the difference between you, me, and country music.

Note on a bottle of root beer left at the Driftwood Tavern downriver of Goodnight

Hey, Hildee,

Jim and I fished this out of the Moses this morning. It was trapped under the surface, dammed under a felled cottonwood. I thought I'd pulled a heck of a blue cat, but no, I caught a bottle tangled in an old lost line. I was about to throw it back when I noticed something in it.

My curiosity got the best of me, so I took it out and came to see it was a letter addressed to an Uncle Casey. I didn't think much of it, until we saw who it was from. Jim said he was sure the carpenter we met drinking downriver at the Driftwood a few weeks back was named Casey. "And come to think of it, didn't he mention something about a little girl by the name of Disco?"

That's not a name you forget, so I told Jim, unless my whiskey was lying, I was sure it had to be the same Casey. I can't recall if he was a regular at the Driftwood, but I'm hoping you might know how to get this to him since we're headed home now. He seemed like a decent man, and a decent man has a right to a bottle with his name in it. Jim said, "What are the chances we'd find a bottle addressed to a stranger we bender'd with?"

"Slim," I said. "Miracle slim. This has got Holy Spirit written all over it."

Praise be,
Davis Pratt

37

How to Save a Ghost Town

Letter in an empty bottle of Jack Daniel's hidden behind the Blue Felony

Dear Disco,

Imagine my surprise when I'm minding my own whiskey and the bartender hands me a bottle that looks like it made the rounds to the underworld and back, and there's a letter in it for me. I keep to myself, and I figured I was lying low enough that no one would ever find me. But there was your letter, handed to me by the only soul in my neck of the woods who knows my name.

It's not lost on me, the distance this universe brought your letter to find me, so I figure I owe the river something for the trouble.

I may be living the sentence of a mistake, like you, but I know a miracle when I see it in a bottle. I trust if your letter found me so far downriver, this one will find its way to you one day.

The way I count it, God answers about half our prayers, so why not this one?

I knew someday you'd count your uncles and put it together you had an extra one in your story, and I hoped you'd come looking for me so I could tell you what this town will never tell you. As I read your letter, I knew it was time for you to know the truth about me, which is the truth about you.

It's not complicated. Matter of fact, it's such a worn route to Midwestern heartbreak, you'd think folks would see it coming, but I didn't.

I met your mother the first night of the America Festival. In those days, my band toured summer fairs, playing old-school country to the last folks listening to it. We made just enough cash and free funnel cakes to stay on the road, which was as much as I was looking for.

Abilene was just a girl in a yellow sundress carrying an accordion by the side of a dirt road when I offered her a ride.

Before the sun went down, the stars were crossed.

I had no idea what kind of farm she was straying from. It didn't occur to me she had a story that began a second before she stepped into that rusted Wanderlodge. Some conversations travel so far, they erase the road behind you. I couldn't tell you what was said, but by the end of that conversation, I was a different person.

It lasted three days before your uncles tracked us down.

Long story short, your trigger-happy grandfather chased me to the Missouri border with a shotgun. I took a convincing grazing from that 12-gauge, and nobody tried to stop him. All the Kennedys and possibly the whole town was afraid of him. I couldn't blame them. I've never seen a man so full of rage, not to mention he owned all the Kennedy farms, so nobody crossed Prescott Steerwell Kennedy.

When I heard you were born, I wasn't gonna let anything stop me. I left the band in Joplin and hitchhiked back to find you.

At the hospital the nurses told me Prescott dropped your mama at the curb and never came back. I promised I'd take care of you, but she said her dad would never let her come home if I hung around. I think she still believes he'll take her back one day.

Your mama said if she ever saw me again, she'd shoot me herself.

I decided to lay roots close enough to keep tabs on you. I even went so far as to tint the windows on my Nova so I could keep watch without taking a bullet.

Since then, I kept up through a waitress friend I made in the drinking days that followed. Everyone knew y'all had it hard, and when you were little, your aunts would sneak away from the farm to bring you coats, socks, and whatnot. I heard one day Prescott caught wind Eileen had been to see you, and he sliced an acre off her inheritance right there in the kitchen, waving his will around like a loaded gun.

From that day on, they stopped bringing socks and started running away from you. That's why you've got a hundred cousins who run for the hills when they see you coming.

That night I gave you my guitar wasn't the first time we'd met.

You spoke to me once.

You couldn't have been more than five. I saw you across Emporia Road, dragging a Radio Flyer down the sidewalk. You left the little red wagon and ran up the steps of the May Day. I don't know how I knew it was you, but I knew. I couldn't stop myself from getting a closer look. I slid my baseball cap low and slipped into the diner without anyone noticing.

I watched you bossing old Curtis around and counting your loose change. I looked down at the menu, and when I looked up, there you were, standing at the Wurlitzer right in front of me, asking for a quarter for the jukebox. I gave you everything in my wallet, every penny I had, and I left weeping like a bad country song.

A few years later, I heard you weren't making friends, and I knew I had to give you what I had to give. That was the night I brought you my guitar.

You were born country. Your eyes were like mine, full of gospel and whiskey, aching for something that doesn't yet exist. It's something you're supposed to bring into the world, but you don't know it yet, so you're dying, and you're just gonna keep on dying until the words spill out of your tinderbox soul and into your guitar.

There are a thousand things to die for, but that is something to live for.

Love,
Your daddy, a.k.a.
"Uncle Casey"

From: Sid Solvang <brooklyncalling@zoomail.com>
To: Tristan Deveraux <NitroGenius@TristanDeveraux.com>

Dear Mr. Deveraux,

I'm sorry to have fled in such a rush that night at the May Day without any explanation. I couldn't explain myself until now. Thank you for your offer. You're right, the terms are extraordinarily generous, and your confidence in me is humbling.

I put everything into Sol's, and when it went down, I swore I'd never cook again. I never imagined I'd be saved by a little weathered truck stop in the middle of Kansas.

It's the gravest act of faith to risk everything you have for a dream and then to share it through some inexplicable impulse, some senseless and reckless need to be heard. It's contrary to every instinct of self-preservation to share a dream with a world that doesn't need another dream and one so hostile to dreamers. There's no practical reason that any art should need an audience, a fourth wall, a table outside your own kitchen, but sometimes it seems to me that a plate hungers to serve like a brushstroke of paint longs to be seen. I've watched how ingredients follow a trajectory beyond me, how each flavor reaches for the next, and how in that mad, magical moment, it all comes together, there is a need to be received.

It makes no sense, the fury of urgency we feel to share something when, tragically, so much art cannot survive the judgment. That beautiful thing that fell from eternity onto your plate can have all its dignity stolen in one bite. One misunderstood bite.

The stifling malice of judging art doesn't sit well with me. For a long time, I could find no joy in a kitchen. I couldn't make a sandwich for my own child without feeling my failure. I didn't intend to ever serve strangers again. In my life I've mastered French technique and molecular gastronomy, but it was a simple pot of soup that saved my soul.

If it hadn't been so cold that day and if the workers hadn't been on strike, I may never have found it again.

Who would've guessed that being reduced to instinct would reduce me to my humanity?

The workers stood along Goodnight Road in a bitter wind. They were bundled up and hunched over frozen signs outside the factory. I knew I had to help the only way I knew how.

We rushed back to the May Day kitchen and went to work on a soup. I wasn't thinking about technique nor critics. I wanted to make something warm and something good.

In all those years of plating Picassos, I guess I lost the truth about why we cook for each other. I forgot serving people is *serving* people. I remembered it that day on that picket line.

When I left that night, I didn't care about stars nor reviews. I didn't care if I was ever remembered for being anything more than a stranger who brought hot soup to cold workers.

But it meant the world to me that they loved that soup.

I didn't use to believe what they say about things happening for a reason, but if anything had gone right in New York, I would've missed this.

I never believed there was such a thing as purpose, but looking back from Emporia Road, every wrong turn I've ever taken seems to be one single arrow, one rusted neon arrow pointing to a little dusty truck stop diner that needed me.

So, to answer your question, thank you, but I have to say I'm sorry, I can't accept your offer in New York. I'm spoken for here in Goodnight, Kansas.

Kindly,

Chef Sid Solvang

EDITOR'S LAST BULLHORN, SUNDAY EDITION

Farewell from departing Editor in Chief Reverend Arlo Foster

Dear Goodnight,

After 20 years of Stills County Fair cannery showdowns and Emporia Road who-said-what, my reign as mystery editor has come to an end, and there's one less mystery in the universe.

Before I was chosen to be your editor, I had scarcely written a word outside my sermons at the Good Shepherd. Most of my days were spent on a tractor, and most of my nights were spent chasing the word of God.

I was startled when I found an unstamped letter in my mailbox inviting me to step up to this soapbox. I thought it was a mistake. I asked why *I* had been chosen. Why not a journalist or someone who had gone to college? I couldn't even afford seminary school.

The former editor said she was told that when she was ready to retire she should find someone who shares the struggles of our readers. The founders never wanted a journalist because there are no journalists in Goodnight. We are farmers. We are workers. Our founders didn't care about looking good nor sounding good. They needed someone who could get out of truth's way. As the mission says, *It's a humble rag for a humble town, and we're not your voice, you're ours.* She said it wasn't easy finding someone humble enough to carry the weight of this town. So I was chosen for my humility.

Ironically, it's what I'm most proud of: the servant's heart.

Nowadays I can write an editorial from my tractor, but you can't imagine the lengths it took to keep this underground before the internet. When I started, we used tunnels from both the Underground Railroad and Prohibition, printing the news from an old speakeasy under Emporia Road. At any point, it wouldn't have taken much to expose the editor, but this town was as determined to keep our secret as we were. Our readers understood the importance of having a pure channel for the truth.

It's been a wild ride keeping up with Emporia Road—the broken church bells and cannery triumphs, the Fourth of July parades, everything lost and everything found, our universal struggles and our loneliest heartbreaks.

I trust there's good to be found behind all things, goodness even in the timing of ends.

That's why I harbor no ill will against those who brought us to this crossroads where I lay down the beautiful burden of your words. I look forward to having more time with my family and for meditation on my sermons. Now that I have a little more time on my hands, maybe I'll find something more to do with words.

One thing's for sure: I could write a book about all of you.

About *us*.

I could write a book with all your kind and wild letters, your back-porch stories, the pictures of grandchildren you've been sending me all these years. Maybe I'd call it *How We Saved Goodnight, Kansas*, because I hope you know we *did* save it.

Your letters, your voices, your prayers saved this town. I know it would be a good story, because it would be *our* story.

I can't imagine how I'd begin to capture all the voices of Goodnight. It would take an act of mysticism and faith beyond me, but maybe I will write that book someday. Some things we don't have a choice about, and I'd like the world to know that Goodnight, Kansas, is still here.

No matter what the map says, *we are still here*.

Rest assured, the *Star*'s inkwell is never dry. I've chosen a new humble servant to offer the quill, someone to tend your lost and found, to mind your misplaced things.

Tomorrow someone else will be keeping watch over your lost Bibles and false teeth, found kittens, keys, and winter coats.

So, friends, keep an eye on your mailbox. One of you has an invitation coming.

Any day now.

READING GROUP GUIDE

1. What do you think it's like to return to your hometown after a prolonged absence? What might or might not have changed?

2. Do you prefer living in the city or in a more rural area? What are the advantages and disadvantages of both?

3. Both Sid and Scarlet struggle with rifts in their families. What causes these kinds of divisions? What are some of the ways to make amends?

4. The May Day Diner is just one example of a small, local institution. Why do you think it was important for Sid to save the May Day? Do you have any examples of small, independently owned businesses that you would save if they were set to close?

5. Do you think Sid's decision to buy the May Day Diner is reckless? Why or why not? If you were in his shoes, what would you have done?

6. What are the pros and cons of both small-town and big-city living? How are they both represented in this novel?

7. For most of the novel, Sid chooses not to cook, despite being very talented. What do you make of his decision?

8. The Solvangs slowly fall in love and find a home in Goodnight. Have you ever fallen in love with a place? What does home look like or mean to you?

9. Is Goodnight, Kansas, too small for Disco? What might make a city or a town the "right" fit for someone?

10. What do you make of the sçandal with GATC? Did you find the company's actions realistic?

11. Did you guess who the editor of the *Goodnight Star* was? What is the importance of a neutral, anonymous editor? Is it even possible to be neutral?

A CONVERSATION WITH THE AUTHOR

Where did the inspiration for this story come from?

When I moved from Kansas to Los Angeles in 1999, I was so homesick, I started writing stories about a fictitious town that captured what I missed, and I never stopped writing them. Over twenty years, Goodnight absorbed everything around me: the New Yorkers I ran with, my extended family of deeply religious Indiana farmers, the Baileys who saved me in small-town twelve-step meetings... My uncle is a missionary who would say *good night* when profanity was called for, and the warm feeling I got from that seemed to build the whole town. A less conscious but pervasive influence was growing up in the world of newspapers. My dad was a columnist for the *Wichita Eagle*. Witnessing how he interacted with readers—rallying to get a heart transplant for a little girl, guilting thieves into giving back a man's stolen Christmas lights—that lesser-told power of the press reverberates through the story.

The broader themes—rural flight, offshoring, environmental and labor justice—these issues leaked into the story from my life. A profound influence was being swept into the UFCW grocery workers' strike as an activist in 2003 and covering labor struggles from sweatshop workers to bellhops as a reporter for five years. It was life-changing to see the solidarity of the labor movement in contrast to my experiences as a worker trying to survive on minimum wage and the hopelessness of managing food insecurity alone. This was a theme I hadn't intended to include, but the issues that matter to us have a way of bending our stories in the shape of our beliefs, the shape of us.

What are the difficulties of writing an epistolary novel?

I could write three pages about a drop of rain, so the epistolary structure reined me in, but I missed the luxury of exposition. I love writing immersive descriptions, layering details with ironic and playful juxtaposition, so it was disorienting to give up my style. In early drafts I tried to push the characters to carry my voice, but ultimately, I had to let go of my usual literary voice, get out of the way, and let the story tell the story. Initially it was liberating to move through the characters' voices so directly. As the narrative developed, it was more challenging to thread each character and not forget anyone along the way. It was tricky to keep track of a whole town, but I had the most fun deciding who should tell what part of the story.

Did you ever consider writing this in a traditional novel format?

This story diverged from a traditional third person novel about Disco in her twenties. As I tried to explain how she became so cynical, one chapter sprawled into a hundred pages of the history of the town, dating back to the Civil War! The backstory was in the way, and I felt the novel failed, but I didn't want to leave Goodnight. I could smell the Eisenhower flapjacks and hear the buzz of the May Day's neon sign. The characters were so real to me, it felt like betrayal to give up on them, so I cut twenty thousand words and used them like one of Scarlet's sourdough starters, creating a new novel centered on the backstory of the town.

I needed a break from Disco, so I experimented with different perspectives. I'd just read a couple of epistolary novels, and I loved how they captured multiple voices, so rather than choose one POV, I chose all of them. It started as an experiment, but when I realized I could blend fiction with my journalism background, I was hooked.

Did anything change in the story from the beginning ideas to the final draft?

I keep a "leftovers" file of everything cut from early drafts. By the last revision, there were 180 pages of leftovers, so it was an entirely different book. My favorite part of writing is the way something unexpected falls onto the page. For me it's an act of mysticism to follow the characters around and see where they take me. I wish I could write a book for every ghost town, and this fascination hijacked the narrative. I'd been circling and collecting stories of Kansas ghost towns for years while my family explored many abandoned mining towns on Gold Country road trips, so it connected and reframed the nebula I was writing from. I think the concept of saving a ghost town was an unconscious metaphor, as I was writing with a mission of saving the town I'd created. I always find there's a moment in writing fiction where you meet yourself—where the arc of the character confronts your arc as a writer in a sort of climactic reckoning.

Where did you get inspiration for all the food?

Around 2007 my cable went out, and I could only get one channel. They kept playing a marathon of cooking competitions. I had no interest, but I always left the TV on for the comfort of voices, and within days of watching nothing but cooking shows, I was addicted. I see so many parallels between the artistic angst of writers and chefs.

The way I use words to layer sensory constellations feels conceptually similar to the way chefs blend flavor elements to create dimension, juxtaposing the senses. I was most inspired by the swagger around molecular gastronomy and challenges that asked chefs to interpret abstract concepts as dishes, which was the essence of Sid's approach to cooking.

I'm a terrible cook, so I had to do a ton of research about culinary arts from recipes to studying the world of chefs to googling what black squid ink tastes like. Unfortunately, none of it has improved my cooking.

What do you want readers to take away from your book?

The short answer is comfort. The darker the world looks, the more I've needed books that feel good, but not in a sentimental way. As this latest iteration began around 2019, my intention for a cozy escape was derailed by my need to reconcile the staggering turmoil around me—political division, rampant racism and classism—as I lived between two disparate California cities in a country that seemed on the brink of civil war. It all leaked into Goodnight, and my intention shifted. I wanted to create a story that imagined in a small way what the other side of that division could look like.

This book draws from so many invisible moments in my life as a worker, as a fish out of water, as someone who regarded themself as a failed artist. I hope it brings a little solace and validation to anyone who has felt unseen, misunderstood, or like their life didn't matter. It's a revelation to recognize how small moments of benevolence matter more than the cruel ways we measure ourselves. There's something extraordinary in realizing, as Sid said, that it's enough to just be the guy who serves warm soup to cold workers.

What are you reading right now?

I'm usually reading two books at once, one at home and a library audiobook for the car. Rebounding from the sadness I felt from reading James Baldwin's *Go Tell It on the Mountain*, I googled something to the effect of *happy books that are not patronizing*, and I found *This Is Happiness* by Irish author Niall Williams. So far the poetic language has blown me away. I also just started *Americanah* by Chimamanda Ngozi Adichie. I came across it researching strong examples of voice in openings to novels for a craft lecture I was giving. From the first page, I was in love. I crave books that reconcile homesickness and diaspora because it's a chronic theme in my life and something I can't reconcile. I also just love being transported to a place I've never been and becoming immersed in an unfamiliar world. I'm savoring every word.

ACKNOWLEDGMENTS

My gratitude starts with Kansas, which has become an invisible friend since I left, and I'm pretty sure we haunt each other. This book is my reckoning, my forgiveness, and my apology.

I'm so grateful to my agent, Jenissa Graham, and BookEnds Literary for championing this story. I'm endlessly thankful for the heart of my editor, MJ Johnston, and everyone at Sourcebooks.

This book would not exist without the support of my family: Jon, Miles, Violet, Lisa, Bob, Chase, Tracy, Emma, Jackson, Mickey, Scott, Nancy, Dave, Sarah, Thom, Duncan, Cora, Matt, Dave, Mary, Clarissa, the Geigers, the Pallos, and all the Austin Ellingers. Thank you to my UBC family: Linda Svendsen, Sheryda Warrener, Alix Olin, Mallory Tater, Sara Graefe, Annabel Lyon, Tanya Kyi, John Vigna, Martin Kinch, Ariane Anantaputri, Jess Goldman, Shaelyn Johnston, Jasmine Ruff, Franka Odenwaelde, Valentina Sierra, Sofia Osborn, and Cara DiGirolamo. So much gratitude to Tracy Archibald, Yvonne, Clarence, Ernie, and all of Metro. Thanks to everyone at Benicia Public Library, especially Alli and Brandi. I am forever grateful to Marlene Howell, Jan Feyen, Rita Younglund, Steve Trollinger, Tricia Murajda, Sarah Ray, Tanya Russell, Nancy Crane, Connie Pride, Scott Scheffer, Maggie Vascassenno, John Parker, MT Karthik, Molly Paige, Maggie LePique, Ernesto Arce, Tony Bates, Lainie Clemensen, Sarah

Yost, Ken D, Rob F, Rick Luther, Zola Fish, Yul Spencer, Charlie, Jack, Robin, Marty Robertson, Matt Thomas, Christina Hauck, Margaret Wheeler, Neal Miller, Max Holtzman, Aimee Leisy, Casey Greer, Quentin Cox, Kara Bryant, Billy Minshall, Heather Pierini, Katy Buckley-Smith, to all the angels of Agape, Parklane, DRU, Moorpark Noon, the Ahlberg family, Bob Wolfe, Deron Haught, and, of course, Oprah.

ABOUT THE AUTHOR

Page Getz is an author, teacher, and journalist who spent half her life in Kansas and the other half in California, working as a reporter for the *Los Angeles Times* and Pacifica Radio. Her work appears in many publications, reconciling themes of diaspora, mysticism, addiction, classism, labor justice, queerness, and small towns. She lives with her family and dogs in Vancouver, where she holds an MFA in creative writing from the University of British Columbia. She is still recovering from the wayward youth and pathological idealism that inspires her work.